Sid Johnson and the Phantom Slave Stealer

Frances Schoonmaker

Auctus Publishers

www.auctuspublishers.com

Published by Auctus Publishers
606 Merion Avenue, First Floor
Havertown, PA 19083

ISBN 978-1-7368278-9-5 (Paperback)
ISBN 978-1-7368278-8-8 (Hardcopy)
ISBN 978-1-7368278-7-1 (Electronic)
Library of Congress Control Number: 2022911499

To Warren and Bruce

CONTENTS

1.
Eavesdropping

Was that a gunshot? Sid Johnson sat upright in bed. Maybe he'd been dreaming. Jimmy lay on the other side of the bed tangled up in the covers. It was no use asking if he heard the shot. His little brother would sleep with the house falling around them. *Maybe it was men huntin' down by the creek.* He slipped out of bed, going to the window.

Dogs bayed off in the distance. He felt sorry for the poor animal they were after. Leaning out of the open window, he breathed in the soft night air. The sound of the dogs faded. Maybe they weren't going to have their kill after all.

A shadow moved on the far side of the orchard. *Too big for a fox.* He'd almost have said a person, except there wasn't any reason for someone to be in the orchard at night. After a while, he gave up watching.

Yawning, Sid shoved Jimmy back onto his half of the bed. Smoothing out the covers, he crawled in, pulling the quilt up to his chin. He could hear Ma and Pa downstairs, talking in muffled voices. Ma had been to see someone who was sick. *She's just now getting home*, he thought, snuggling into the warm spot where Jimmy had been. He let himself drift back to sleep—but not for long.

Downstairs a woman moaned. *Ma? Was she hurt?* Goose bumps prickling the back of his neck, Sid threw off the covers, jumped out of bed, and flew down the stairs.

A candle burned on the kitchen table. Ma was on her hands and knees scrubbing up something that looked like blood. She looked up as calmly as if she were merely wiping up crumbs after supper. "Why, Sid, whatever are you doin' out of bed this time of night?"

"I heard a gunshot."

"Oh, that. Never mind. Your Pa is determined to catch the fox that's been botherin' the hens."

"Did he get hurt?" Sid looked at the blood. "I heard someone moanin'—"

"Must be the house talkin'." Ma didn't give him time to finish. "Old houses make night sounds. Nothin' for you to worry about.

You'd best get back to bed. Just wanted to wipe this up so it doesn't dry on the floor."

Sid went back to bed. He was not convinced. If this had been the first time, he might not have worried so much. But he had been awakened in the night before by strange sounds coming from downstairs. Ma always said old houses make sounds. Pa said he was probably having nightmares. Sid wasn't so sure, not now, not with blood on the floor. Ma and Pa were hiding something from him. If they wouldn't talk about it, he'd have to find out another way.

The following night, Sid slipped out of bed and stood at the top of the stairs listening. Ma and Pa usually sat at the kitchen table talking after everyone else was in bed. If they saw him, he'd say he was on his way to get a drink of water.

All Sid wanted to know was what the two of them were up to. Unfortunately, Pa was in the middle of a rant. "Abe Lincoln is right. Steven Douglas got his Kansas-Nebraska bill through Congress by caving in to slaveholders. Dumbest thing Illinois ever did was let Abe retire from Congress back in '49."

Sid knew what was coming next. Pa couldn't get over it when the popular Stephen Douglas was elected to the U.S. Senate instead of Abraham Lincoln. "Folks keep saying Douglas should run for President. Hen's teeth! Far as I'm concerned, Honest Abe would make a far better President. Lord knows we need somebody who amounts to something in that office. Mark my word. We are getting closer and closer to a war over the slave question."

"You don't think it will come to that?" said Ma, undisguised worry in her voice.

"What did you expect from the Compromise of 1850?" said Pa. "Whoever named it the 'Bloodhound Bill' had it right. Being in a free state stands for nothing, not when any slaveholder in the country can come in and arrest people."

There wasn't anything more to learn. Sid knew about the Fugitive Slave Act. Pa was likely to go on about it for another hour. Sighing, he started for bed.

"I keep thinkin' of that poor woman," said Ma. "God bless her. I hope she made it to safety—"Sid stopped in his tracks, listening—"Leastwise you got her as far as Alton this mornin'. Travelin' alone and hunted down like an animal! Thank God that gunshot just grazed her. I didn't think I'd ever get the bleedin' stopped."

The gunshot. Sid strained to hear every word.

"They wouldn't want to harm her now, would they?" Pa said. Sarcasm rang in his voice. "It would reduce her value."

Sid took in a sharp breath. The dogs he heard baying in the night were after a woman and that woman had been in their house. The realization hit him like a punch in the stomach. He knew that people searching for slaves on the run often used dogs, but he'd never actually let himself think about what it would be like to be the one who was hunted.

"President Pierce would say we're breaking the law," said Pa. "Folk like him try to hide behind the Good Book. Reckon they did have slaves back in Bible days. Doesn't make it right. They thought the earth was flat then, too. This is 1855. We ought to know better."

"I'm afraid, Ben," said Ma. "Sid is gettin' older. He's bound to find out. He might let somethin' slip at school. He saw me moppin' up the blood last night."

Sid held his breath, hardly able to believe what he was hearing.

"I'm not worried about Sid," said Pa.

"We're going to have to tell the boy sooner or later. He can keep his own counsel. It's the young ones. Little Cora would blurt out everything she knows to the first person who asks. Jimmy never met a stranger he couldn't talk to."

So, they've been sheltering runaways. The idea slowly sank in. Any guilt Sid might have felt at eavesdropping vanished. He hoped Ma and Pa would take him into their confidence. Until they did, he had to be prepared. If Ma and Pa got into trouble for helping freedom seekers, he'd have to take care of Jimmy and Cora. It wasn't that he approved of slavery but breaking the law was another matter.

Pa carried on about politics for nearly a week. There weren't any gunshots or muffled voices in the night. Worried about what might happen, Sid listened anyway. He couldn't afford to miss anything.

"They call it states' rights," Pa was going on again one night. "It's nothing but varnishing over the fact that these slave states don't want to give up their cheap labor. That's the plain truth of it."

Sid sat on the steps at the top of the stairs, head in his hands. He was getting weary of politics.

"But, Ben, it isn't as if Illinois has clean hands," said Ma. "We have neighbors around Alton who still have indentured servants."

"No, we don't have clean hands," said Pa. "That's another burr under my saddle. When people move into Illinois with slaves, the law says they can keep them for a year as indentured servants. Some of these people just refuse to obey the law. Now they're pushing to make it legal to keep your slaves if you move into a free state."

"Mrs. Harold's anniversary is comin' up," said Ma. "It's almost 20 years since Mr. Harold was killed."

"They knew the risks, Sadie," said Pa. "When Harold started working on that abolitionist newspaper with Reverend Lovejoy it was only a matter of time. Anti-abolitionists kept destroying his press; I don't think anybody expected them to murder Lovejoy and Harold—not in a *free state*. I don't know, Sadie. Makes you wonder about a lot of things."

Sid sighed inwardly. It wasn't that he didn't care about their neighbor, Mrs. Harold. He wasn't learning anything new. Besides, it was hard to stay awake at school when he didn't get to bed on time. *Guess I'll give it up for the night*, he thought. He turned toward his bedroom as Ma said, "What we're doin' isn't risk-free, Ben. Sometimes I worry about the chil'ren. What will happen if they come for us?"

Sid whipped back around. *Come for us*— he supposed she meant if slaveholders came after them or maybe anti-abolitionists like the ones who killed Mr. Harold. *It's about time they thought about that.*

"I'm not sayin' I'm sorry to be part of the Railroad," said Ma.

Railroad? Does that mean the Underground Railroad? Sid was stunned. Was there really such a thing? *Are we a part of it?* There were vague rumors about how people managed to escape from slavery. He didn't think anybody really believed there was a train running underground, though.

Ma sighed. "I don't know as I'd have had enough courage to get involved if it wasn't for Mrs. Harold. But I worry. I worry about you, Ben. You could get a big SS branded on your hand, like that sea captain back East, or worse."

Branded? with SS? Sid caught his breath. Who would do such a thing?

"Walker was caught," said Pa. "The thing is not to be caught."

"Ben Johnson! I don't reckon Jonathan Walker planned on bein' caught. Bein' branded as a slave stealer may be a mark of pride for him now; he's a famous abolitionist. But think what the man went through. And think of people who are caught, and nobody comes to their rescue."

Sid felt a chill go up his spine. The more he learned, the more frightened he was.

"Don't think I don't worry, Sadie," said Pa. "I worry about the children, too. And you, going out all hours of the night. Then about the time I start to question, there's somebody who needs a safe place and I know we're doing the right thing."

"I know, Ben." Ma sighed. "Risk or no risk, we can't sit by and do nothin'. And yet, what we do is such a small drop in the bucket. For every person who gets away from slavery, how many hundred are left with no hope of ever bein' free?" She heaved another big sigh. "The risks we take are nothin' compared to the risks they take."

There was a long pause downstairs before Ma spoke again. "On another matter, what did Luke have to say in his letter?"

A letter from Uncle Luke in California? All thought of the Underground Railroad and slave stealing flew out of his head. His uncle in far-away California was a larger-than-life figure to Sid, a real hero.

Pa had been to town, making a stop at the post office. "I thought my little brother had lost his good sense when he took off for California back in '49. Seemed like every third man was talking about striking it rich, unless they found Coronado's gold on the way."

"Well, Luke didn't strike it rich," said Ma matter of factly.

"No. He didn't find the lost Seven Cities of Gold, either." Pa chuckled.

Seven Cities of Gold? Sid's imagination ran away with him. They studied about Coronado in school, Coronado and the conquistadors who traveled all the way to Kansas looking for the fabled cities. The Spaniards found turquoise, silver, and people who already lived there. *They took them, too, like they were gold for the havin'*, he thought.

"Luke ended up with a nice piece of land, though," said Pa. "Thinks we should go out. California's a free state."

Go to California? Sid listened intently.

"If there's a war, we'd be in a good place," said Pa. "It's not likely to spill over into California. I've been thinking on it for some time. Luke says there's a piece of land right next to his that's come up for sale. Says it would make a fine orchard."

"Oh, Ben," Ma said. "I just don't think I could do it. I know this isn't the best piece of land in Illinois but think of how hard we've worked on it. It would be that hard to leave, too."

Going to California sounded exciting, especially with Uncle Luke there. But Sid agreed with Ma. He wasn't so sure he'd really want to go west, not if it meant leaving home.

"And what would happen to our stop on the Railroad and the people who need us here?" Ma asked.

Stop on the Railroad? There it is again. Sid's thoughts bounced between Uncle Luke and his growing understanding of what it meant to have Ma and Pa breaking the law to help people trying to get away from slavery.

"I don't know, Sadie," Pa sighed. "Our folk are all gone now. Luke's our only family. I'd like the children to grow up knowing family. It's getting crowded here, too. Next thing you know, they'll be gobbling up all this good farmland to build factories. It's already happening. Anyway, it'd be a whale of a lot better going to California than sitting here in the middle of a battleground. If we end up in a war, there won't be any more slave stealer or Underground Railroad."

"It's getting more and more dangerous," said Ma, "I'll grant you that."

"Safe stops have to shift anyway, Sadie. We've seen that before. It's just these new laws make it so much harder. Our place is getting to be a crossroad for slave trackers and bounty hunters. The word trespassing means nothing to some of them. That bounty hunter I caught today was out there searching the barn. Took a pitchfork to the hay. God help anybody who tried to hide in the hayloft."

"Thank God Sid and Jimmy were at school," said Ma.

Bounty hunters, here? Sid was jolted into action. He needed to know some things. He walked downstairs like he was going for a drink of water. He hoped Ma and Pa would take the opportunity to bring him into their confidence. If there had been any chance of it, loud knocking at the door ended the possibility.

2.
A Foot in the Hay

A man with a coat thrown over his pajamas stood at the door. "Doc Short sent me for Miz Johnson. Baby's on the way. He's over to the Miller place tending old man Miller. Can she come?"

Ma had already gone for her valise. It wasn't unusual for the doctor to send for her—sometimes in the middle of the night. She didn't have any formal medical training, but Ma had brought many a baby into the world. When Dr. Short was busy, she'd done everything from setting broken arms to treating colic. The only thing she refused to do was surgery, but Dr. Short allowed he'd rather have her cut him open than a lot of men he knew who'd studied medicine.

Ma was out of the house in a flash. "Best get on to bed, Son," said Pa. "No use us waiting up for your Ma. May take her the rest of the night."

Sid wanted to ask Pa about what he'd heard. He wanted to tell Pa that he didn't think it was right to break the law, that he didn't want him branded with SS or put in jail. He didn't like the idea of going to California, either, not really. *Why can't Uncle Luke move back home? Then we'd have family here.* But he didn't know how to say what he wanted to say. It was a long time before he was able to go to sleep.

At breakfast the next morning Pa announced, "This is the day you've been waiting for, Cora. The kittens have their eyes open. Sid, you can take Cora and Jimmy up in the loft to see them, if everyone promises to be real careful. Mind, you three have to finish your chores first."

Serena, a feral grey tabby, found the barn one day, liked it, and stayed. Ma named her "Serena" because of the gentle, serene look on her face. Sid agreed. It suited her. Cora had been wild with excitement ever since he discovered that Serena had given birth to a litter of four kittens in the hayloft.

"Cora, you must promise to be careful with those kittens," Ma advised as they helped her clear the table. "They aren't like your rag doll. You love on 'em too hard, you can hurt 'em."

The tea kettle was singing. Ma took it from the stove and poured hot water into two large, gray-speckled enamel pans.

Jimmy, who usually put up a fuss about helping with the dishes, didn't complain. Once the table was clear, he took up his post next to the worktable. Ma washed in one pan, Jimmy rinsed in the second pan; Cora and Sid dried. Sid did most of the drying, but Cora was learning. Once the dishes were put away and beds made, they headed for the barn.

The barn was a long, gray, weather-bleached wooden building. It stood at the end of a winding driveway that led past the house. Sid loved the fresh smell of hay greeting them as they opened its big doors. He could have found his way inside with his eyes closed. A wide space in the middle was where their wagon, buggy, and the plow were stored. All along the right side of the barn, the roof sloped downward where it ended over an open, fenced-in area adjacent to the pasture. This is where the cows were held before milking, and where they sheltered during the winter. A door at the far end let the cows inside. Wooden stanchions stood all along one wall. The stanchions could be locked in place so the cows couldn't escape during milking. Their cows were so gentle that it wasn't necessary.

"Where's Buttercup?" Cora asked, looking around. Gentle Buttercup was a special friend. Sid had watched her grow from a calf. Now he milked her twice a day. In fact, all their animals were special. They were like members of a large family. Each one had a name. *If we went to California, we'd have to sell all the animals*; the thought came unbidden and unwelcome. It was one more reason not to go.

"Where's the horses?" She sounded disappointed. They kept three gentle horses—two workhorses and one for pulling the buggy and riding. Their stable extended along the left side of the barn.

"They're out to pasture," said Jimmy. "Don't you know nothin'?"

Sid gave Jimmy a look the way Pa would have. "They wouldn't want to stay in the barn all day, not if the weather's nice." He tried not to lose patience with Jimmy. But sometimes he felt like giving his little brother a good, hard punch.

Jimmy looked up at the hayloft that ran the entire length of the barn above the stable. "How come we got so much hay?"

"The cows and horses will eat some this winter, and we'll put some of it on the floor for their beddin'," said Sid. "They'll eat corn, too." He nodded toward the corn crib at the far end. "We'll take some of the corn to the mill in Alton, so it can be ground up for the chickens—"

He didn't have a chance to finish. Jimmy sped toward the ladder that led to the hayloft, Cora right behind him. "Wait," he called, hurrying to catch up.

"Jimmy, climb up first; wait for Cora. I'll come up last. Then I'll show you where to find Serena and the kittens. Mind you, nobody picks up a kitten unless Serena says so."

"She ain't gonna tell us nothin'," said Jimmy scrambling up the ladder. "She's just a cat."

"Not 'posed to say ain't," Cora scolded.

"Serena has her ways," said Sid, before a fuss started. "You just have to know what to look for. Up you go, Cora. Use both hands." Once they were all in the loft, Sid cautioned, "Remember where the edge of the loft is, so nobody falls off. Serena is just back here. We'll move slowly so as not to alarm her."

Crawling over the hay, Sid motioned the other two to follow. Serena lay stretched out in the hay to one side, near a large, shuttered vent that let air into the back of the hayloft. Four little kittens eagerly suckled. "How come they're pushin' Serena?" Cora asked.

"They push with their paws to get her milk flowin'," Sid explained. "Kittens do that."

"Look at their stubby little tails!" laughed Jimmy. "Can I pick one up?"

"Best let them finish breakfast," said Sid. He held out his hand to Serena. She let him rub around her ears. "See, she's purrin'. She's proud of her little family."

They watched quietly. Cora and Jimmy lay on their stomachs, elbows propping them up. After a while, Cora got up to explore along the wall where there was less hay. When the last of the hay was gathered, all along the back wall would be filled in. There wouldn't be room to walk. "Just stay back there where it's safe," Sid cautioned. He had to keep a careful watch over her, but he wanted her to have the fun of exploring. She'd be back in a flash as soon as the kittens quit suckling. She threw herself on the hay, laughing.

Jimmy was transfixed by the kittens. "Their tummies are gettin' fatter, 'n fatter," he said. "Reckon one of 'em will explode?"

"No, they'll quit when they're full. Serena will get up directly when she thinks they've had enough." Sid kept an eye on Cora all the while. She pulled herself up and stood looking wide-eyed at the hay, her mouth hanging open.

"What is it, Cora?"

"A foot."

He got to her just as she reached down and tickled a brown foot that was sticking out of the hay. A boy about his age sat up, wide-eyed with terror. "It's okay," said Sid. "We won't hurt you. We don't hold with slavery. You a runaway?"

The boy stood, looking from one to another. His coarse cloth shirt was in tatters. He wore trousers held up by a rope that was tied at the waist. The trouser legs ended about half-way up his shins.

Sid looked at Cora and Jimmy. "This has to be a secret. You must solemnly promise not to tell." They gravely shook their heads in agreement.

"You got folks with you?" Sid asked.

The boy swallowed, looking down at his feet. "Posed to meet up with my mamma. Can't find her."

"I don't know what to tell you about your mamma," said Sid. "My ma and pa might know. We help folk who are runnin' away from slavery. You're safe here. I can get you some food and water. You travelin' at night?"

The boy nodded.

The sound of horses and voices outside ended the conversation. Looking through the vent, Sid saw Pa talking with two men on horseback. "You Johnson?" One of them waved a paper, shouting at Pa. "Name's Mean, August Mean. I got a warrant for the arrest of Lula and her son Elijah, property of Salias Pugworth of Banner, Kentucky. Been missin' for near a week. You seen 'em?"

"Nah," Pa let his speech slide into the way the men were talking, as if he were one of them. "From what I hear runaways comin' up this way follow the Illinois or they's headin' over to the Wabash River. Don't see 'em 'round here. Reckon we're a little off the path. Besides, if I seen one of 'em, I'd be claimin' the reward for myself, now wouldn' I?"

"That ain't what we hear," said the second man. "The way we hear it, you been harborin' runaways—"

Mean interrupted, "There's a federal law agin it. If you know somethin' about Lula and Elijah, you'd best own up. Turn 'em over, and we'll look the other way. We haveta look for 'em, we'll have the law on you. You can count on it."

"Well, Mr. Mean," said Pa. "Can't think who woulda told you that. Maybe somebody as was tryin' to steer y'all in the wrong direction. Aimin' to waste yer time here, whilst the runaways hightail it up the Wabash River."

The men dismounted. "This here paper gives us the right to search your property," said Mean. "That's what we're goina do. You got a storm cellar, Miz Johnson?" He tipped his hat to Ma, who stepped out into the yard with Pa.

"Yessir," said Ma. "Did I hear y'all say Banner, Kentucky? I'm Kentucky-born myself. Grew up there. Y'all are sure welcome to look. We don't hold with breakin' the law."

"This here is Roscoe Bones," said August Mean, nodding toward the other bounty hunter. "He's gonna need to inspect the house and cellar, Miz Johnson."

Roscoe Bones tipped his hat to Ma.

"Looks like there's a smokehouse out back of the house, Roscoe," said Mean, "and don't forget to look in the privy. I'll check the barn and henhouse."

Sid flew into action. "Everybody quiet. Here's what we're goina do. We have to move slowly, so as not to frighten Serena. We need her help."

He didn't stop to think about breaking the law.

3.
Bounty Hunters

Sid watched nervously when August Mean got to the barn. Mean searched the feeding troughs behind the stanchions, the horse stable, the manger that held their hay, inspected the buggy, and looked under the wagon.

Pa was right behind, offering advice in the same slow drawl. It was funny. Pa prided himself on his crisp "Yankee" speech. Now he sounded like somebody from the South, like Ma. He was so helpful and friendly that if Sid hadn't known better, he'd have thought Pa wanted nothing more than to cooperate.

"Course there's the hayloft. Kids is up there playin' with some kittens," Pa said.

Sid cringed inwardly with every step the bounty hunter took up the ladder. Cora and Jimmy sat on a small pile of hay holding a kitten each. Cora was sucking her thumb. Ma was trying to break her of the habit, but now wasn't the time to say anything. Sid played with another, while beside him Serena groomed the fourth. The boy was nowhere to be seen. Sid silently prayed his plan would work. He was terrified that it wouldn't.

Taking her thumb from her mouth, Cora looked up at the bounty hunter. Sid nearly stopped breathing. *We're done for—there's no tellin' what she'll say.* He didn't dare try to stop her for fear of making it worse.

"You better be careful Mister, or Serena will get scared and move her kittens," Cora said. Sid silently let out a breath of relief.

"Well, little missy, we wouldn't want that now, would we," Mean said kindly. When he smiled, he looked as nice as anybody you would ever meet. "You youngens seen anybody crawl up here?"

They shook their heads. "No sir, we can't help you," said Sid. "Been up here near an hour, too."

Grabbing a pitchfork, Mean said, "I'm just goina fork this hay to make sure there ain't any runaways holed up for the day. Haylofts is one of their favorite hidin' places. They sleep in the day and travel by night. Reckon there could be somebody here as you don't know about. They can be plenty dangerous.

You youngens stay right where you are. I won't let you get hurt."

Sid watched tensely. August Mean gripped the pitchfork and stabbed the hay vigorously where Elijah had been only moments before.

"Nobody here," he said after a while, disappointment ringing in his voice. "Well, you youngens enjoy the kittens. And you, Son," he bent down, putting his hand on Sid's shoulder, "if your pa is tryin' to put somethin' over on the law, you'd best warn him agin it. I'd hate to see a fine boy like you haveta be head of the family 'cause his pa's in jail or been shot by some angry slave holder tryin' to claim his rightful property. There's real nice folk like your pa that think slaves is better off free. Truth of it is, slaves don't know the first thing about carin' for themselves. Slaves is better off with somebody to look after 'em. And it's *the law.* Remember that, you hear?"

"Yessir," said Sid, trying to stay calm as the man climbed down. He put his finger to his mouth, signaling Jimmy and Cora to be quiet and stay put.

"Whatcha' hidin' in here, Johnson?" Mean grabbed the latch to the corn crib door.

"Best not open that," Pa was right behind him. "Corn's dried on the cob. It'll fly out on ya. Once it's full, I take what I need from this here small door at the bottom. Ain't room in there for nothin' or nobody."

"Reckon that's why I'd better have a look," said Mean, grimly. "I caught more 'n one of 'em hidin' in a corn crib." He yanked the door open. Pa stepped aside as corncobs came raining down. Jumping to get out of the way, Mean let out a string of oaths, slipped, and landed on the floor. Corncobs pelted him.

Pa forced the door shut and gave the bounty hunter a hand to help him up.

August Mean didn't even say thank you. Nor did he volunteer to help clean up. Limping from the barn, he yelled angrily, "Find anything, Roscoe?"

Roscoe Bones called from the smokehouse. "Nobody here. I already searched the house top to bottom."

"Stay put, everybody," Sid said. "They might come back." He watched through the vent. Mean stormed into the chicken house. Chickens flew out of his way, flapping their wings and squawking.

The two men were grim-faced as they mounted their horses. "Consider this fair warnin', Johnson," yelled Mean. "Man with a fine family like yours oughta be more careful. You ain't heard the last of us. I mean to find those runaways. You been reported. Where there's smoke, there's fire, if you get my meanin'. Fire could do a lot of damage to a nice place like this."

As soon as the bounty hunters rode off, Sid told Cora and Jimmy to stand up. "Are you Elijah?" he asked, helping the boy out from under the hay where they had been sitting.

The boy nodded, ducking down again as Pa returned to the barn.

"You youngsters better come in the house," Pa called, pausing at the foot of the ladder. "Here, I'll help Cora down. Come here, Sugar Plum."

"Come up here a minute, Pa, please?" Sid asked.

Elijah cowered in the corner behind Cora and Jimmy as Pa's head reached the top of the ladder. "We found Elijah," said Sid.

"Thank God!" said Pa. "Elijah, your mamma's with us, got here last night. She's worried sick about you. You'd best stay here till it gets dark, though. Those bounty hunters will be watching the place. They know you're here; they just don't know where.

We'll get you some food and water. Soon as your mamma says so, we'll help you on your way. You may have to lie low tonight."

"Yessir," said Elijah, still wide-eyed.

"Jimmy, take Cora back to the house," said Pa, lifting her from the ladder. "Sid and I will get this corn picked up. Have to say it was worth it to see that bounty hunter dance. Happens every time. They insist on opening that door. That man's language would fry bacon. I'm sorry you had to hear him."

"I can hep, Sir," said Elijah. He looked down from the loft, as if he were waiting for permission.

"Come on down," said Pa, "I appreciate your offer, but I don't want to risk you being in sight. You try to get some rest. I'm going to make a place for you down here. It will be safer. Those two scoundrels won't give up so easily. Somebody's reported us. They'll watch every move we make."

As Elijah came down the ladder, Pa took in a sharp breath. Sid gasped. For the first time, he noticed that Elijah's torn shirt was in strips across the back, sticking to him in places. They had piled hay over him, and Cora and Jimmy sat on it to hide him from the bounty hunters. He hadn't let out a sound. It must have hurt terribly.

"Let me have a look, Son." Pa inspected Elijah's back, shaking his head. "There's no fire in hell too hot for the person who'd do a thing like this. We need to get those wounds cleaned up. I'll get the Missus out here to take care of you. Sid, fetch a bucket of water from the pump. Bring it through the front. Leave the barn doors open. Won't look so much like we're trying to hide something."

Elijah was nowhere in sight when Sid returned with a bucket of water. Pa was busy shoveling corn into a bushel basket.

As soon as he saw Sid, Pa let himself into the stable and lifted the top of the manger where they kept fresh hay for the horses. He set it on the floor of the pen. Sid was flabbergasted. There was Elijah on his stomach resting on a bed of clean hay in a space Sid didn't even know existed. Pa lifted his hand to silence him before he could say anything.

He had a box of clean rags, too. "Give him a drink first," Pa said softly. "I'm going back to work where I can be seen." He gently placed his hand on Elijah's shoulder. "Sid will put some wet rags on your back, Son.

We have to soften up those places where your shirt is stuck.

"Sid, when Elijah's had a good drink, wet a few rags in the bucket, enough to cover his back. Lay them on gently over the shirt. It's bound to hurt, but it will hurt a whole lot less if that shirt can come off nice and easy when Ma cleans the wounds. Then come help me get this corn cleared up."

Elijah had a good long drink from the bucket. Following Pa's directions, he lay back down on his stomach.

"I'm sorry, Elijah," Sid apologized as he placed the first wet rag. Elijah didn't flinch. When he had a layer of wet rags covering Elijah's back, Sid picked up a shovel and went to work with Pa. His eyes burned with tears. Whatever had been used on him had left Elijah's back marked with long gashes. Sid had never seen anything like it.

"I know, Sid," said Pa. "A person can see a wagon load of terrible things, and still, something like this brings tears to his eyes."

"But Pa," said Sid, sniffling, "that man spoke so kindly to Cora. He looked like a real nice man. How could he think Elijah would be better off with somebody who'd do that to 'em?"

"Money. They collect a lot of reward money. It's not just bounty hunters. The whole slave system is based on money. That's why it's so hard to get rid of it." Pa paused, leaning on his shovel for a moment. "But you know, Sid, there's usually good in the worst of us. I reckon most of the mischief and a lot of the evil in this world is done by people who think they're doing good. You can't reason with them. They figure out a way to turn things around so they can feel like they're doing the right thing."

"Like sayin' that slaves are better off with their masters," said Sid.

As they cleared away the last of the corn, Pa said in a low voice, "Sid, your ma and I have been meaning to tell you. I don't hold with breaking the law. But the law that says one man can own another is wrong. Doesn't matter if a slaveholder treats slaves with kindness; if they were really kind, they'd free them and pay them wages for their work."

"I'm glad you're helpin' people," said Sid, and he meant it. "It's the right thing to do."

"There are so many slaves in this country. So few ever escape from it," said Pa, shaking his head. Sid had never heard him sound so discouraged.

"The law doesn't protect people like Elijah. A slaveholder can do what he likes, and the law is on his side."

"Why can't we change the law?"

"We keep trying," said Pa. "You're a good boy, Sid. You have a kind heart. That was a smart thing you did to save Elijah."

Pa went over to the manger, "We'll keep a watch over you, Elijah. I'm putting the top to this manger back in place. You'll be safe. Hasn't been a bounty hunter find it yet. Try to rest. The Missus will be out directly to bring you some food and take care of your back. She'll be singing 'Amazing Grace'. You know it?"

"Yessir," said Elijah.

"If she's singing, you're safe. If she stops, don't make a sound. She'll be back when she can. If anybody knocks on the manger or calls to say you're safe, don't believe it. If I come for you, I'll sing 'Amazing Grace,' too, though it won't be as pretty."

"I never guessed, Pa," Sid said as they left for the house, "all the times I put hay in that manger, I never suspected. And, Pa . . ." Sid confessed that he had been eavesdropping.

"Should have told you sooner," said Pa. "Just as well you knew. Otherwise, that young man would have been caught. I just hope Jimmy and Cora can keep this to themselves."

Gathering his courage, Sid said, "So we're part of the Underground Railroad. Is it really underground?"

"It's not really a railroad, Son. It's places people can hide and rest on their way to freedom. So yes, we are one of those places."

They washed up on the back porch. "Who's the slave stealer?" asked Sid, drying his face on a rough, cotton hand towel—it was one Ma had made from a flour sack.

Pa furrowed his brow, "Where did you hear about a slave stealer?"

"I dunno, maybe at school?" Sid hedged. He wasn't sure he should say how much he'd heard when he listened to Ma and Pa. "Like Captain Walker, but somebody else, somebody who steals slaves and brings 'em across the Illinois border. It's just a name I heard."

"Hmm," said Pa. "First of all, it isn't stealing to give somebody back what was theirs in the first place. Second, it might be a person, might be more than one person. We don't ask questions, Son. And we don't pass on names." He closed the door to the porch behind them.

The welcoming smell of a pot of ham and beans simmering on the stove greeted them. "Sadie, we've found Elijah."

"Thank God!" said Ma. She looked at Sid, then at Pa, her eyes asking a silent question.

"I've told him, Sadie. Best he knows as little as possible, though."

"I've already told Lula," said Ma. "Cora and Jimmy couldn't wait to tell. They're playin' inside. I don't want 'em out where a bounty hunter could find 'em. I wish they didn't know."

"Can't be helped," said Pa. "That young man's back looks bad. He's taken a beating. May be why he and his mamma left."

"Reckon I'd better kill a chicken for dinner," said Ma, like she wasn't paying any attention.

It didn't make any sense. Why would Ma kill a chicken with a pot of ham and beans already cooking? *Maybe she's changed her mind.*

"Sid, fetch me a cabbage from the root cellar, please?" Ma began putting some things in a gray-speckled enamel pail: milk, bread, a slice of ham. "While you're out there, I need you to get a pan of rainwater and set it on the stove to boil, *if* you can get to the rain barrel. I don't know when you plan to get those weeds cleared out like I asked. That whole patch is dryin' up and goin' to seed. You'll have twice as much work to do next summer."

Sid cringed. He hated chopping weeds. They brushed against him as he made his way to the rain barrel, some almost too tall to see over. Had it been that long since he promised to clear them out?

"What worries me is somebody has reported us," Pa was saying as Sid returned to the kitchen. "Those bounty hunters had the legal papers to search our place. That means they had to be able to show good cause. When I was in town, Sherriff McDown told me we'd best be minding our P's and Q's. Course he wouldn't say more than that, but I knew something was up." Turning to Sid, he added, "He couldn't deny their warrant. That means he had the sworn testimony of somebody who has seen something—"

"Or says they've seen somethin'," said Ma, pulling several large leaves from the cabbage. She washed them off.

Sid's jaw dropped, "Who would do that?"

"I don't care to speculate, Son," said Pa.

"Wouldn't want to start feeling ill toward any of our neighbors. Best to be tight-lipped anyway."

Ma laid the cabbage leaves out on a clean rag and began rolling them with her rolling pin.

"Make a fire under the iron kettle, Sid. Your Ma will need hot water if she's going to pluck a chicken."

"What about Elijah?" Sid asked.

Ma didn't answer his question. She rolled up the soppy cloth that held the crushed cabbage leaves and put it along with the things she was collecting in the speckled pail. She poured the boiling rainwater into a jar.

"Whatcha put a knife in the jar for?" Jimmy asked, on his way through the kitchen.

"Keeps the jar from breaking as I pour in hot water," said Ma. "I need you to make sure Cora stays in the house while I'm out dressin' a chicken, Jimmy. Reckon you can do that without gettin' into a fuss? It's very, very important or I wouldn't ask."

"Sure, Ma," said Jimmy, swelling with pride. "How come it's dressin' a chicken? Looks like you're undressin' it to me." He didn't wait for an answer. Grinning, he was off to the next thing.

Sid gathered and piled wood under the cast iron cauldron kept near the barn. They used the cauldron to heat water for laundry and jobs requiring more than a teakettle could hold. By the time he had filled it from the pump by the stock tank and had the fire going, Pa had killed a hen. Ma would plunge the chicken into a bucket of boiling water and pluck off the feathers. Sometimes Sid plucked the chicken for her.

"Not today, Sid," Ma said. "I need you to keep an eye on Jimmy and Cora. We can't have 'em out talkin' to the world. I'll take care of things here."

"But I thought—"

Ma interrupted before he could finish. "When you're busy doin' somethin' regular, people who are watchin' lose interest. They don't watch so close. It's the best way to do what needs to be done without bein' noticed. Now run along." She began humming "Amazing Grace."

Sid reluctantly obeyed. He wanted to be where Elijah was, but he knew he had to follow orders. If he didn't, something might go wrong. Elijah could be captured.

Somehow, in the middle of plucking and dressing a chicken, Ma was going to make her way into the barn. She would clean Elijah's back with the warm rainwater. Then she would lay the juicy cabbage leaves over his wounds, leaving them there to draw out any infection. How many times had she done this very thing right under his nose?

That afternoon at dinner, Pa told Jimmy and Cora that they must never tell anybody about finding Elijah. "Not even the preacher?" asked Jimmy.

"Nobody, not even the preacher, or your teacher, or your friends," said Pa. "Anybody we tell is in danger."

4.
Buying Some Time

Cora and Jimmy were in bed, fast asleep, when Sid finally met Elijah's mother. She was a tall, graceful woman with hair cropped close to her head. Dressed in a man's shirt and trousers, she sat at the kitchen table with Ma.

Pa said he thought they ought to stay out of sight a couple of nights. "Elijah's back needs some time to heal. I can take you to a safe place up in Alton on Monday; they'll get you on up-river. My wagon has gone past many a bounty hunter."

Lula was determined to leave. "I sure appreciate what you've done. I know the boy is in bad shape. I did the best I could, but there wasn't time. Our guide came and we had to run. We can't stop running now. We were told we'd be safe here, that you could give the boy the care he needs. We're supposed to meet up again, where the

Mississippi joins the Illinois River, by dawn tomorrow. If we aren't there, we'll be left behind. I'm afraid we have to take the risk."

"That's a fair piece up the road. If you miss your connection, we can get you to the next safe place on the way up to British North America," said Pa.

Lula shook her head. "No, Sir. My family will meet us there with the guide. We could lose track of them. We can't afford to take that risk."

Sid couldn't help noticing the way Lula spoke, more like Pa than Ma. He wondered if she'd been to school. It was illegal to educate slaves in some states. Some kids at school said the way slaves talked was ignorant. Ma said kids at school didn't know what they were talking about. "How you talk depends on lots of things, like where you come from. Your Pa and I don't talk the same. You chil'ren talk in-between both of us."

"Lula, I'm puttin' up some food for you to take," said Ma. "No tellin' when you'll get a real meal again. I got Elijah's back cleaned up. There's some infection, but I think the poultice I put on will take care of that. It is goina need some more attention, though. I'll give you somethin' you can use when you have a chance.

"Ben, I reckon you should take some butter and eggs over to the widow."

"Mrs. Harold?" Sid asked, regretting it immediately. Ma and Pa both frowned at him.

"Here's what we do," Pa explained. "When it gets dark, I'll take the buggy and draw the bounty hunters off by heading out to our neighbor's house in the opposite direction. They'll think I'm taking you over to the Wabash. That will buy you some time."

Lula nodded.

Pa continued, "When I hitch up the buggy, I'll tell Elijah to wait till Sadie throws a pan of dishwater on the nasturtiums at the back door. That will be his signal to meet you in the garden. Make your way back through the orchard, then follow the creek going north. It will take you up to Alton. If you run into trouble, take shelter in the smokehouse behind that big brick house that overlooks the creek a ways up. It backs up against the church yard on the edge of Alton. It's about four miles up the road."

"Folk there will help you," said Ma. There's no dogs to worry about."

"When you see the church steeple," said Pa, "you'll know you're in the right place. There's a mill along the creek where you can shelter. There's also a Friends Meeting House near the Mississippi. That's a safe place, too."

"We know of these places," said Lula.

"Good," said Pa. "Sid, bring me the butter and eggs when I pull the buggy up to the house."

Sid didn't get to see Elijah or where Lula had hidden. "Better that you don't know, Sid," said Ma. "If you don't know, then you can answer honestly if you're ever asked."

"I shouldn't have said Mrs. Harold's name," said Sid.

"No, you shouldn't. We use names, but only given names or code names. Lula and Elijah wouldn't mean to tell. We wouldn't either, but, Sid, people do some awful things to get information."

The autumn nights were getting cooler. Elijah's thin cotton shirt was in tatters, and he was barefoot. "Elijah needs some new clothes," said Sid. "Reckon he's about my size." He got a pair of his trousers, a heavier shirt, and a pair of shoes and socks for Elijah.

As he gathered up the clothes, Sid acted on an impulse. He wrote on a piece of paper, "Good luck." Then he added, "We're praying for you." He didn't write his name or Elijah's on it. He figured Elijah would know. If Elijah couldn't read it, Sid felt sure his mamma could. He put the paper and the stub of a pencil in one of the pockets. Pa said he'd take the clothes when he went to hitch up the buggy.

Ma gave Lula a work shirt to put over her shirt. "It's darker, and heavier. It'll protect you from the underbrush and the cold."

Their plan worked like a well-oiled machine. It was nearly dark when Pa went to the barn. The clothes for Elijah made a big lump under his coat. They watched from the kitchen window. "He's tryin' to look suspicious, but not too suspicious. Those two bounty hunters will be watchin'," said Ma.

They could barely see Pa in the fading light. He looked to right and left, then quietly opened the barn door. He was gone for what seemed an age before he reappeared leading their horse, Sandy, hitched to the buggy. He left the barn door open. When the buggy stopped by the back porch, Sid carried out a bowl of butter and small basket of eggs. Pa put them in the buggy and hopped in.

When Sid stepped back into the house, Lula was not there. He never saw her or Elijah again. He had a sunken feeling, wishing he could have said goodbye.

It was pitch dark outside when Ma threw a pan of water out the back door. Sid watched, but there was no sign of Elijah leaving the barn, or of Lula leaving the house. Ma said if they were lucky, they'd get a riverboat all the way to Chicago, or even into British North America. Now that it was illegal to give sanctuary to freedom seekers, they had to go all the way to British North America to be safe.

When Pa returned, Ma let Sid run out to help him unharness Sandy. Pa didn't have anything to say until they were back in the house.

Ma had hot cocoa waiting. "Why, Sid, where are your shoes?" she asked. "It's too cold to run around barefoot. And at night, too."

Pa looked at him, then at Ma. He didn't say anything.

Sid swallowed hard. "He didn't have any shoes."

Ma set the steaming cocoa on the table, kissing him on the top of the head. "How did

Widow Harold like her butter and eggs?" she asked, turning to Pa.

Pa grinned. "Sandy gave those two bounty hunters a good run for it before they forced us off the road. They gave the buggy a work-over. I figured the longer they took, the more distance between them and Lula and Elijah.

"They were plenty angry. Like I told them, all I had with me was butter and eggs for my poor widow neighbor. They headed back toward the creek, lickety-split. God help them, Lula and Elijah will need every inch of distance we could give them.

"Mrs. Harold sent you some pound cake."

Sid wasn't sure how things worked, but it sounded like Mrs. Harold must be in on it. He hadn't given much thought to it when Pa took butter and eggs to their neighbor, but now, as he thought about it, there wasn't any predictable schedule. Sometimes they went weeks without taking her anything, then two or three times in a row. *Why would she need butter and eggs anyway? She has her own farm. And she sure isn't helpless.* Mrs. Harold had two grown sons.

Pa looked at him as if he knew what Sid was thinking. "Don't ask questions, Son. Nobody knows any more than they have to." Reaching for a piece of pound cake, he added, "You can't tell what you don't know."

That wasn't all, either. Once he was on the alert, Sid made another discovery. Nobody said any more about a slave stealer, but sometimes Pa left the house at night carrying his gun. When that happened, he didn't get home until nearly dawn. Sid wondered what else was going on right under his nose. He couldn't fault them any longer for breaking the law, not after seeing Elijah. *But what will I do if they're caught?*

5.

Where There's Smoke

Sid was in the middle of a game of tag in the churchyard when he noticed the tall brick house facing the creek. He had seen it every Sunday for as long as he could remember. It was different now. His eyes searched out the smokehouse behind, wondering. *Did Elijah and Lula take shelter there?* He sighed. *I'll never know.* He looked down at his new shoes. They weren't broken in yet. They pinched his feet.

"Sid! You're 'It.' What are you waitin' for?" somebody called.

It was a balmy autumn afternoon, perfect weather for Dinner on the Grounds Sunday. After the morning church service, the men set up tables outdoors under graceful chestnut oak trees that surrounded the churchyard. The leaves were beginning to turn. In a few weeks, the first hard frost would send them to carpet the ground in gold. As he carried their picnic hamper from the buggy, Sid thought maybe fall was his favorite time of year. *I hope Pa wasn't serious about goin' to California.* He was curious about Uncle Luke and faraway places. Even so, Sid didn't think he'd want to live anywhere else in the world.

His mouth watered as the women set out one delicious looking dish after another. He hoped some of Ma's fried chicken would be left after the men finished serving them-selves. He was glad he was old enough to go through the line with the older boys, right after the men. Some of the girls said it wasn't fair, *but that's just girls for you*, he thought.

"Anybody hear tell of that slave steeler who's been operating down along the other side of the border?" One of the men sitting at a table nearby asked between bites. "My brother-in-law down in Missouri says he's lost two of his best to a slave stealer. Disap-peared just like that. Couldn't find a trace of them. He's not the only one to report losing slaves, either. Slave stealer follows the same pattern, but they can't catch him at it."

Sid caught his breath. He carried his heaping plate past the table, listening, and walking as slowly as he dared.

"Then I say more power to the slave stealer," said another man, waving the drumstick he'd been eating, as if he were trying to emphasize his point.

"Now you all know we don't talk politics at church," said another, changing the subject. "Anybody been to that barber who just set up shop in town? I hear he's chargin' 15 cents a cut and a dime for a shave."

"I'll tell you what!" somebody else said. "Prices are goin' sky high these days."

After dinner, the girls walked around the church in a long line with their arms around each other, while some of the boys had a competition to see who was best with the slingshot. Sid won the competition hands down. "Sid, I think you could take down Goliath with that sling," laughed one of the men. Sid curled the long, loose ends of his sling around its pouch and put it in his pocket. There wasn't any prize, but it felt good to win. There were more games before people returned to the church for a hymn-sing and another sermon.

The sun had not yet made its final drop behind the hills when they started home. As they got closer, Pa said, "I smell smoke.

Wonder if somebody's burning brush along the creek."

"I wouldn't think so, not on the Lord's Day," said Ma. "Just look at that sunset, all gold and pink. Isn't it a glory?"

"There's a fire somewhere," said Pa, urging Sandy ahead. "Better find out where; we might be able to help. As dry as it's been, somebody could be in real trouble."

As they topped the low hill that led down into the valley, where their farm began, Ma let out a startled cry, "It's our place, Ben! Please, God, not the house!"

The buggy careened down the road, Sandy at a full gallop. "It's the barn," screamed Jimmy. Cora burst into tears, burying her head in Ma's lap.

As they pulled into the broad driveway that led up to the house and farmyard, they could see fire licking around one side of the barn. "Sid," said Pa, handing him the reins, "leave Sandy hitched up. Tie her to the garden fence. Then come help me. We've got to stop it before it spreads. If it reaches the hay, we've lost the barn.

"Sadie, get Cora inside. Jimmy, get the milk buckets. Fill them at the stock tank. We'll make a bucket brigade. Sid, you throw water on the fire till your Ma can help. I'm going to try and get the wagon out."

"Don't you dare, Ben Johnson," said Ma, her voice as hard as steel. "There's nothin' in that barn worth your life."

The fire rapidly spread along the foundation, reaching the front of the barn. Flames licked at the barn doors, lighting them up. Sid thought his heart would stop. For an instant, flames leapt up, making it look like the letters SS were written in flames on the barn door.

There wasn't time to look twice. Pa handed him the reins. Sid turned Sandy toward the house. She was terrified. Her eyes bulged, and her nostrils flared as he tied her to the fence. It took a few precious minutes to settle her. When he looked again, the letters were no longer there. The doors to the barn were covered in flame. *Did I imagine it?* Flames ran around the foundation of the barn and along the back, too, as if the fire were being led along a path.

Before he could get to the wooden tank where the livestock were watered, a buggy came full speed into the yard. It was Mrs. Harold and her grown sons Jacob and Daniel. The men jumped from the buggy almost before Mrs. Harold pulled it to a stop near Sandy. Each of the men had a bucket and shovel. Without asking what to do, they handed the buckets to Sid and began shoveling dirt on the fire where they could reach it.

"Saw the smoke," said Mrs. Harold as she joined Ma at the watering tank. Jimmy filled the buckets with water, keeping Ma, Mrs. Harold, and Sid relaying it to Pa. Dousing the fire with water didn't seem to slow it down. It sputtered and flared. Like some living creature, it began climbing up the barn walls on all sides.

"There's a spade in the smokehouse, Jimmy. Get it!" yelled Pa. "Water is just making things worse. Sadie, move the water brigade over by the pasture back of the barn. Give it a good wetting along the fence."

The Davis family, neighbors to the north, drove in right after Mrs. Harold. They were on their way back from church, too, saw the flames, and didn't even stop at home. Mrs. Davis directed their daughter to stay in the house and keep watch over Cora, who stood on the porch crying.

Mr. Davis set up another bucket brigade to help keep the fire from spreading to the pasture. He put one of his two sons, both older than Sid, to pumping water from the well to replace what they were taking from the watering tank. It seemed hopeless, but the fight went on. The water brigades wet a long swath of grass and weeds along the back fence to the pasture. Sid's arms ached as he took bucket after bucket of water from Mrs. Harold.

Mr. Davis redirected his bucket brigade to water down the chicken house, so it wouldn't catch fire. The chickens had been asleep since sunset. Now they staggered out into the yard, too sleepy to protest the water splashing on them through their windows. They settled in a dazed heap along the side of the stock tank away from the water brigades.

Despite their best efforts, arms of flame appeared at the barn windows, orange against the night sky. Sid gasped as a column of black smoke and a sudden burst of flame shot out of the vent in the hayloft. A blazing inferno covered the roof in seconds. The whole barn was alight. "We've lost it," Pa said wearily. "All we can do now is protect the house and pasture."

Sid stood frozen, watching as the flames claimed the barn. The cattle had broken through their pen in terror. Now they milled around the yard with the few chickens that hadn't found their place in the heap by the watering tank. "Boys, round up these cows," Mr. Davis ordered, jarring Sid back into action. "Head 'em into the pasture."

Sid turned to help with the cattle when he saw Cora. Unseen in the confusion, she had escaped from the Davis girl. Running at full speed, she headed straight for the barn. "Serena! Kitty, kitty," she screamed. "Serena! Get Serena and the kittens!" Tears gushed down her face.

The Davis girl was right behind her. "No, no, Cora! Come back," she cried, grabbing her hand as Cora crossed the driveway.

Cora pulled free.

"No, Cora," Sid yelled, running to intercept her. A burning beam crashed ahead, sending sparks dangerously close. But Cora kept going.

Sid threw himself at her, tackling her around the waist. She tried to wrench free, kicking and screaming as they fell to the ground. "Serena! Serena!" she sobbed.

"Cora, we can't get Serena," Sid panted, pinning her to the ground, holding her as tightly as he could. "When she smelled the smoke, I'll bet she got the kittens out." He wasn't at all confident that she had, but he had to calm Cora down. In her state, he couldn't be sure that she wouldn't run straight into the fire to try and save the cat.

"I tried to keep her inside, Sid," cried the Davis girl.

Suddenly Mrs. Harold was there. "Don't you worry, little darling," she said, bending over them. Sid could feel Cora relax. She quit fighting him. Reaching down, Mrs. Harold lifted Cora from his arms. Nodding to the Davis girl, who stood nearby with tears running down her cheeks, Mrs. Harold said, "Come here, Cora. We'll go looking for kitty, us three. Cats are real smart. I'll bet she will be somewhere away from the fire with every one of her kittens, safe and sound."

Sid pulled himself up, still out of breath. Cora slid down from Mrs. Harold's arms and took her hand. They walked back toward the house and away from the fire, Mrs. Harold on one side and the Davis girl on the other. "We will look for hiding places around the house. That's where I'd expect a smart cat like Serena to take her babies," Mrs. Harold said. She gave Sid a look that told him she wasn't so sure about Serena either.

More neighbors came. Some of them, like the Davis family, were on their way home from church. Others lived close enough to see the red glow from the barn. They offered sympathy, doing what they could to help. The biggest problem now was putting out fires that flared up in the farmyard as pieces of blazing wood fell from the barn, sending sparks everywhere. The barn was far enough from the house that it would not pose an extreme threat unless the wind whipped up.

Sid looked around for what to do next. Smoke hung in the air like a heavy black fog, burning his eyes, making it harder to see as night settled in.

With a loud crash, the barn collapsed in a blazing heap. It looked like a volcano as burning fragments and sparks erupted into the air.

The wind whipped up. No longer a breeze, it cleared the air. But it also sent sparks and burning bits of wood dangerously close to the house and the dry lawn in front. Jimmy's bucket brigade was redirected to relay water to the lawn to contain the threat. Somebody produced a ladder and climbed up on the roof of the house to make sure it was protected.

Sid was refilling his buckets at the stock tank when he saw a curl of smoke rising from the patch of weeds by the smokehouse. Nobody else seemed to notice. "There's a fire startin' over by the smokehouse," he called. Heading toward it, he tried to stifle the panic that seized him. Nobody seemed to hear him. Smoldering weeds now burst into flames. He had to put the fire out before it spread to the smokehouse. If the smokehouse caught fire, it would be nearly impossible to protect the house.

6.
The Smell of Burning

By the time Sid reached the weed patch, flames were rapidly eating their way toward the smokehouse. The fire hissed and sputtered when his first bucket of water hit. He barely phased it; the weeds were too dry. The second bucket wasn't going to be enough either. He was too late.

Thinking quickly, he raced ahead of the fire to the path by the smokehouse. *Got to slow it down. If I can just get to the rain barrel.* He splashed the second bucket of water across the top of the dry weeds as he ran. His only hope was that somebody would see and come to help. Flames fanned out across the tops of the weeds. His face tingled from the heat. The fire crackled and spit as it reached the wet weeds along the path. Helped along by the wind, it found dry spots, licking its way closer and closer to the smokehouse wall. In that awful moment, Sid realized there wasn't enough time to dip water out of the rain barrel and throw it on the fire, one bucket at a time.

He could never say afterward how he did it, but in those crucial seconds, Sid pulled the lid from the rain barrel. With every ounce of strength he could throw into it—strength he didn't even know he had—Sid tipped the half-full barrel over onto the weed patch. Water flooded through the weeds, pushing them over and away from the path itself, drenching the oncoming fire. He stood, shaking all over as Daniel Harold ran up to help, pouring two buckets of water out over the tops of the weeds where the fire still blazed. The fire sizzled and sputtered to a smoldering halt.

"You just saved the smokehouse, Sid," said Daniel, throwing an arm around him. "Good thinking. By the time I saw the blaze, I thought sure we'd lost it, too. Let me help you tip that barrel back up in place."

Sid felt too weak to move. He didn't have to. One of the Davis boys joined them, throwing water on the smoldering weeds as he came. "I'll give you a hand, Mr. Harold."

Sid watched the two of them right the barrel. "We were all focused on the house,

Sid," the Davis boy said. "I was on this end of the water brigade and just happened to look this way. That was really something you did. We'll have to get you a place as strong man in the circus when it comes to town."

Smiling weakly, Sid managed to get as far as the back steps of the porch, where he gratefully sat down. It was hard to feel like a hero when he knew the threat to the smokehouse was his fault. *It wouldna happened if I'd cleared the weed patch like I promised Ma.* He watched as flames devoured what remained of the barn. Like the last few kernels of popcorn in a pan, sparks began bouncing up at irregular intervals. Finally, they quit flying about.

With the house no longer in danger, people began leaving. Those who had been to Dinner on the Grounds left the remains of their picnic baskets. "The last thing you need to be worryin' about is cookin' supper," one of the women said to Ma.

Everyone but the Davis family, Mrs. Harold, Jacob, and Daniel had gone home when Sheriff McDown rode up on horseback. The women were clustered in the kitchen organizing left over potato salad, baked beans, and a generous supply of other delicious leftovers for a cold supper. The men huddled in a group near the back steps to the house where Sid still sat. Somebody put a cup of cocoa in his hand.

Sandy was in the pasture with the workhorses now. Sid had no idea who had unhitched her from the buggy, or when. The cows and calves were all accounted for. The Davis boys were doing the evening milking. The chickens had been returned to their house. But Serena and her kittens were still unaccounted for. Sid ached inside with worry. The fire moved so quickly. *Did she have time to escape? And what about the kittens?*

"I don't want to be an alarmist, Ben, but I reckon you know that fire didn't just happen," said Mr. Davis. "The way it spread around the foundation all at once and exploded, straight up to the roof—"

"It brought the barn down mighty quick," said Jacob Harold.

Sid listened intently.

"Black smoke and sputtering when we threw water on it—sure signs in my book," Mr. Davis said. "Anybody else smell turpentine?"

"I'd say the foundation was laced with it," said Daniel Harold. "We could stop it with dirt, but we weren't fast enough. It got ahead of us."

Maybe somebody painted S.S. on the barn doors with turpentine. The thought occurred to Sid. But it didn't make sense.

Sheriff McDown spoke up, "Some of these bounty hunters and trackers are getting real aggressive. They seem to think anybody with a barn could be harboring runaways. They'll do just about anything to smoke 'em out. But this is the first time I've seen anything like this around here, Ben. I'll come back in the morning and have a good look. My guess is nothing will tie this to anybody. They're too careful."

"Times are getting real tense." Mr. Davis said.

Daniel Harold mopped his brow with a large handkerchief. "We're too close to Missouri," he said. Lifting his hat, he ran the handkerchief over his curly black hair. "Slaveholders over there are ruthless in tracking down people who get away. Shoot, Jacob and me carry our papers with us all the time. If we're caught without them, we could be sold to the highest bidder. Bounty hunter would take us in a minute, too, if they had a chance."

Jacob shook his head. "Time was when Missouri held to the principle of 'once free always free,' but that day is gone. I won't let the wife and youngens off the place unless one of us is with 'em."

"That's just playing it smart, Jacob," said Sheriff McDown. "They wouldn't be asking to see your papers. Free Negroes are kidnapped and sold down South all the time."

"All they'd have to do is drag us back across the Missouri state line," said Daniel. "Wouldn't matter what we had to say."

Sheriff McDown frowned. "The State of Illinois won't accept the testimony of a Negro anyway. They would accept your adoption papers, but not if a bounty hunter burned them."

"They'd burn them, too." Mr. Davis shook his head, looking at the barn. "Can't think of a worse time for a fire, Ben, with winter coming on."

*How **are** we gonna take care of the animals this winter?* Sid hadn't thought that far ahead.

"I'll have a word with the preacher," Mr. Davis said. "Maybe we can organize an old-fashioned barn raising."

"It won't replace the feed for your livestock, but I expect there's plenty of other neighbors who will help out," said Jacob Harold. "We still have to bring in the rest of the corn in that field across the creek. You're welcome to share it."

"I don't know," said Pa. "It's mighty good of you, but Sadie and I have been thinking about joining my brother out in California. I might just sell off the cattle this fall and move on when spring comes."

California. Sid felt it like a slap in the face. He hoped Pa wasn't serious.

"Well, I can't say as I'd blame you," Mr. Davis said. "A war over slavery is staring us in the face. Slave states aren't going to budge so long as they're making money from it. Still, we'd sure hate to lose good neighbors."

Sid didn't hear the rest of the conversation. Something brushed against his leg. He looked down to see Serena. "Did you move your kittens in time, Serena?" he asked. She must not be too troubled. She was purring. He scooped her up into his arms and rushed into the house to tell Cora.

Cora already knew. She was all smiles. "We found Serena. She was in a cozy place under the smokehouse."

"With her kittens," the Davis girl added. "They are so cute, all cuddled up there on the far side of the smokehouse."

Sid shuddered at the thought. A few seconds and Serena's safe place wouldn't have been so safe.

The next morning, he awoke to the smell of burning. The barn was still smoldering. Pa said it would smolder for days. Sid figured he'd have to go after the cows and bring them in for milking. He didn't. The cows were waiting at the fence. He wondered how they felt about not having a barn.

He and Jimmy stayed home from school. They weren't allowed to go near the barn, though.

Sheriff McDown came early. As Sid and Pa walked around the barn site with him, he said "Some ugly things have been happening. I've been pretty successful at looking the other way at what goes on down here with you and over at Widow Harold's. It's getting harder and harder to get around enforcing the law. You have to stop, Ben. You need to think about the safety of your family. And you need to look to the safety of those you've been helping. Anybody looking to you for shelter is sure to get caught. I expect the

Harold men will know how to get word out on the Grapevine. God help 'em, I hope so."

"You didn't hear about a woman and her son being caught a night or two ago, did you?" asked Pa.

Sheriff McDown's face relaxed. "Not on my watch. August Mean and Roscoe Bones after them? They've been through here more than once. But I know these woods better than they do. So do my dogs. We just happened to be down at the creek the other night. Didn't see the woman and her son, but we ran into Mean and Bones. My dogs are real good at taking the lead. I'll leave the rest to your imagination.

"Fact is, I wouldn't put something like burning your barn past that pair. You gotta admit, Mean and Bones are the right names—they're mean to the bone, both of 'em."

Suddenly he bent down. "Just what I figured." Sheriff McDown held up a stick. One end was covered with something thick and black. "Pine tar. I expect they threw a few of these around the barn. That and a little turpentine would do it."

When the sheriff left, Sid asked, "Do you think Lula and Elijah got away?"

"Son, in this business, we can only do our bit along the way and pray it comes out right. We never know for sure."

"Pa," Sid worked up his courage, "did you see S.S. in the flames on the barn doors before they burned up?"

Pa gave him a puzzled look. "No, I didn't, or I would have told Sheriff McDown. Maybe it was a trick of the light."

"I don't think it was a trick of the light," said Sid. "Why would anybody do that?"

"If they did, it would be to terrorize anybody trying to help people to freedom. It would be like saying, 'This is what you can expect.'"

Pa was convinced that it was time to move west. Ma might not have ever agreed to pack up and go to California if the barn hadn't burned. But Sheriff McDown was right. They could no longer be a safe house for people on their way to freedom, not for some time to come. They thought it was time to move on. Sid wasn't so sure.

7.
Sounds in the Night

It wasn't a gunshot that made Sid sit up in bed. Nor could he hear dogs baying in the distance. A quiet shuffling sound—a sound he'd heard before—roused him. It was the sound Ma said was the language of an old house at night. This time he bolted downstairs before it stopped, compelled to be a part of what was happening. He didn't ask himself if it was a good idea or he might have waited.

A single candle burned on the table. Ma and Pa were helping a man through the kitchen. Startled, Ma looked up, a frown crossing her face when she saw Sid. Pa gave him a look that said he hadn't any business being there. "The boy's seen us, Sadie. We might as well take care of things right here. Just stay out of the way, Sid."

Sid couldn't understand why they were so peeved with him. *It's not like I didn't help with Elijah.*

They eased the man into a chair. It was then that Sid noticed Pa was carrying an iron ball attached to a long chain shackled to the man's ankle. Pa set it down carefully and got the man a glass of water. Ma began dabbing the man's forehead with a wet rag where a gash was crusted over with dried blood. "Put the kettle on, Sid," she said. "You may as well be helpful." Sid was relieved to have something to do.

The man was breathing hard. Pa took off what remained of his shoes. Far too big for him, they were worn through at the soles and without laces. "That was close," said Pa. "Glad you made it. You can see the barn's gone. It's still smoldering. Bounty hunters. There hasn't been time to get the word out on the Grapevine. Maybe you can help pass it along. You meeting someone?"

"On my own," said the man. "Didn' plan on leavin' 'fore next week"—he winced as if somebody had just smacked him in the face—"somethin' happen. Met folk headin up to de Illinois. Couldn't go fast 'nough to keep up. Guide said y'all could hep."

"Don't worry," said Pa. "Folk tell us it's hard to make it on your own. We'll get you to the next place where you can wait for a guide, or they can help you catch a boat. We lost our wagon in the fire, so we have some figuring to do. We'll make it work. Meanwhile, we have to get this shackle off. Unfortunately, it will have to wait until tomorrow." Pa sighed. "All my equipment was lost in the fire."

Equipment? Sid wondered, but he knew better than to ask.

"You can stay here as long as you need," Ma said. "Couple of months ago we had a family stay for near a month before it was safe for 'em to leave.

"What would you like us to call you?"

"Joseph," the man said. Sid hardly heard him. *A family in the house for a month without me knowing anything about it?*

The tea kettle began singing. "Sid, would you chop up an onion for me?" asked Ma. "Small bits. I don't have a cabbage in the house. There's an onion in the basket under the worktable. Be careful. I don't like the way your ankles look, Joseph, 'specially the right one. Wish those shackles could come off. I'm puttin' an onion poultice on it."

The man smiled faintly. "My Missus woulda done..." The sad, pained look returned to his face.

Meanwhile, Pa poured boiling water into one of the speckled pans, cooling it down with a couple of dippers of drinking water from the bucket that sat on the worktable. He had the man put his feet in the pan to soak and began unwinding rags Joseph had wrapped around the shackle to protect his ankle. Joseph winced. "Must hurt," said Pa. "Looks like it's pretty raw in places. I don't see how you managed to run, having to carry that thing." He nodded at the iron ball. "Give your feet a good soak then the Misses can get them doctored up. I'm gonna scramble you an egg. Want some ham with it?"

"Yessir," said Joseph, wincing as Ma worked on his ankles.

Sid poured boiling water over the chopped onion. While the bits soaked, Pa had him cut a couple of slices of Ma's good bread and butter them.

"You want some coffee, or would you rather have cocoa?" asked Pa.

Joseph asked for cocoa.

By this time Ma had cleaned the wounds on Joseph's shackled ankles. "The poultice will help, so will a good night's rest. We'll see how it looks tomorrow when the shackles come off."

"Yessum," said Joseph. "Shore 'ppreciate it."

"Now Sid," said Pa, "as soon as Joseph has something to eat, we're going to move him. I want you to go back upstairs. I don't want you to know anything you don't have to know. Joseph's life depends on it."

"Good night, Sir," said Sid reluctantly. "And good luck." He didn't know what else to say. Part of him felt like bursting into tears. Another part felt grateful they could help Joseph. It was all mixed up with disappointment in not being allowed to know more, fear of being caught, and anger that any human being would be chained.

He'd heard about shackles. Sometimes bounty hunters made their way through Alton with captured slaves, but he rarely actually saw them and then only at a distance.

As Sid climbed the stairs, he wondered where in the world they were going to put Joseph and where they'd kept a whole family. He wondered, too, what people like Joseph would do if there wasn't a safe place to stop. And he wondered if Elijah had made it to safety. *There's no way to know,* he reminded himself. There was still the pressing question about slave stealers, too. What did Pa have to do with them? Why did he slip out at night sometimes, carrying his gun? *Is that why SS was on the barn door?*

There was no trace of Joseph when Sid came downstairs the next morning. Nor were there any tell-tale sounds in the house. Nobody said anything. It was as if it had never happened.

When they'd finished the morning milking, Sid couldn't hold back any longer. "How are you goina get him to the next place?"

"I haven't figured that out yet, Son," said Pa. "That ball must weigh at least 20 pounds. Someone was on his heels. It won't take them long to be back with dogs."

"How did you know he was here?" asked Sid.

"I can't tell you that," said Pa. "I will tell you that we had a double wagon bed on that wagon we lost in the fire. It was a narrow fit, but I could carry up to four people if I had to. I've thought of borrowing Mrs. Harold's wagon, but that would signal anybody watching us. Unfortunately, the buggy isn't equipped to handle that kind of work."

Sid puzzled over it all day at school, so much so that the teacher had to say something. He thought Sid was still distracted because of the fire. That evening well after Jimmy and Cora were in bed, Sid asked Ma if he could have some cocoa. She made a pan of cocoa—enough for all three of them.

"I have an idea," said Sid. "What if you had Joseph climb in one of the feed sacks in the smokehouse and put something around him, like you were goin' to the mill or to do trade. You could haul that in the buggy."

Pa seemed to consider it before answering. "Not a bad idea, Son, but if I'm stopped—and I'd expect to be—they'll run one of those thin spikes through the bag to make sure it's what I say it is. I don't think it would work."

"What if it was me drivin' Sandy?" Sid asked.

"I wouldn't want to take that risk," said Pa, "besides, they'd stop you, too."

Ma intervened. "Ben, what about some of that corn in the crib out behind the chicken house? It escaped the fire. What if Sid takes that to the mill to have it ground?"

Pa gave her a puzzled look.

"Well, he could take more than one trip," said Ma. "About the time he made his third trip, they'd probably let him pass. And he's a boy. I think he can get away with it, even if you can't. He might not even be stopped. People don't think chil'ren can do anything important."

"Let me think on it," said Pa. "It would still be risky to Joseph."

Friday evening after chores, Pa said, "Sid, we need to get some sacks filled with corn if you're going to get it to the mill tomorrow morning." Sid didn't know if he was more thrilled at being taken into Ma and Pa's confidence or frightened by what it meant. They carried three sacks of corn dried on the cob to the side of the smokehouse, where they propped them up in plain sight. Pa sewed two of them closed with a big needle and heavy string.

As they washed up on the back porch, Sid asked, "What do I do once I get to the mill?"

"I was about to get to that. Liam Robinson will know what to do. Tell him, 'Pa says to tell you he wants the usual grind but with a return.'"

"The miller is in on it?" Sid marveled. It was like a whole world existed that he didn't know anything about.

Pa didn't give him a direct answer. "If one of his boys meets the buggy, tell him your pa asked for you to see their pa. And remember to address Liam Robinson by his given and family names."

Sid knew that. He had known the miller and his family for as long as he could remember. But Pa still reminded him. "They don't hold with titles that put any man or woman ahead of another. Not a bad idea, if you think about it."

Sid could hardly sleep that night. He'd never expected to be in on a plot to help somebody to freedom. He wondered what he'd do if he were stopped, if he'd done the right thing in volunteering, if Ma and Pa were wise to have that much confidence in him. But morning came and he had to go on, fearful or not. *If I don't do this, they'll never think I can do anything*, he told himself.

Getting his chores done felt like trying to pour molasses on a cold day. Everything seemed to be in slow motion. It was all leading to the moment when Sandy was hitched to the buggy.

8.

A Dangerous Mission

Sid helped Pa put the first sack of corn on the floor next to the back seat of the buggy. "Be careful, Sid," said Ma.

He was off for the mill in Alton by half past nine o'clock. He'd driven alone to the Harold farm and up as far as the church, but never as far as the mill. It was a warm, sunny morning with just enough crispness in the air to remind Sid that it was late autumn. Once they turned out of the drive and uphill toward Alton, Sid began to relax. It wasn't long, though, before horses began following him. "Steady, Sandy," he called. "Just riders," though he was pretty sure that Sandy didn't need steadying as much as he did.

Three riders followed for a while before one of them came up alongside the buggy. The other two rode ahead, turning around and stopping in the middle of the road. They faced the buggy where they could block Sid from going forward. He slowed Sandy. The rider beside him tipped his hat. Sid tipped his hat in return, trying to look unconcerned, "Good day, Sir," he said.

"And a good day to you, Son." Unlike the bounty hunters after Elijah and his mamma, this man looked like a perfect gentleman. He was wearing a fancy coat, riding breeches, and leather boots that came to his knees. "Might I trouble you to pull over for a moment?" the man asked. "My name's Alfred Pedigrew. I'm a landowner out of Crittenden County, Kentucky. I'm on the lookout for my slave Joseph—ran away near a week ago. He's a dangerous man, violent. I tracked him to the Kentucky border, where he met up with a group of runaways. I tracked them up to the other side of that creek over yonder. The trail vanishes right around here. Looks like the work of some slave stealer to me. We are checkin' everyone goin' up toward the Illinois."

Sid brought Sandy to a halt; Pa had told him exactly what he must do. "Yessir, Mr. Pedigrew. Would you like me to get down?"

Mr. Pedigrew nodded. "What do you have in that bag? It's big enough to hide a grown man."

"I'm haulin' corn to the mill today, Sir," said Sid. "Our barn just burned down this week and we lost our wagon. Fortunately, we didn't lose any livestock. But we need some more feed."

"Sorry to hear about your barn," said Mr. Pedigrew, "you'll forgive me for checkin' the bag."

Even though he knew that he wasn't carrying Joseph on this trip, Sid held his breath.

Mr. Pedigrew drew a long, thin spike from a scabbard at his side. He drove it into the bag, wiggling it past corn cobs, getting it stuck, pulling it out, and stabbing again. Sid flinched with every stab. Mr. Pedigrew examined the buggy. He didn't take out the seats, but he did inspect them carefully. He looked under the buggy, tapping with his long spike. "Just the one bag today?"

"Yessir, for this trip, Mr. Pedigrew. We could have put another up on the seats, but Ma was against it. She doesn't want the seats all marked up." Sid said his rehearsed lines, trying to sound casual. He didn't feel casual.

"Leave it to the women folk," said Mr. Pedigrew, smiling. "You're all clear. You needn't worry, Son. If you aren't doin' anything illegal there is nothin' to fear."

"Yessir, Mr. Pedigrew, but there is somethin' scary about havin' your things searched." Pa hadn't told him to say that. It just came out.

Mr. Pedigrew laughed, a kind, almost musical laugh. "Yes, I suppose there is. Run along to the mill then."

It was just as Pa had predicted. Even so, Sid was in a cold sweat as he and Sandy moved on. When they got to the mill, Liam Robinson was the one who greeted him. "Welcome, Sid Johnson. Thee is getting to be a man now, driving into Alton by thyself." Liam Robinson spoke the plain speech of the Quakers. "Thee is taller than when I saw thee last. What can I do for thee today?"

"Pa said to tell you that he couldn't get in, Liam Robinson. He wants the usual grind, but with a return."

"Pull the buggy on inside then," said Liam Robinson. "It won't take long."

A stone archway allowed wagons to be drawn into the building where grain was unloaded and livestock and chicken feed or cornmeal, oat, and wheat flour were loaded. It wasn't until then that Sid realized one of the riders had followed him all the way to the mill.

The mill was a stone building built out over a fast-flowing creek that emptied into the Mississippi, not far from the place that the great Mississippi and Missouri Rivers met. *Elijah and his mamma may have stopped here*, he thought.

The man on horseback dismounted. "What can I do for thee, Friend?" Liam Robinson asked.

"I'd like to watch you unload that buggy," said the man, matter of factly. "Man I work for lost a slave yesterday, name of Joseph. He's a dangerous man. Wouldn't want him to escape and hurt somebody. He'd as soon kill ya as look atcha."

"Thee is a bounty hunter, then?" asked Liam Robinson.

"No. I've worked for Alfred Pedigrew for near 20 year. Good man."

"Thee can watch the whole process of milling, start to finish if it suits thee."

The man looked at Liam Robinson skeptically. Sid understood. It was well known that members of the Society of Friends were often deeply involved in helping people escape from slavery. "I want to see what's in the sack," the man said. "Runaways can squeeze into all kinds of shapes, like they was made of bread dough. Ain't natural."

Liam Robinson did not reply. He nodded toward his two boys. The Robinson boys were almost as tall as their father. One pushed a wheelbarrow. The other went straight to the buggy to get the sack. "Dump that in the wheelbarrow where this Friend can see what's in the sack," said Liam Robinson. "We've nothing to hide."

One boy hoisted the sack out of the back of the buggy. He cut the yarn lacing with his pocketknife. Then the two boys dumped the dried corn on the cob into the wheelbarrow. Satisfied, Mr. Pedigrew's hired hand nodded, thanked Liam Robinson, and left.

"Followed thee all the way, did he?" asked Liam Robinson.

"Mr. Pedigrew stopped me right after I took the main road," said Sid, feeling more confident.

"Best thing for thee to do is to go along; if thee can. We may oppose what they do, but the law is on their side."

"There's somethin' I don't understand," said Sid.

"What would that be, Sid Johnson?"

"Well, I never met a slaveholder before. Mr. Pedigrew seemed like a real nice man. How could he be a nice man and own slaves?"

"There's the rub," said Liam Robinson. "There's a bit of God in everyone, Sid Johnson, but some things cannot be reconciled. An answer to thy question is beyond me."

The men on horseback were nowhere to be seen on the return trip until Sid got to the turn-off to the farm. He waved to them as he left the main road. They waved back, apparently uninterested in his sack of ground corn.

The second trip went as Ma predicted. Sid was stopped. He exchanged friendly greetings as Mr. Pedigrew inspected the buggy and ran the spike through the sack of corn. By the third trip, Sid was beginning wonder if it would work. Pa had already loaded the sack with Joseph hidden inside when it was time to leave. Sid didn't even get to see him.

Mr. Pedigrew was waiting. Sid prayed that he would wave him on. Pa said that if they stopped him, he must act as if nothing was amiss, no matter what happened. He said it twice, "No matter what." Pa seemed to feel confident Joseph would be safe. Sid was to tell Liam Robinson, "Course grind this time, no return." He said Liam Robinson would know what that meant.

Unfortunately, Mr. Pedigrew held up his hand for Sid to stop. He pulled Sandy to a halt and hopped out of the buggy, hoping Mr. Pedigrew would have no more than the quick look Ma predicted. "Well, Son, looks like you've had a good day's work haulin' corn. This won't take long."

Sid had no more than breathed an inward sigh of relief when, to his horror, Mr. Pedigrew pulled out the steel spike. He nearly bit his tongue in agony as the man plunged it into the sack where Joseph lay.

There was no cry. There wasn't even any blood on the spike as Mr. Pedigrew withdrew it.

At least he just made one stab. Sid prayed that Joseph really could squeeze out of the way like bread dough.

"What's the matter, young man? You look like you've seen a ghost," said Mr. Pedigrew, putting away the spike.

"I was just thinkin' how awful it would be if somebody really was in the bag," he said, shaken. "I reckon they'd be dead."

Mr. Pedigrew gave him a hard look, "No more than they would deserve. Sometimes, unfortunate though it is, you must make an example. Glad there wasn't anybody in there for your sake." His features softened as he said, "You're a fine boy. Don't let yourself get mixed up in somethin' illegal. If your daddy is protectin' runaways, I daresay he means it to be for good. But it will bring him down. Best thing you could do is come clean. If you do, I'll reclaim my property and look the other way."

Mr. Pedigrew returned the steel spike to its scabbard and mounted his horse. "If he's harborin' Joseph, his life and the life of every member of your family is in danger. I can't count how many times do-gooders have been murdered by ruthless runaways. It is a constant danger."

Sid didn't know what to say. He was terrified that Joseph was injured and needed attention, but he didn't dare rush Mr. Pedigrew.

"If your pa's caught—and he will be—he will go to jail. Harborin' runaways is breakin' the law, the law of the United States government and God's law. The Good Book says, 'Thou shalt not steal.' This is your chance to do somethin' really big for your family and for your future." He looked at Sid expectantly.

Pa hadn't prepared him for this. Sid looked Mr. Pedigrew straight in the eyes. "Thank you, Mr. Pedigrew," he said politely, hoping that the fear he felt didn't show in his voice. "All I can tell you is that I'm just a boy. I reckon if my pa is protectin' runaways, he wouldn't tell me about it. If he's hidin' 'em, I can't think where, except the barn, and it's gone. So, I don't know how I can help you."

"God help me, I hope you're tellin' the truth," said Mr. Pedigrew. "Be a shame for a fine young man like you to have to be head of the house. Go on then. If you hear anything or see anything, we'll be around. You can come tell me. I'll never let anybody know. That's a promise. I'm a man of my word." With that, Mr. Pedigrew waved him on.

Sid put Sandy to a trot. He was so upset he thought he'd throw up. He couldn't imagine how Joseph had managed to wiggle around the spike. *What if he's dead?* The thought haunted him the rest of the way to the mill. He wanted to pull over and check the sack, but Pa was very firm, "No matter what happens, you absolutely must go on. You understand? No matter what."

At least the man wasn't following him this time. Maybe they thought there wasn't anything in the sack. It was small comfort.

"Course grind, no return," he said when Liam Robinson appeared.

"Thee is white as a sheet, Sid Johnson. Come on inside the mill and have a glass of cider. It's our first cider of the season. It's mighty tasty, too."

"They stabbed the sack," Sid said, trying not to break down and cry. He wasn't sure how much he could say. "I was worried ..."

Liam Robinson nodded. "Never you mind about that, Sid Johnson. Sometimes they stab the seats, ruin the upholstery. Priscilla Robinson sent some gingerbread cookies out for thee to go with the cider. Thought thee might need a little something."

"Please tell Priscilla Robinson I said thank you," said Sid.

He ate the gingerbread cookies and sipped cider, unable to appreciate either in his anxiety. After a while, Liam Robinson reappeared. "Got your feed loaded up, Sid Johnson. Tell Ben Johnson I said everything is fine and I appreciate his business. Thee need not worry thyself, Sid Johnson."

Sid wanted to ask; he knew he shouldn't. He didn't know if he ought to be relieved or worried. Turning back on to the farm road, he waved to the men, trying to look cheerful. They waved back.

When he had a chance, Sid told Pa what had happened. "It was fine, Son," said Pa, "Joseph wasn't in the bag."

"He wasn't? Where was he?" Sid knew the minute he asked: there would be no answer. "You aren't going to tell me, are you."

"Suffice it to say that we came up with an alternative," said Pa.

"You mean I was going back and forth all that time for nothin'?" Sid didn't know whether to be relieved or angry.

"I didn't say that," said Pa. "I'm right proud of you. You helped save a man's life. Let's pray he makes it up to British North America."

After that, Sid got up and helped if he heard sounds in the night. But as winter wore on and word spread along the Grapevine, they were less frequent. Still, Ma and Pa were on the alert. Still, Sid was not allowed to see where people escaping to freedom were hidden, or how Ma and Pa knew they were there. Still, Pa slipped out of the house at night sometimes, returning just before dawn. And still, he knew nothing more about the slave stealer.

Sometimes, after he had heard Pa slip out of the house at night, he was tempted to follow and see what was happening for himself. But Pa's words, "I don't want you to know anything you don't have to know. Joseph's life depends on it," came back to him, every time. It was too big a risk to take just to satisfy his curiosity.

One day Ma and Pa went to Alton, taking Jimmy and Cora with them. Sid had a wonderful afternoon being by himself. One thing he wanted to do was explore the old barn site. Pa had warned everyone away from it, but Sid figured Pa didn't want Jimmy and Cora playing there. He was much older and knew how to be careful. The temptation to have a look was too much to resist.

Aided by a sturdy stick, he cautiously poked in the ashes around beams that hadn't burned entirely. Pa had already salvaged the wagon wheels and tools that survived the fire. Some were melted into interesting shapes and still lay in the ashes. He found an axe head that was intact. Pa would be pleased. He set it down where it could be found. The barn seemed smaller when reduced to its foundation. He stood about where the corn crib had been, remembering the cow stalls, the hayloft where he'd found Serena's kittens, Elijah, and the time August Mean opened the corn crib after Pa warned him against it. He was smiling to himself, remembering how Mean had danced under a rain of corncobs, when the stick he was leaning on suddenly began collapsing. Part of the barn floor was folding in on itself. Thrown off balance, he nearly fell. He jumped to the side. Panting, he watched the dust and ash settle.

That was close! He stared down at a bowl-shaped space where he had been standing seconds before. It looked like a sinkhole, where the top layer of the ground collapses into a cave or large hole underneath. *Must be about four or five feet across.* It made him wonder. Maybe it wasn't a natural thing. The safe place in the manger had been there without him knowing it. *Was there a cellar under the barn that I didn't know about?* Maybe the avalanche of corn cobs deflected attention from a secret entrance to an underground chamber. He determined to explore the sink hole a little more when he had a chance. But it was getting late. He had to get cleaned up before everyone came home. He didn't want to be found covered with ashes. *I don't want to set a bad example for Jimmy and Cora*, he told himself. In his heart, he knew it was because he had disobeyed.

By the time Sid had a chance to explore the sinkhole it wasn't there. It looked like it had been filled in. Nothing was said about it; he didn't dare ask.

It came up several weeks later when he and Pa were alone. "Son, I don't want you exploring in the ashes or anywhere else around that barn site. Daniel and Jacob are buying the farm. Jacob and his family will live here. You could compromise their safety, especially if there's a war."

"Yessir," said Sid, feeling his face go hot with embarrassment. "I didn't mean—"

"I know, Son," interrupted Pa. "But that doesn't change the facts."

9.
Hard Choices

All winter long they prepared for the trip west. Letters came from Uncle Luke filled with useful information. Pa did a lot of studying about the trip. Ma did a lot of worrying and studying. Planning how to pare down their belongings to practically nothing was a mind-boggling job. Hard choices had to be made about what to keep and what to sell or give away. Ma didn't want an auction with people tramping around all over the place. Sid figured she didn't want people accidentally happening on where they'd hidden fugitives. *Or where they're hiding them.* Sid wasn't so sure that he knew everything that went on. *There's no tellin' what happens when I'm at school.*

Things began to disappear from the house. One day when he and Jimmy got home from school there was a big empty spot in the parlor. "What happened to the sofa?" Jimmy demanded. "What are we supposed to sit on?"

"There are plenty of chairs in the kitchen and there's the rocking chair," said Ma, unruffled. Jimmy rolled his eyes. "If you need a secret place, we can put a quilt over a couple of chairs." That seemed to console him.

More empty spots appeared as Ma sold off or gave away pieces of furniture. Jacob and his wife bought some of the furniture, but they wouldn't need it until they moved in. *Good thing, or there won't be anything left to sit on*, Sid thought.

He was starting to resign himself to going to California. "Just think, Jimmy, we'll see American Indians and hunt buffalo. Maybe we'll even meet Kit Carson," he said, trying to convince himself as much as Jimmy.

Jimmy's eyes widened, "Kit Carson! Really and truly?"

"Maybe. It's goina be one big adventure, like camping out along the creek with Pa in the summer." From the moment he mentioned the famous frontiersman, Sid was talking to the air. Jimmy tore through the house yelling, "Gonna see Kit Carson!" Ma put a stop to it by sending him outside.

At night, after Jimmy fell asleep, Sid lay awake wondering. Some of the kids at school envied him. Others thought his family was just plain crazy. He tried not to let it dampen his spirits even more. He thought about what they'd see, and about leaving behind bounty hunters and arguments over slavery with friends at school. There would be no more worries that Ma and Pa would be caught helping freedom seekers—that was a good thing, too. Maybe they would meet the famous Kit Carson. No matter how hard he tried to convince himself, though, Sid couldn't feel truly excited about making the trip.

Pa read aloud each new letter from Uncle Luke. Ma had them shelling dried beans or some other chore as they listened. "Let's see what Uncle Luke has to say," Pa said one evening when an especially fat letter arrived. "You know I'm partial to the Santa Fe Trail," Pa read. "There's so much trade along the Santa Fe that it's well protected. There are trading spots, now. You can get about any-thing you need in Santa Fe—"

"Then why do we have to take all this stuff?" Jimmy interrupted, waving to the sacks of supplies that were starting to accu-mulate in the kitchen.

"Manners, Jimmy," Ma raised her eyebrows and gave him a stern look.

"It's a long way from here to Santa Fe," Sid said. "We'll need all these things."

Pa read on, "Folks leave all times of the year now. They say the trails are busy as city streets. Don't leave too early. You could get caught in a blizzard on the mountain passes, especially on the California and Oregon trails. I've enclosed a note from Eliza."

Pa handed the note to Ma. "Looks like another one of Eliza's lists."

"Oh good," said Ma, reaching for the note. They had never met Aunt Eliza, Uncle Luke's wife. Sometimes she wrote, too, with advice for Ma about what to pack.

Pa read on. "Find a good wagon master. Folk tell me that most of the trains don't get organized until they get to Council Grove these days. Folks just show up in Council Grove with their wagon and find a group going where they want to go. I think that's a bad idea."

"That's way out in Kansas Territory, isn't it?" Ma asked. "I'm not sure I'd want to do that. I agree with Uncle Luke."

"I agree with Unka Luke," said Cora, beaming at everyone as if that settled it.

"Council Grove's a little less than two weeks out of Westport," said Pa. "I think Uncle Luke's right. Best pick up what we don't take with us in Kansas City." He read on:

There's a fellow named Bill Stokes who lives out here. He knows how to run a wagon train. I told him about you. He'll be in Kansas City in early March. If you can travel with him, that is my best recommendation. It won't cost that much extra, and it will be well worth the money. He likes to start early so his wagon company doesn't face that desert from Santa Fe to California in July.

"Huh?" Jimmy looked puzzled. "He just said we shouldn't start early."

"I guess he means not just any old time of year," Sid explained.

Later, Sid and Jimmy helped Ma organize a list. Jimmy read from Aunt Eliza's letter. She said some things were better bought in Kansas. Ma wrote down what they would take with them from home. Sid wrote down what they'd buy in Kansas.

"A family of four will need about 600 pounds of flour," Jimmy read, "Wow! That's a whole bunch of flour."

"Kansas," said Ma. Sid put it on his list.

"120 pounds of hard tack?" Jimmy made a face. "Ewww! Nobody likes hard tack."

"Hard tack crackers may not be the tastiest, but they will keep," said Ma. "My list. I know the ones I like. They may not have them in Kansas."

"I don't like any of 'em," said Jimmy under his breath.

"Keep reading," said Sid.

"400 pounds of bacon. Yum-m." They went through the entire list. Sid added 60 pounds of coffee beans, 4 pounds of tea and 100 pounds of sugar to the list to be bought in Kansas along with a sack of rice. Ma put 200 pounds of lard on her list with a question mark. "We have to decide if it will be cheaper to ship it to Kansas from here or buy it there," she explained. She added dried peaches, apples, and beans to her list. They always had a good supply from the orchard and garden.

"There ain't goina be any room for us in the wagon," said Jimmy, "not with all this stuff!"

Aunt Eliza advised them to put their bacon in a barrel with bran. "The bran keeps the sun from melting the fat," she wrote.

To Jimmy's apparent relief, Ma agreed with Aunt Eliza that drying vegetables for the trip wasn't worth the effort. He read with a satisfied expression, "They aren't that good, and you can find plenty of greens on the way. But a sack of onions will stead you well." Jimmy made no objection to onions.

Ma pinned lists up on the kitchen curtains where she could refer to them.

Pa kept Sid busy, too, when he wasn't in school. They sharpened the plow, scythe, hoe, shovel, broad axe, and saw. The plow survived the fire. Pa was especially pleased when he found the axe head. Sid felt a pang of guilt when whenever he saw it.

"We'll need all these tools when we get to California," said Pa. "Luke says they're priced higher than a kite out there."

Pa's hunting knife and gun would be needed on the trip. That went without saying.

Pa started taking Sid with him to hunt along the creek more regularly than in years gone by. "You're good with a gun, Sid. But good isn't good enough. You have to be better than good. If we're ever in a tight spot, I want you to know exactly what to do without having to stop and think about it."

One day there was a surprise when he came home from school. "Your own gun, Sid," said Pa, "You're almost a man now. See that you use it responsibly."

Sid looked at the gun Pa handed him, hardly believing it could be his. It was a musket rifle, a new model, one that was lighter weight than Pa's. He spent as much time as he could taking it apart, cleaning, and polishing it. From then on, he took it with him when they went hunting.

Ma was always thinking ahead, trying to mentally rehearse their steps and what they were likely to need that Uncle Luke and Aunt Eliza hadn't thought of. One evening at supper, she said, "Shoes!"

"Shoes what?" asked Jimmy.

"We'll be walkin' most of the time," said Ma. "We're bound to wear out our shoes and you chil'ren are growin' like weeds. You'll outgrow your shoes before we get to California. We'll need to buy new shoes for everybody and in larger sizes for you chil'ren."

"We haven't been buying ready-made shoes that long, Sadie," said Pa. "I haven't forgotten how to make a shoe. But you're right. Best pack my last and awl. I'll set aside leather for repairs and for making new shoes as we need 'em. That will take up less space than ready-made shoes, and we'll get the size right."

"And my cornbread pan," said Ma. "I'm takin' my cornbread pan." Sid was a bit surprised. Ma made such a thing of taking cooking pots that she could use in different ways. She wouldn't tolerate anything else being cooked in the cornbread pan. Ma made cornbread with butter. Most people used bacon grease. "I took me years to get that pan seasoned just right. I'm not makin' cornbread in a pan that's had lard in it."

"You bring that pan, Sadie," laughed Pa. "The thought of your cornbread on the trail is enough to put hope in any man."

"How you gonna bake cornbread without an oven?" asked Jimmy.

"You wait and see," said Ma. "I have my ways."

It was like that every night. Right after the fire, when Ma and Pa made up their minds to go to California, they sold the cattle. It was like saying good-bye to family.

The only consolation was that they kept Buttercup and Mr. Davis bought the rest. They would be loved and cared for.

Sid hoped they would take Buttercup to California, but Pa wouldn't promise.

"We need the milk and butter for now," said Pa. "I'm keeping a yearling to butcher. Daniel and Jake Harold have put their name in for the work horses. We need Sandy for the trip."

"Eliza says some people take hens," said Ma. "I haven't decided. We can leave them for Jacob and Seraphina if we decide not to take 'em. A chicken coop would take up a lot of room in the wagon."

Just before Christmas Sid got to drive over to the Harold farm to pick up sides of bacon and ham. They usually bought a whole pig, but Pa said that ham and bacon would make the trip better than other cuts of pork. Mrs. Harold hurried out to the buggy as Daniel helped Sid load up the meat. Miriam, the oldest of Jacob and Seraphina's little girls, was with her. "Uncle Daniel be gone a l-o-n-g time, Sid."

Daniel picked her up. "You're getting so tall I can hardly pick you up anymore." Turning to Sid he said, "Missy Miriam doesn't like it when I work down at the docks in Alton or on one of the steamboats."

"I don't either," said Mrs. Harold. "It's too risky. But you didn't come for a family argument, Sid. Tell your mother not to worry about having enough fat to make soap. Seraphina and I are making enough extra soap to send with you."

"Tell Cora to come play," Miriam said. The two were fast friends, though Miriam was Jimmy's age. She didn't go to school, though. She was taught at home.

As soon as Sid got back with the meat, Ma called Jimmy to come help. She was holding one of the large blue speckled pans. "We're goina rub the meat with this mixture."

Jimmy scrunched up his nose. "Ewww."

Ma gave him a look. "Don't be silly. It is mostly salt and brown sugar. Every crevice has to be filled."

They had to use their bare hands. Jimmy complained most of the time, made faces, and said his hands hurt too much from the salt.

"One more reason to quit biting your fingernails," Sid told him.

"Why can't we just go and shoot buffalos on the way? There's plenty of buffalos out

West," Jimmy whined. "I don't wanna go to California anyway. Injuns is sure to scalp us!"

"Indians *are*," Ma corrected. "And where did you ever get an idea like that?"

"Everybody at school says Injuns attack wagon trains," he said.

"Well, everybody is wrong," said Ma firmly. "Uncle Luke says Indians rarely attack wagon trains. I don't want to hear you say 'Injuns' again, either. It's disrespectful."

They put the meat into wooden tubs and covered it up with more salt. "Now," said Ma, "it has to sit like that in the smokehouse for six weeks."

"I ain't never eatin' none of that stuff," Jimmy said.

"You will if you get hungry enough," said Sid. It wasn't that he liked the work any more than Jimmy did, but some jobs have to be done.

The yearling was butchered shortly after. "Oh no, not again!" Jimmy groaned when he learned the whole process of preparing meat had to be repeated with the beef.

"The salt draws out the water," Ma explained. "It's the water that causes it to go bad. Believe me, you'll be glad we have this once we're on the Santa Fe Trail."

When Ma's back was turned, Jimmy made a face and mouthed, "Won't neither." Sid pretended he didn't see.

By mid-winter, the rafters of the pyramid-shaped roof in the smokehouse were hung with ham, sides of bacon, and beef. One of Sid's jobs was to keep a low hardwood fire burning so that the meat would cure. It wasn't too different from other winters that he could remember, except for the feeling of urgency.

One evening Pa said, "Tomorrow morning I want you up well before sunrise, Son. See if you can bring in some game."

"We huntin' turkey?" Sid asked.

"Not we, *you*," said Pa. "You're better than good now. Time you tried on your own close to home where it's safe. Just remember to stick with small game. There are plenty of prairie hens and turkeys. Don't shoot anything larger unless you have to. Stay this side of the creek."

"I'll take my slingshot," said Sid. "Daniel Harold says there's a lot of quail movin' up into the cornfield now."

"You don't need practice with your slingshot," Ma said somewhat cryptically. "Don't kill anything needlessly."

10.

Hunting Alone

It was well before sunrise on what promised to be a glorious early winter morning. It was unusually warm for February. Sid set out through the orchard. From there, he picked up a path that followed along the edge of the woods bordering the creek. There was enough bite in the air to frost his breath. Dark outside, it was even darker in the shadow of the woods. He took his time, enjoying the feeling of freedom and responsibility as he followed the familiar curve of the trees. *I'm gonna miss this old woods. I'll probably never see it again once we leave for California.* A feeling of deep sadness welled up.

He was so caught up in thought that he was nearly on top of two horses before he realized it. They were tethered just before the path took a sharp bend to the right where the Harold property began. The horses looked vaguely familiar, though he couldn't think who they belonged to or why they'd be out so early. *Unless somebody's trappin' down along the creek.* Pa would be furious. Pa neither trapped nor permitted it where the creek cut through the farm. Neither did the Harold family.

The horses looked at him with curiosity rather than fear, their ears forward, heads down. He took some time to study their tracks beyond the bend to see what it might tell him about where they had come from and who rode them. It was still too dark to tell much.

Just ahead, corn shocks loomed in the softening dark of dawn like tents pitched along a battlefield. It was an ideal place for wintering quail and wild turkey. Hunting would have to wait until he figured out why the horses were there.

Even before dawn, there was enough broken brush to follow where two people had dismounted and led the horses around the bend. *Why?* Whoever it was had made no pretense of hiding their tracks. Sid followed broken brush where the trespassers had made their way toward the creek. If somebody was checking traps, they knew they were trespassing. It could be dangerous. Drawing closer to the creek, he slipped into the undergrowth—just in time. Ahead, two men were talking in low voices. Dropping to the ground, Sid eased himself up to look. He was closer that he thought. If he so much as sneezed, he would give himself away. The men were flat on their bellies, stretched out on massive rocks that overlooked the creek. Guns at hand, they were waiting for something. Sid couldn't see it, but he knew that down below the rocks was a shallow stretch in the creek where it widened as it cut its way toward a deep ravine and a little waterfall. They seemed to be fixed on the Harold's cornfield that continued on the other side of the creek.

Despite the dark, he recognized them: bounty hunters, August Mean and Roscoe Bones. Sid's hand tightened on his gun. *No wonder the horses looked familiar.*

The two were arguing. Aided by the wind coming from the direction of the creek, he could hear snatches of their conversation above the sound of the water. "Missed 'em"—Mean's back was to him—"don't travel by day."

"It's still dark." Roscoe was turned slightly in Sid's direction. His voice carried. "We ain't gonna get another chance like this. I'm tellin' ya on good authority; slave stealer is headed this way with half a dozen runaways comin' up outa Missouri."

Mean was harder to hear, but it was clear enough that he disagreed with Roscoe, he was tired of waiting, and he didn't want to risk getting tangled up with other bounty hunters.

"But we catches 'em, we got the ticket," said Roscoe. "I ain't talkin' 'bout *any* slave stealer. I'm talkin' 'bout *the* slave stealer, that phantom slave stealer that's been terrorizin' three states. Slaves calls him Belteshazzar."

Sid's blood ran cold. *A phantom slave stealer, headed this way?* What could Roscoe mean by phantom? In his mind, slave stealers were in the right. Roscoe made the slave stealer sound like some evil, ghostly creature.

Mean raised his voice. "Slaves ain't that organized." As he sat up, the wind carried his voice in Sid's direction. "—don't believe it. What kinda name is Belt-shaver whatcha call 'em anyway?"

"*Belte-shaz-zar*, it's from the Bible," said Roscoe. "Dontcha know your Bible? Cousin of mine tracks up the Missouri. He beat it out of a runaway. Slave was meetin' this Belteshazzar. He steals slaves and disappears with 'em into thin air. Ain't nobody been able to catch 'em or the slaves he steals."

"Sh-h-h," said Mean, suddenly dropping back onto the rock. "Somethin's movin'—"

A tall black figure appeared out of the mist that clung to the cornfield beyond the creek. Roscoe dropped down on his stomach. The figure, a man, strode across the field. As he neared the creek, he slowed, paused, and looked both ways. He paused again before he reached the creek bank.

"Give 'em time," said Mean, "—he signals the slaves—our move." Sid wished he could hear better.

Roscoe began to slip upstream along the high bank, so close Sid could have reached out and touched him. Mean turned and called to Roscoe in a firm, but low voice, "We'll have 'em covered from two angles. If they scatter, shoot one of 'em. It'll put the fear in the rest."

Sid's chest tightened. He hardly breathed as Roscoe moved past. His hand gripped his gun so hard his knuckles were white. But, like Sid, Roscoe was fixed on the black man across the creek. The first hint of light hit him. The man carried a gun in one hand and a turkey in the other. He looked up; the light hit him full in the face. Sid gasped. It was Daniel Harold. *I have to warn him.*

If he cried out, Daniel wouldn't be able to hear him over the sound of the water. The wind was in the wrong direction, too. But, if he didn't warn him, Daniel could be captured or killed.

"Damnation!" said Roscoe. "It's one of them that lives back over the hill. Nothin' we can do. He's on his own property and he's got papers."

Mean turned toward Roscoe again. Sid could hear him perfectly. "They don't know that in Missouri, now do they. Big one like him? He'll bring a pretty penny."

"If the devil don't cross it," Roscoe said. "He's big all right. I seen him workin' for hire down to the Alton docks. This ain't goina be easy."

"Gives any trouble, shoot him," said Mean, turning back to watch Daniel.

No! Terrified of what might happen, Sid's mind raced. He hadn't loaded his gun. The minute he tried Roscoe would be on him.

He could try to call their bluff—pretend it was loaded—but he knew he couldn't do it. He had his slingshot, but the men were too far apart now and there was too much brush to allow for two good, clean shots in succession.

Then he remembered: *the horses*. In a matter of seconds, Daniel would start across the creek. There wasn't much time.

The bounty hunters were so focused on Daniel they didn't see Sid hurriedly ease his way back to the path. Once away, he rounded the bend at a run. Stopping where the horses waited, he loaded his gun, hands shaking. Quickly, he untethered the horses. With one hand he aimed his gun toward one of the corn shocks on the near side of the creek and shot. Yelling, 'Hi!" at the top of his lungs, he slapped the nearest horse on the rump with his game bag. The horses took off at a gallop. *If they catch him anyway, it won't be so easy for them on foot.* He had to get back to the house and tell Pa before the bounty hunters got away with Daniel.

Hurriedly, he reloaded his gun. *One more warning shot.*

He wasn't fast enough. Arms as strong as a steel trap suddenly snapped around him from behind. "Whatcha think you're doin', sonny-boy?" Roscoe Bones growled.

"Pa sent me out huntin'," he gasped, terrified.

"What'n the devil did you go shootin' for, Roscoe?" called August Mean, crawling through the brush where the horses had stood. "Scared him off. I don't know why I let you talk me into this. Now all we got to show for a night perched on a rock is bein' on a rock. I'm durn near too stiff to move." He pulled himself up to his full height, suddenly noticing Sid. "Well, well. What have we here?"

"He done scared him off," said Roscoe, tightening his grip. "Run off our horses, too."

"I thought you were trappers," said Sid, truthfully. He tried to sound calmer than he felt. He wasn't sure what they would do to him.

"You ain't much of a liar," growled Roscoe.

"Interferin' with the legal work of bounty hunters?" sneered Mean.

"But this is our farm," gasped Sid.

Mean slapped him across the face, hard. It stung so badly tears burned his eyes. Picking up Sid's gun, Mean stepped back, propping it against a tree next to Roscoe's gun. He took several more paces back. Leaning on his rifle like it was a walking stick, he eyed Sid as if he were trying to decide what to do with him. "You workin with that—?" Mean used some words for Daniel that made Sid sick to the stomach. "Tell us what you know, and I'll let you go. Or maybe you'd like some more of this?" He held up his hand as if he were going to slap Sid again.

Sid flinched. He couldn't help it. Mean laughed. "You know what happens to boys who think they can do a man's work?"

"I wouldn't do that if I were you," Daniel Harold spoke calmly as he stepped from the woods, a revolver pointed at Mean, "because, unless your friend lets my friend go nice and easy, and you get off this property, I'm going to have to shoot you both." Rifle slung across his shoulder, Daniel sounded as cool as lemonade on a hot day. Roscoe's grip tightened.

"Go ahead, shoot me," said Mean just as calmly. He kept talking, looking straight at Daniel while his hand gradually eased down the barrel of his gun, lifting it ever so slightly from the ground. "Shoot me and you don't have a chance this side of hell. They'll hang you. Roscoe, this big boy drops that fancy revolver, or you knife that young weasel."

Sid could see what Mean was trying to do, distract Daniel, then suddenly whip his gun into place and shoot, but he was too frozen to cry out and warn Daniel.

Sid felt one of Roscoe's arms go loose as he reached for his knife. The other was still locked around him so firmly that he couldn't move.

A shot cracked the air. Daniel knew exactly what August Mean was trying to do. He knew what he was doing, too. He shot just past the bounty hunter's head, aiming where the bullet would hit a corn shock instead of scattering rocks or ricocheting. It was so close that Mean dropped his gun, wildly jumping to the side. Letting fly a string of curses, he staggered to keep his balance, tripped over his gun, and fell backward to the ground.

Startled by the shot, Roscoe loosened his grip ever so slightly. Putting all his strength into it, Sid brought his elbows up, twisted his body, and rammed Roscoe in the stomach with one elbow.

Roscoe let go, doubling over in pain. Sid lost his balance and fell flat on his face.

"Roll, Sid!" Daniel yelled.

Sid rolled away as fast as he could. A knife flashed in Roscoe's hand, barely missing him.

"Drop the knife," Daniel ordered, his voice deadly calm. "Stay right where you are, Mean." A second shot came so close Sid felt like an explosion had gone off in his head. Hitting the grassy turf just behind Roscoe, the bullet sent dirt flying. Roscoe dropped the knife.

"Next shot counts," said Daniel. His voice was measured, deadly, terrifying. "Get those hands back of your head, both of you, *now*.

"Get your gun, Sid. These two seem to have trouble following directions."

Sid pulled himself up. It felt like stars were flickering inside his head.

"Men, nice thing about this fancy new Third Model Colt Revolver is that I can fire six rounds without reloading," Daniel spoke as if he were talking with thick headed schoolboys, "That means I have four more bullets, two left for each of you. I don't see anybody around to hang me. You will be floating down to the Mississippi before you're seen again."

Sid picked up his gun, hoping he wouldn't have to shoot anybody.

"Draw a bead on Roscoe Bones, Sid," said Daniel. "He so much as flinches, take off his right leg. The boy's that good, Bones. Don't make him nervous. As your friend said, we can't expect the boy to do a man's work.

"Don't try to get up Mean. You can stay right there until I decide if I'm going to shoot you. Don't make the decision for me."

The sound of a horse coming at a gallop sent a look of relief over Roscoe Bones' face, that is, until he saw who it was. Pa, rifle in hand, reigned in Sandy a few yards away. Sid could see Pa out of the corner of his eye, but he kept his gun aimed at Roscoe and didn't look away.

"I was starting to worry about you, Son," said Pa, dismounting. He nodded at Daniel. "Morning, neighbor. I see you've been busy."

"Morning, Mr. Johnson," Daniel said, as casually as if he'd just dropped by the house to visit.

August Mean lay in an undignified position on the ground, hands behind his head. Roscoe's eyes darted between Daniel and Pa.

"Reckon we should have this one stand up so we can put a rope on him?" Pa asked, picking up Mean's gun.

Sid was shocked. It didn't sound like Pa to suggest hanging anybody.

"Nah, wouldn't want these two hanging around my property," said Daniel, without so much as cracking a smile at his own pun. "I was just considering whether to introduce them to Sheriff McDown or float them down the creek and have it done."

"I'll save you the trouble of deciding," said Pa. "Go get your breakfast. I've met these two before. It will be my pleasure to deliver them to the sheriff for trespassing on our property, threatening the life of my son, and confessing to setting fire to my barn."

Roscoe made sputtering sounds. "Shut your fool mouth," said Mean. "They ain't got nothin' on us."

"Sid, maybe you can round up their horses," said Pa, ignoring Mean. "These men will need a way to leave town once they're out of jail."

Sid collected their guns while the bounty hunters were bound, hands behind their backs. "I don't reckon they'll mind walking," said Pa. "It's no more than they've done for so many others. I've never known a bounty hunter yet, who walks while his captives ride."

Pa left, riding behind the bounty hunters who were on foot. Daniel gave Sid a pat on the back. "Those two try anything and they'll find out that your father is not to be trifled with." A broad smile seemed to take up his whole face. "Out hunting this morning, too?"

"Yeah. Reckon I'd better get on home and find those horses. Guess it's too late to get a turkey now."

"I'd say you caught something bigger than turkey," said Daniel. "If you hadn't fired that shot, I'd be on the way to Missouri. Mamma Harold doesn't like it when I go out hunting by myself. I reckon she's right." He sighed. "But I can't live trapped up. I might as well be a slave." He paused a minute as if he was deciding if he should say something. "Sid, folks think the worst part of being a slave is the back-breaking work most slaves endure. I think it's being kept like you're a piece of property and have no right to your own hopes and dreams." With that, he handed Sid the turkey he'd been carrying when he crossed the creek. "Take this. Don't want you to go home empty handed."

Sid protested. "Thank you, Mr. Harold, but I couldn't take your turkey."

"No arguing with your elders," said Daniel, grinning. "And you're old enough to call me Daniel now. After all, we're like family and now we've fought together."

Sid took the turkey, grinning back. "Thank you, Daniel." It felt awkward and good at the same time.

Ma was anxiously waiting when he got to the house. Sid handed her the turkey, telling her what had happened. "And they said there was a phantom slave stealer named Belt-something."

"There are men and women who go into slave states to help slaves get away," Ma said. "Slaveholders call them stealers. Some of them have been slaves. They take a terrible risk."

"But are they really phantoms? I mean, is there a phantom slave stealer?" Sid almost bit his tongue after he said it. He didn't believe in ghosts. Still, it was plenty scary.

"No, Son," said Ma. "I wouldn't go much on names anyway. I expect phantom's somethin' made up to explain when people get away to freedom. If you're a slave tracker who has agreed to catch somebody, and they get away, what are you to do? You can't be blamed if some phantom spirited them away."

"It makes it sound like the slave stealers are the bad ones," said Sid.

"It's supposed to," said Ma. "I reckon it's a way to scare people held in slavery, too.

Make 'em afraid of the folk who are tryin' to help."

"You mean scare the slaves, so they won't want to leave?"

"Like the folk who threaten chil'ren with the boogey-man. 'Slave stealer's goina' get you.' Even worse, if the stealer sounds like some kind of ghost goina make you disappear forever." Ma sighed. "Best not to repeat anything you hear like that anyway.

"I know it's hard when your Pa and I are so tight-lipped, but rumors are dangerous. If you pass along the wrong information, somebody could get killed. You did a brave thing, Sid. I'm not sure we'd have ever been able to find Daniel again if they'd made off with him. And he did a brave thing in rescuin' you."

Sid had a feeling she knew more. He made up his mind to find out what Ma and Pa were keeping from him. It was more than curiosity. Something inside seemed to compel him to know if there really was a phantom slave stealer, and if so, who it could be. *Maybe if I know, I can do more than just chop onions when they're tryin' to help somebody.* Admittedly, it didn't happen often now. Once they left for California, there wouldn't be any reason to know. *Except maybe if I knew, I could ask 'em what happened to Elijah, if he made it to safety*. It had been months since they'd found Elijah in the hay, but he couldn't get the image of the boy's tattered shirt and wounded back out of his mind.

"Pa said they confessed to burnin' the barn," said Sid. "But they didn't."

"Your Pa was just puttin' the fear into 'em." Ma didn't smile, but there was a twinkle in her eyes.

He didn't have any trouble rounding up the bounty hunters' horses. They were standing in the orchard looking confused.

It seemed like every day the house looked simultaneously like an empty cavern and a store. Provisions were stacking up in the kitchen and the parlor. Most of the upstairs furniture was gone. He, Jimmy, and Cora slept on their featherbeds on the floor. Their beds had been sold. The only pieces of furniture Ma wanted to keep were the cherry wood rocking chair made by her great grandfather and a walnut cradle that Pa's father made for him before he was born. "I know people take too much with them and end up leavin' things along the trail. I'm only askin' to take two pieces of furniture."

Pa said, "Sadie, if you want that rocking chair and the cradle, we'll find a way to keep them."

"I'm gonna have all the heartbreak now," said Ma. "I keep tellin' myself all these things are only things. I take comfort in knowin' Seraphina Harold is gettin' my good china and the china cupboard. She's takin' the four-poster bed. Featherbeds are goin' with us. Eliza says we can tuck them up under the hoops on our covered wagon."

It didn't strike home until Ma told Sid he had to choose two of his toys to take along. "That's all we'll have room for. You decide."

He'd outgrown most of his toys, but it was harder than he thought it would be. He chose his toy soldiers, a set made by Grandpa Johnson. They had their own little wooden box. He no longer played with them, but they were precious to him. He settled on his bag of marbles, too. Patting his pocket where he kept his slingshot, he thought, *It doesn't count. It's a weapon.*

One night at dinner they were talking about Jacob Harold and his family moving in once they left for Kansas. "People at school say Jacob can't buy a house," Jimmy said.

"Oh, do they?" said Pa. "Why would they say that?"

"Cause he's black," said Jimmy. "They said Daniel and Jacob are black and Mrs. Harold is white."

"Mr. to you," said Ma firmly, "Mr. Daniel and Mr. Jacob."

"And? What do you reckon people at school mean?" said Pa, patiently.

"And they're her slaves," said Jimmy. "Slaves don't own stuff."

"I see," said Pa. "Well, people at school have it wrong. When they were boys about your age, Daniel and Jacob were slaves. Their parents were killed trying to escape with the boys to keep them from being sold. Mr. and Mrs. Harold bought them at an auction. But they didn't keep Jacob and Daniel as slaves; they adopted them. They brought them up as their own children. Now they own the farm along with Mrs. Harold."

"But people at school say black people's supposed to be slaves," said Jimmy. He seemed genuinely confused. "They say Mr. Jacob and Mr. Daniel are uppity, they don't talk like—" he stopped himself, covering his mouth.

"Not everybody at school says that Jimmy," said Sid. "You've been listenin' to some people who don't know what they're talkin' about."

11.
The Loulabelle

It was a crisp day in early March when they set out for Kansas City. The whole Harold family came to the farm to see them off along with a bunch of neighbors. Mrs. Harold, Jacob, and Daniel took them to catch a steamboat from Alton. Ma and Cora rode with Mrs. Harold in her buggy with their hand luggage and a picnic basket. Cora, to everyone's surprise, insisted on sitting in the back seat with an old basket filled with her things. She usually wanted to sit by Ma.

Jacob and Daniel drove a big wagon loaded with everything the Johnsons still owned. To Sid's relief, Buttercup was tied on behind. He and Jimmy got to ride in the wagon. Pa brought up the rear on Sandy.

The wagon was unloaded, its contents waiting on the dock in Alton by the time their steamboat, the *Loulabelle*, came into sight. The *Loulabelle* looked like one of Ma's three-layered cakes, with one deck stacked on another, the top layer smaller than the lower two. The lower deck was already lined with barrels, crates, sacks, trunks, and boxes of all sizes carrying everything from family possessions to rice, calico, wagon parts, and farm equipment.

"Reckon we'll be buying some of that when we get to Kansas," said Pa, laughing.

"What a beautiful boat!" said Ma.

"I wouldn't be one to say, 'I told you so,' but I knew you would like her," Daniel gave Ma an ear-to-ear smile. "Captain and the man who heads the lower deck crew know me. Jacob and I are going to go help load and get y'all a nice safe place before it gets crowded."

"You be careful," Mrs. Harold cautioned. It was why Jacob's wife and children had to stay at home.

"Careful?" Jimmy looked puzzled.

Sid explained, "Sometimes freed and born free black people are kidnapped. Daniel and Jacob always have to be careful."

"Huh?" said Jimmy.

Sid didn't know how to explain what happened all along the border states, making it unsafe for free black people. It was impossible for him to understand why people who wanted to get rid of slavery didn't want to live near people who had been freed from slavery. But he didn't have a chance to try. Jimmy was curious about the next thing, offering a commentary as the cargo was loaded, "There goes Mr. Daniel with Sandy and Buttercup," he called. The animals looked so terrified Sid almost wished they didn't have to go along.

"Keep an eye on your things," Jacob advised when he returned. "Some folks will make off with anything they can get their hands on. We got your trunks and barrels backed up against some big crates where you'll be out of the wind. Daniel's holding your place. Make your beds right up there on your trunks with your backs up against those crates. It will be safer, and you'll be protected from the river if she decides to take a mean turn. The Missouri's not a tame river. Things can get mighty rough on the deck, especially if there's a thunderstorm. Mind, it may take you awhile to get your sea legs."

Mrs. Harold wiped her eyes. "You're like family, Sadie. We're going to miss you something awful. What y'all have done over the years—we won't ever forget that."

Sid figured she meant helping freedom seekers. But nobody said it directly. Nothing was ever said in public. It occurred to him that it was the last he'd ever hear about the Underground Railroad and people escaping to freedom. *I guess I won't ever find out any more about Elijah or the phantom slave stealer. I wish I could have.* It was a mystery unsolved. It felt sad, like when he said good-bye to his friends and everybody who came to the house to see them off.

Ma was all teary as she hugged Mrs. Harold. "We couldn't of asked for better neighbors, Leona." Their goodbyes were disrupted by a loud meow from the old, covered basket Cora was carrying.

"What have you got in there, Cora?" asked Sid. The answer was obvious. It shouldn't have surprised anyone. The surprising thing was how quiet Serena had been.

Ever since the fire, Cora had been nearly inseparable from Serena. She hadn't made nearly the fuss they'd expected when she learned the kittens had to be given away. She didn't even protest when Ma and Pa said that Serena would be Miriam's cat. Now Sid knew why.

"Sweetheart, you're gonna haveta let Mrs. Harold take her," said Ma. "Cats like bein' in the same place. Serena won't be happy leavin' her home territory."

"Miriam will take good care of her," said Jacob. "Besides, we're keeping two of her kittens. She'll like being with her youngens."

Cora frowned. "Serena wants to go to Cal-forna."

Ma looked at Pa in desperation.

Pa picked Cora up, basket and all. "Sugar Plum, you wouldn't want Serena to get lost. It's a long way to California. Cats don't like to ride in a wagon."

"Serena likes ridin' in wagons," Cora insisted.

The last of the passengers for the top deck were boarding. "Y'all best be moving with the line," said Jacob. "If the lower deck gets too full, they won't let everybody on, even with a ticket. Steamboats make money from freight."

Pa frowned. "We don't have time to fuss over a cat. But mark my word, Cora, she may decide to take off and head for home."

As the boarding line began to move, Sid looked up at the top deck. People leaned over the rail looking out over Alton. They would have a very different experience on the Loulabelle. On the upper decks people had private cabins and a crew to serve their every need. Some of the bigger, fancier boats had gambling on the upper decks. But Robert Sterling, captain of the Loulabelle, was a Methodist who didn't hold with gambling. Ma thought that was in his favor.

"I don't have any objection to Captain Sterling being a Methodist," Pa had said. "My first concern is whether or not he knows how to run a steamboat and if he has a pilot worth his salt. Daniel says he's the best. That's good enough for me."

Ma frowned. "He doesn't hold with slave labor, either. I won't take passage on a boat where slaves are kept in ankle chains and made to clean the decks. I don't care how good the pilot is."

The lower deck began boarding. "You'll see Daniel once you're on deck," Jacob said. With that, he and Mrs. Harold had to leave them. Other passengers closed in behind.

"There must be at least a hundred deck passengers," said Pa as the line moved forward, "not counting those already on board."

Once they stepped on board, people scurried to find the best spots. Daniel waved to them from across the deck. "Over here. Y'all stand right here by your goods. You're close enough to the rail to get plenty of air, but not too close." He shook hands with Pa and Jimmy. Cora reached out and hugged him. He took her from Pa, giving her a hug and setting her atop their trunk. "Now you can see everything. Mind you stay put, Missy. Don't go and get lost in this crowd."

Suddenly Cora's eyes widened. "I want Miriam to come on the steamboat."

"Miriam's goina miss you," said Daniel, "but tell you what. You write a letter to her, and I'll see that she writes back. How about that? You can mail it in Kansas." He tipped his hat to Ma and shook hands with Sid. "You're almost a man now, Sid. Take care of these folks. We both know you can do it." With that he was off. They watched him make his way through the boarding crowd like a fish swimming upstream.

As the gate to the deck closed, the *Loulabelle* sounded her whistle. Suddenly a man ran up the dock, a small bag in one hand, waving his ticket with the other. He was dressed in a fine suit like passengers on the upper deck. The men at the gate opened it slightly. He leapt on as the *Loulabelle* pulled away from the dock. "That was close!" laughed Pa.

The crowd at the dock melted away, but Mrs. Harold, Jake, and Daniel stood waving to them. Near where they stood, two men rode up to the dock at a gallop, reigning in their horses. One of them jumped off his horse, throwing his black hat to the ground and stamping his foot. "Looks like he isn't too happy about missing the *Loulabelle*," said Pa.

Sid waved his cap until Mrs. Harold, Jacob, and Daniel became no more than dots on the far-away shore. He let out a sigh that felt as if it had started in his toes.

"It won't be the most pleasant trip," said Pa. They couldn't afford to pay for a cabin on the upper deck where tickets cost twice as much. "Those folks above are paying for a fancy floating hotel."

Cora opened Serena's basket, bursting into tears as the cat bolted, disappearing over the crates. "Don't worry, Sugar Plum," said Pa. "She knows where her family is. She won't leave the boat. Cats don't like to swim."

"Told you so," said Jimmy. Pa gave him a severe look.

"Can I go see Buttercup and Sandy?" asked Sid. "They're just over there."

"May I," corrected Ma. "Be careful. Some of those animals are real upset."

"I wanna go, too," begged Jimmy.

"We don't know our way around the boat yet, Jimmy," said Pa. "Sid's tall enough to get through the crowd and see where he's going. You're barely out of knee britches. You could get lost."

"I never get to do nothin'," Jimmy protested.

Sid eased his way around the crowded livestock pen. Frightened animals called out above the sound of the engine. Buttercup and Sandy were wild-eyed. He rubbed Buttercup's nose gently. "Pa says it will be a dirty, hot, smelly ride, but we'll get there." He reached over, patting Sandy. Her eyes were bulging, and nostrils flared. "Good girl," he said.

The boat sounded its whistle as it rounded the bend where the Mississippi and Missouri Rivers met, startling the animals. Suddenly, a calm came over them. Sid could feel Buttercup and Sandy relax as the calm reached them like a ripple on the water. He looked up to see a man making his way around the penned-up animals, speaking softly to them. "Hello," the man said when he reached Buttercup and Sandy. "This is a hard trip for animals. They don't always know what's happening to them. These two yours?" Sandy's ears went forward as the man gave her a pat on the neck. Buttercup looked at him as if she expected her turn. He gave her a scratch behind the ears.

"Yessir," said Sid, "My name's Sid Johnson." He extended his hand the way Pa did as they met other passengers.

"I think you have a way with animals, Sid Johnson," said the man, smiling as he shook hands. "Folk around here call me Bright, C'lestin Bright." He had the kindest eyes Sid had ever seen. There was a sparkle in them, too, that suggested he could appreciate a good laugh. "Animals aren't so different from the rest of us. We all need a little kindness." With that, Mr. Bright made his way on around the circle of animals, speaking softly, patting those he could reach.

Sid took a longer route back, going past the boilers that powered the paddle wheel at the rear of the boat. Ma would probably disapprove, but she hadn't actually *said* to take the direct route back. Besides, he wanted to have a look. As he got closer, he could feel the heat. Men added wood to the fire as the boat picked up steam.

Seeing him recoil from the heat, some men lounging near the rail burst into laughter. "Can't stand the heat, young fella? This ain't nothin'." They acted like it was a great joke.

"Yeah, wait till we hit full steam—"

Another man interrupted, winking at his friends, "That is if the boilers don't explode and send us up-river in pieces."

Sid didn't think it was anything to laugh about. He didn't like the way the men looked at him either, as if he were something they could step on.

"Heck, the Big Muddy would like that," chuckled still another man. "She's a real boat-eater. Life of one of these tubs is three-four years at the most. How old is the *Loulabelle*, anyway?"

"Bout five 'n a half year," laughed a man at the back.

"Yep, the Big Muddy's a graveyard for steamboats. She's just a waitin' fer us." Sid couldn't keep track of who was talking. He wanted away, but the men had gradually hemmed him in.

"'Spect this is your first and last trip on a steamboat," laughed one of them.

"Yeah, last trip ever," somebody said, sending the others into peals of laughter.

"Afternoon, Gentlemen." It was the man who had boarded at the last minute. The men parted as he stepped into the circle. Putting his hand on Sid's shoulder, he nodded to them. "Don't let these fellows get to you, Sid. They're just trying to have some fun. They're right. The Missouri's a dangerous river because she's so shallow and full of sand banks, but we've had good rains, so she isn't running low. If they were a mind to, they'd tell you we have one of the best pilots on the Missouri. I doubt any of them boarded the *Loulabelle* because they wanted to drown. Now if you gentlemen will excuse us ..."

The men stepped aside in silence.

When they were well away from them the man said, "I expect they're good men at heart, Sid. They just get carried away, usually at someone's expense, I suspect."

"How did you know my name?" Sid blurted out the question before he could stop himself. He regretted it immediately. He didn't mean to be rude.

The man gave him a big, reassuring smile. "When you're in close quarters like on the *Loulabelle*, there are many ears. That's a good thing to remember. It isn't a good idea to let everybody know your business. My name's Gallagher, William Gallagher." They shook hands.

"Thank you, Mr. Gallagher. I didn't think those men would hurt me, but I didn't know how to get out." Before Sid had time to ask him anything else, Mr. Gallagher was on his way around the crowded deck.

Most people sat now that they were underway. Some sat on small kegs or folding stools, others on the deck. Ma's rocking chair was piled up on the crates above them. It took up too much room to put on the deck, but they had folding stools Pa had made especially for the trip west. The scenery went past slowly but steadily. It wasn't the most comfortable ride. The river was rough and rocked the steamer.

Meals were served on the upper decks. People below had to fend for themselves. It wasn't so bad. You could pay for a little stove to cook on, but Ma had a picnic supper prepared for their first night out. They sat on a quilt in front of the trunks. "This is quite lovely," Ma said, "eatin' while evenin' falls on the river."

It wasn't lovely for everyone. They had just finished supper when a little boy nearby began vomiting. His frantic mother stood frozen, holding a crying baby. "Get me some ginger root, Sid," said Ma. "It's in my valise. Daniel said we'd better be prepared."

By the time Sid was there to help, Ma and the boy's father had the deck clean. Pale and wide-eyed, the boy leaned up against his mother looking as if he could heave again at any minute. "He doesn't have a fever," said Ma. "Like as not it's the rough water. I'll just need some hot water to make him some ginger tea."

She looked around to see if anybody had a stove she could use. It wasn't necessary, though. A man from the deck crew brought a kettle of boiling water. "Little'en ain't got his sea legs," he said kindly. "Best make him some ginger tea if you can. Don't worry, lad, it will get better on up ahead where the water is smoother." He poured water into a tin cup, nodding approval as Ma sprinkled some bits of ginger root on top.

"We'll let that steep a bit," said Ma. "If you have some crackers, you can try givin' him some a bit later when the tea's cool enough to drink.

The boy wasn't the only one aboard the lower deck who had trouble with the choppy waters. Several people on their end of the deck were seasick. Like the Johnsons, it was the first trip by steamboat many of the passengers had taken. Ma was kept busy. Sid carried the kettle for her, pouring hot water for ginger tea. It wasn't until the *Loulabelle* entered calmer waters nearly an hour later, that stomachs seemed to settle down. As Sid walked with Ma back to their spot on the deck, he couldn't get the smell of vomit out of his head. Suddenly it felt as though his stomach was turning inside out. He barely had time to get to the rail.

"Let's get you back to our spot," said Ma. "Put your arm around my neck. We'll take it slow."

He couldn't. Every time Sid stood upright, another explosion hit him. All he could do was hang over the rail, his head swimming.

"Have him smell this newspaper, ma'am," said a man's voice. "Hold it over your face and breathe in, Son. Nice big breaths. Let them out easy."

"Thank you, Captain Sterling," said Ma.

Strange as it seemed, the newspaper worked. The churning in Sid's stomach stopped. Later, he was sorry that he didn't have a chance to see the captain up close. At the time, he was too sick to care. Ma said the deck crew had reported an unusually large number of people who were seasick. Captain Sterling made a point to check for himself. "He is real nice. He even took time to thank me for helpin' out. Who would of thought of smellin' a newspaper? Goes to show you can learn somethin' new every day."

By bedtime, Sid felt more like himself. Like other deck passengers, they made their own beds. He was able to help Ma make a palate for Jimmy, Cora, and himself atop their trunks. He slept on the outside, with Jimmy and Cora next to the crates where they wouldn't fall. Ma and Pa slept on a palate on the deck next to the trunks.

Cora didn't want to go to sleep without Serena. Pa convinced her to leave the basket on the trunk at her feet, "Serena will probably return in the night, Sugar Plum."

Sid awoke in the night. Serena wasn't in her basket. The boat wasn't moving. Everyone seemed to be fast asleep. Getting up, he wedged the quilt against Jimmy so he wouldn't roll off on top of Ma and Pa. Sliding off the end of the trunk, he made his way through sleeping passengers to the rail where he could feel the fresh air on his face. It was pitch dark out on the water.

"Can't sleep, Son?"

Sid jumped, startled at the low voice that seemed to come from nowhere. It was Mr. Bright.

"Do they always stop the boat at night?" Sid asked.

"Sometimes, when there isn't enough moon. The pilot holds the boat overnight if he thinks it isn't safe. My guess is there's a sandbar ahead and getting around it is too dangerous without a full view. That's one of the things about the Missouri. The sandbanks are always shifting. The river is never quite the same one day to the next. I've been on board many a time when we've had to get out and lighten the boat so it could get around a sandbank. The Missouri is a hard river and full of challenges. That's why we can be thankful for a good pilot."

The call of an owl in the distance broke the quiet on the river. "If you keep looking and listening, you'll see and hear a busy world out there," said Mr. Bright. Across the river, a log slipped into the water making a soft plopping noise. Ripples spread out into the river.

"Traffic on the river has made it easier for people," said Mr. Bright, "but it hasn't been so kind to the creatures who live here."

Sid hadn't ever thought of that. He didn't know what to say, so he didn't say anything. He looked and listened. Foxes barked in the distance. He flinched at the cry of some little animal that was probably going to be a fox dinner.

"Sometimes Mother Nature seems unkind," said Mr. Bright.

"I reckon foxes have to eat, too," said Sid. "I just feel sorry for their prey. Pa says we shouldn't kill another creature if we can help it, except for food, and we should be quick and merciful about it."

"Your Pa is a wise man."

"Do you work on the river?" Sid asked, regretting it immediately. Ma said it was rude to ask people what they did for a living.

"Sometimes, when I get a chance," Mr. Bright said. "I like to know what's going on, how the river is changing, what's happening to all those who depend on her. We depend on her. She was alive thousands of years before people ever asked her to carry them.

Now she depends on us." Sid wasn't exactly sure what he meant. Mr. Bright spoke of the river as if it were a living thing.

Across the river, the log floated along the shore. Instead of being caught up in the current and driven back to the bank, it seemed to be gradually moving toward them. As it drew close to the steamer, a head as dark as the river came up, then another. Open mouths gasped for air, then submerged. Mr. Bright looked at him, "Sometimes it is better not to see. Best not mention this to anyone, Sid."

"Will they be all right?" Sid asked in a whisper.

"We can hope so. I expect they'll drift for a piece, then get on over to the other side of the river where they have a chance of disappearing safely."

"I hope they make it," said Sid.

"So do I," said Mr. Bright.

How long they stood there looking and listening, Sid couldn't have said. He wasn't aware of time passing until he yawned, covering his mouth. "You'd best turn in," said Mr. Bright. "Morning will be here before we know it. I'm very happy to have shared this time on the river."

"Me too," said Sid.

12.

A Curious Request

Sid awoke with Cora calling for him to move over. It was daylight. The boat was moving again. She wanted down. "I'm writin' a letter to Miriam," she declared. Soon she was bent over her slate making marks. Sid figured he wouldn't break the news that she couldn't send the slate like it was a postcard.

After breakfast, Ma let Sid take Jimmy and Cora around the deck to explore on condition that they didn't bother anyone or climb on the rail. Sid looked for Mr. Bright but didn't see him anywhere.

As they returned, he spotted a woman seated on the deck not far from where their trunks were located. She leaned over a large carpet bag that sat on the floor in front of her. She took out first one thing then another, putting them on the deck beside her. A breeze sweeping across the deck picked up a paper among her things and pushed it along toward the railing. Sid acted quickly, intercepting the paper. It was a five dollar note issued by a bank in St. Louis. Still searching in her bag, the woman didn't seem to notice. "Excuse me, Ma'am," he said. "This just fell from your bag."

She looked up, startled. Taking the bill, she caught her breath and held it to her chest, "Oh, my! I've been looking for it. I thought I'd lost it. Thank you. I can't thank you enough." Sid understood. Five dollars was a lot of money to lose.

In the afternoon, they watched as the riverbank drifted past. They listened to the crew sounding the depth of the river and visited Buttercup and Sandy. Later, they played hopscotch with some other children in a bare spot on the deck.

Serena appeared at the edge of the crates above their trunks; she stayed there all day. She wouldn't come down, even at Cora's coaxing. Sid took her scraps of food and a tin cup of water. By the second morning, Sid awoke with Serena sitting at his head, trying to groom him. She didn't like the way his hair felt in her mouth, shaking her head as if it left a bad taste. To Cora's delight, Serena stayed down, taking a long nap in her basket.

The river was full of drama. Sometimes they saw frogs singing on the bank, jaws puffing out like balloons. Water rats scurried above the water line, looking for food. Dragonflies skimmed the surface, their wings flashing blue in the sunlight. Occasionally a fish jumped from a still pool.

Late in the afternoon, they passed a field where black men plowed with horses. A white man on horseback watched over them. *Slaves.* The sight gave Sid a sick feeling in the pit of his stomach. Pa said most slaves worked in the fields. He wondered if these men working in the fields would ever be free, and if there really was a phantom slave stealer who would help them escape. He thought of Elijah and his mother. *I hope, hope, hope they got away.* He thought of the people floating with the log, trying to find freedom. He thought of the bounty hunters. *How can anybody try to make a bad thing sound like it is the right thing to do?* Sometimes the world seemed nonsensical.

The *Loulabelle* eased around sandbanks and dead tree branches, passed whirlpools, and swirling water. At one stop, they took on pigs squealing with fright. "More slave food," said one of the men. "Some of these plantation owners won't give their slaves beef; feed 'em pork. Cheaper."

"You mean the pork they don't want for themselves," said a second man, dryly.

"I think they like fatback and salt pork bettern anything," said the first man. "Thrive on it. Heck, they'll even eat the offals. Love 'em."

"You could be right," said the second man. "On the other hand, maybe they're makin' the best out of what they can get. I don't reckon black folk are that much different than the rest of us. If we was the ones in chains, we'd have to make do, too."

"You one of them abolitionists or somethin'?" asked the first man.

It was troubling, but Sid didn't hear the rest. *Maybe we didn't leave all that behind.* It was a disquieting thought.

The sun began its arc toward the western horizon, sending a path of gold along the river that turned to pink near the riverbanks. Above, fluffy clouds blushed a lighter shade of pink. As the *Loulabelle* slowed down to dock at one of its many stopping points, Sid took Jimmy and Cora to watch. Some of the men were fishing from the side of the boat. They had no more than docked when one of the fishermen let out a startled cry, "Got a big one on the line!" His float disappeared under water.

"Big catfish!" said a bystander. "They'll take a fishing line under like that." As the man hauled in his catch, the bystanders around burst into laughter. At the end of his line was a snapping turtle.

"Don't let him get you!" said one of the men, grinning at Cora and Jimmy. "Snappin' turtle gets you he won't let go till it thunders." Cora and Jimmy looked wide-eyed.

"Yes, he will," said Jimmy, tentatively. "I seen plenty of turtles."

"Reckon those was ordinary turtles," said the man who had caught the turtle. "Snappin' turtles is in their own league."

"Never was a truer word spoken," said another bystander. It was one of the men who had teased Sid about the boilers. "Snappin' turtles is just waitin' to getcha."

Sid could feel Cora flinch. He would have liked to have a better look at the snapping turtle. He'd seen snappers on the creek at home, but this one was larger. He didn't want Cora getting any more upset than she was, though. He steered them away to another part of the deck. "Don't believe that man, Cora," he assured her. "Those are just old made-up stories. No turtle is gonna hang on to somethin' that long. He'd be wantin' to find a fish or somethin' good to eat."

"Nobody's afraid of an old snappin' turtle, anyway," said Jimmy.

As the *Loulabelle* pulled away from the dock, Cora climbed up on the trunk by Serena, who was curled up in her basket fast asleep. A man, who looked as if he belonged on the upper deck, made his way toward them. He nodded politely, "Hello, Sid." It was Mr. Gallagher, who had rescued him from the men by the engine.

Looking at Cora, Mr. Gallagher said, "When I was a little boy, I liked to go barefoot in the summer. Somebody told me that a snapping turtle was after my big toe, and if he got it, he wouldn't let go until it thundered. It scared the daylights out of me. I was afraid to go barefoot after that. I was even afraid there might be a snapper under my bed at night. Of course, a snapping turtle would get awfully hungry between thunderstorms if he didn't let go of my big toe. Snapping turtles are a whole lot smarter than that. So don't you worry, little Miss. Those men were just having a bit of fun at your expense. In the whole history of steamboat travel, I've never heard of a snapping turtle holding on to somebody's toe." He smiled at her. Looking down at Serena, he said. "What a nice way to travel. Is she your kitty?"

Cora nodded, thumb in her mouth.

"Do you think she'd mind if I gave her a pat?" Mr. Gallagher asked politely.

Cora looked at Ma, who came over to the trunk to join them.

"Evening, Ma'am," he said, tipping his hat, "name's William Gallagher. You have three youngsters with mighty fine manners, as I had occasion to notice."

"Thank you," said Ma. "We're the Johnson family." She smiled reassuringly at Cora.

Cora took her thumb from her mouth. "Serena is goin' to Cal'forna, Mr. Gal'ger."

"Good for Serena. I suppose you'll be going with her?" Mr. Gallagher stretched out his hand so Serena could sniff it. She sleepily raised her head, gave his hand a sniff, and rubbed her face against it. "You're a fine cat, Serena. I hope you have a safe trip to California."

"Serena never been on the Santa Fe Trail," said Cora. She seemed to take a liking to Mr. Gallagher.

"Then she is in for a great adventure. I have traveled the Santa Fe Trail many times, Serena, and it is always full of surprises," he said to the cat. Tipping his hat to Ma again, he said, "Good-evening, Mrs. Johnson," and went on his way.

Before bedtime Sid liked to visit Sandy and Buttercup. He was giving them their evening pat when someone said, "Sid, could I have a word?" It was Mr. Gallagher. "I understand you and your family are on the way to California and you'll be following the Santa Fe Trail."

"Yes sir."

"Santa Fe's my home. The man who heads the lower deck crew tells me your family is well spoken of. I confess that I made a point to ask. I am wondering if you would kindly deliver a letter to my wife for me? I may not get to Santa Fe for some time yet. I hesitate to send it by post. With bandits on the trails these days, it will be a lot safer with you than with the postal riders. Perhaps you could keep it with your things? When you get to Santa Fe, you can leave word for Mrs. Gallagher at the Gallagher Trading Company. It will be easy to find. It's right on the plaza."

"Yessir," Sid said. "I'll give it to my Pa for safekeeping."

"I would like for you to keep it. I think it will be safe enough with you. Your Pa will have a lot on his mind. Besides, I've noticed how responsible you are. You know, a lot of boys would have kept the five-dollar bank note you returned to that woman. She was so distracted she didn't even notice when the very thing she was looking for slipped out of her bag."

Sid didn't know what to say. He hadn't realized anyone had noticed.

Mr. Gallagher looked around before reaching into the breast pocket of his coat and handing him an envelope. It was addressed to a string of names. Sid wasn't sure he could pronounce any of them but Gallagher and Santa Fe, New Mexico Territory.

"What a lot of names—and all one person." Mr. Gallagher smiled, reading them to Sid, "Señora Catalina Lucía Esteban-Valdéz Gallagher, Santa Fe, New Mexico Territory. It's the old Spanish custom. Señora is Mrs. in Spanish. Catalina Lucía are her given names. Esteban-Valdéz is her family name. I married her and gave her my name. Now put that in your coat pocket and when you have a chance, tuck it away with your things where it will be safe. I'd be grateful if you didn't tell anyone else about it. It's personal. I'd just as soon nobody else knew my business."

Sid often wondered afterward why he agreed so easily. It was something he couldn't quite name that made him trust Mr. Gallagher. He tucked the letter away in the wooden box with his toy soldiers, where it was soon forgotten.

Despite all his reassurance about the snapping turtle, Cora awoke Sid in the night, sure that a snapping turtle had her by the toe. He had to take off the blanket and show her that there was nothing in the bed before she would go back to sleep. *Some people seem to take delight in tormentin' others*, he thought. *No matter how hard you try, you can't undo the damage they do*. Then he thought of how Mr. Gallagher had stopped to reassure Cora. Ma liked to say, "Sometimes the smallest bit of kindness makes a big difference."

Unable to get back to sleep, he got up, partly hoping he would see Mr. Bright and talk about the river. By the rail where they had stood, the reflection of a full moon danced on the water. The *Loulabelle* was flooded with moonlight. Clouds began to drift in, leaving pools of dark shadow on the deck.

13.
Hiding in the Shadows

Voices floated Sid's way. Men seemed to be coming along the path between the railing and piles of sacks that reached nearly to the deck above. The voices came closer, low and urgent. Not wanting to be in the way, Sid slipped into the shadows behind some barrels that stood by the rail. Three men appeared, dark silhouettes against the fading moonlight.

"Don't try to play games with me." The speaker's drawn-out drawl and patient tone belied threatening words. "Thought you gave us the slip in Alton, did you? Hand it over. We know you got it."

"What is it that you want from me, Bayless?" It was Mr. Gallagher. He paused by the rail, uncomfortably close to where Sid hunkered in the shadows.

"Me 'n J.J. ain't got time fer parlor games." The man called Bayless sounded as if he were explaining a troublesome arithmetic problem. The faint light glinted on a silver piece attached to his hat band and his silver belt buckle as he turned, blocking Mr. Gallagher's way. "J.J.'s more than a little annoyed at havin' to ride halfway to Kansas to catch this here steamer. Don't do for a body to annoy J.J. He might be inclined to hurt you."

Clouds briefly parted from the moon. The man called J.J. stood behind Mr. Gallagher. A big man, he towered over the other two. Frizzy red hair stuck out from under his hat in all directions. An unruly red beard ended just below his neck. His coarsely woven suit looked as if it had been slept in.

They were a mismatched pair. J.J. looked like a big, friendly giant. Bayless looked like a snake, coiled and ready to strike.

The clouds swept back over the moon like curtains closing at the end of a play. "Like I said, Bayless, you need to explain what you're talking about," said Mr. Gallagher, politely.

"You can call me *Mr.* Sly now, Gallagher," said Bayless, a sneer in his voice. "I don't work for you anymore. You ain't any fancier 'n me. Makin' some money on the Santa Fe Trail don't mean you're some Irish swell."

Sid tried to make himself as small as possible. He hoped the moon would stay behind the clouds.

Suddenly Bayless Sly pushed Mr. Gallagher up against the sacks, pinning his arms down. "I'm getting' fed up," he said. "I'm a reasonable man, Gallagher. Better hand it over or we'll have to take it. I can't hold J.J. back much longer. He's gettin' plum wore down. We ain't followed you all the way from St. Louis to be taken fer fools. Don't reckon you expected us to find you on the *Loulabelle*, but you ain't so clever as ya think." He released his hold on Mr. Gallagher.

"Mr. Bayless Sly," said Mr. Gallagher, straightening his topcoat. There wasn't the slightest quaver in his voice. "Never was a man more well named. If I had anything on my person that you could possibly lay claim to, I would oblige. But I am at a loss."

"Let me refresh your memory, Gallagher. I'm – *we* are – lookin' for the letter you bought off that thief in St. Louis. Paid him a pretty sum for it."

"J.J. Gordon, I'm disappointed to see you take up with Bayless Sly," said Mr. Gallagher, ignoring Sly. "Unlike Mr. Sly, you did good work. You know I always treated you right. Paid you well. Taught you how to save your money and make it grow. I doubt Mr. Sly will do the same. I expect he'll take you for every dime you've saved if he hasn't already."

"Tryin' to get J.J. distracted?" sneered Bayless Sly. "Ain't goina work. This is your last chance, Gallagher." Sly's voice was threatening now. "No more discussion. You hand it over or I'm gonna have J.J. mess up your face. Shame to ruin that fancy suit you're wearin'. But I don't reckon you'll care if you're dead."

The dim light of a half-covered moon fell on J.J. Gordon as he leaned against the rail. He looked at his boots, like he was embarrassed. It didn't seem like he was interested in messing up anybody's face.

The boat lurched. Sid grabbed on to the railing, afraid he might fall. Shrinking back into the shadows, he breathed a prayer of thanks as his grip held.

Caught by surprise when the boat lurched, J.J. stumbled toward Mr. Gallagher. "Sorry, J.J.," he said, giving J.J. a mighty shove. It sent J.J. reeling into Bayless Sly, knocking them both to the floor.

Sly let out a string of curses the likes of which Sid had never heard before, except maybe when the bounty hunter opened the door to the corn crib. He was terrified they'd stumble into the barrels and see him as they scrambled to get up in the dark.

Gallagher was off at a run. The boat lurched again, sloshing water onto the deck. "After him," ordered Sly. He tripped over J.J. as he tried to get up, flattening them both again. "Get up, you useless oaf! He gets off the boat, we'll have hell to pay findin' 'em."

"I don't see no sense in followin'," J.J. puffed, getting up. "Mr. Gallager said he don't have the letter."

Sly steadied himself. "You take his word? Then you're dumber than you look." He took off at a run. J.J. followed, though not in any great rush.

Heart pounding, Sid hunkered in the shadows until the two men were gone and the sound of running died away. He hoped Mr. Gallagher got away. He waited until he was sure the men weren't coming back. *Did Mr. Gallagher give me the letter they want?* Maybe it was some other letter. *It must be some other letter because the one he gave me is addressed to Mrs. Gallagher.* Puzzling over what he'd heard, he returned to his bed atop the trunk.

The next thing he knew, the eastern sky was beginning to show a blush of pink behind them on the river. The last of the stars still sprinkled the sky. The *Loulabelle* was slowing down. "We'll be in Kansas soon," said Pa. "Independence is coming up. Then it's Westport Landing where we get off. Jake said most of this cargo is marked for Independence, so I reckon we'll be here for a bit while they unload."

"Ridin' in a wagon doesn't sound near half so bad after this trip," said Ma. "I don't know as I ever felt so dirty in my life. Not a place for decent folk to wash up proper and so many gettin' sick from the rough waters. I never made so much ginger tea in my life. Sid, we'll have to add ginger root to our list to buy in Kansas."

Sid stood at the rail watching as Independence Landing came into view. The *Loulabelle* glided into dock amidst a bustle of activity on the deck as the crew got ready to unload cargo. The few passengers getting off from the upper deck were first to leave. Sid didn't see anybody who looked like Mr. Gallagher or the men who were after him.

He asked if he could go stand with Buttercup and Sandy while the cargo was unloaded. They were sure to be stressed by the change. Pa went with him. Some other men were there, too, talking to the frightened animals and making sure that nobody took the opportunity to help themselves to the livestock in all the confusion.

The wall of crates and bags that had taken up almost an entire end of the deck began to disappear onto the dock. Kegs, barrels, sacks, and wooden boxes were unloaded or reshuffled to balance the load. In a shorter time than Sid thought possible, the pilot began calling out orders, guiding the ship away from the dock and on its way up the Missouri. A cool breeze swept through the deck where the cargo had been, clearing the stench of animals and people all crammed together for over a week.

A hillside heaving with shanties marked the beginning of Kansas, now called Kansas City. As his eyes followed the shoreline, Sid thought about the river. He wondered what had happened to all the little animals living along its banks before there was a Kansas. He thought about home in Illinois and wondered if he would ever see it again.

A wave of sadness swept over him. Friends at school; dinner on the grounds at church; Mrs. Harold; Daniel; Jacob, Seraphina, and their children; the Davis family; Elijah and his Mamma—it seemed like when you looked forward to one good thing, a whole bunch of other good things were left behind. *Is that how the world works?* he wondered. *At least I have Pa and Ma and Cora and Jimmy. I have Serena and Buttercup and Sandy. Maybe that's enough.* But he couldn't shake the feeling of sadness at the loss of almost everything he had ever known.

He felt as though something big was happening inside, something so big he might explode. He couldn't quite name it, but he realized that he would never be the same after this trip. Nothing would ever be the same. *But that doesn't have to be bad*, he told himself.

As the Loulabelle docked at Westport, Sid looked around to see if he could spot Mr. Bright. He wasn't with passengers from the upper deck. Nor was he anywhere below. Sid hoped he would see him again. He knew he would never forget that night, looking out over the water and thinking about the balance of life in and on the river.

Mr. Gallagher wasn't among the passengers who got off at Westport, either, nor was J.J., or Bayless Sly. It was as if the struggle and escape he had witnessed never happened.

If pressed to describe it, Sid would have said that getting from the docks in Westport to the hotel where they spent the first night was too full of new sights and sounds to take in. At the docks, Pa hired a man with a wagon to haul their things. He took them to the place where Mr. Stokes, the wagon master Uncle Luke had recommended, said they could safely store them until they had their own wagon. Afterward, the wagon driver dropped them off at the Gillis Hotel overlooking the Missouri River. It was a two-story brick building. Mr. Stokes had written that it was a clean, safe place to stay.

Even so, Ma asked to see their room before they paid. She ran her fingers along the edge of the mattress. "No bedbugs," she said. "I'm not payin' to stay in a hotel with bedbugs. We'll take the room." It wasn't fancy, but there were two beds, the first beds they'd seen since they left home. "And the last we're likely to see till we get to California," said Ma.

Cora let Serena out of her basket. "Sid, take Serena's basket outside and give her blanket a good shake, please," said Ma. "Clean out the basket, too. The fur is all matted down in there."

Cora took her thumb from her mouth, grabbing the basket handle. "Serena likes fur in her basket."

"Oh Cora, I wish you wouldn't do that," said Ma. "You've got to quit suckin' that thumb. The Lord only knows what's on your hands. You're far too old to be doin' that anyway."

"Cora's gonna look like a Santa Fe mule with big teeth stickin' out," said Jimmy. He hadn't ever seen a Santa Fe mule, but he seemed to think it was funny.

Ma ignored him.

"I'm goin' with Sid," said Jimmy. Pa overruled him.

"I don't never get to do nothin'," Jimmy whined. He was starting to show the effects of the long boat trip.

"Both of you two mischiefs are gonna have a good wash and go to bed," said Ma, firmly. "Sid, walk a ways past the hotel steps. Wouldn't be fair to other guests to have a blanket shook in their faces."

Sid walked along the road, farther than he needed to. After a week on the *Loulabelle*, he finally had his sea legs. Now it felt odd to be walking on a surface that didn't move under him. Stepping to the side of the road, he set about giving Serena's blanket a good shake. He was brushing the accumulated hair out of her basket when a horse and buggy passed him by, stopping in front of the hotel.

As he walked back to the hotel, a man stepped out of the buggy. Sid caught his breath. It was J.J. Gordon, all cleaned up, red beard trimmed, and wearing clean clothes. Following him was Bayless Sly. Still dressed all in black, his clothing looked spanking new. His hair was trimmed. His hat shaded a handsome, clean-shaven, but hard face. He looked as tough as beef jerky.

They don't know me, Sid told himself. Even so, he was scared. He stepped behind a big evergreen shrub that stood near the entrance, waiting for them to go inside.

The men lingered in front of the hotel, arguing as the buggy pulled away. Sid froze in place, wishing he hadn't stopped. *What will I do if they see me hidin' in the shrubs?* He wished he knew another way inside.

"You aims to *what*?" Sly's voice was like a growl.

"I'm hirin' on with teamsters headin' back to Santa Fe," J.J. said.

"We ain't done," said Sly. "Man can't disappear into thin air like that."

"Scent's done gone cold," J.J. said. "Shouldna let you talk me into leavin' Santa Fe in the first place."

"You gettin' cold feet on me?" Sly sounded so threatening a chill went down Sid's spine.

"What he said got me thinkin'," said J.J. "Gallagher always done right by me."

"Thinkin' ain't your strong point," said Sly. "You do all his grunt work. He gets the money. You call that right? I ain't spendin' my life grubbin' to make somebody else rich."

"I ain't seen much difference workin' for you." J.J.'s face looked like a storm cloud. "Gallagher was right. You done spent up mosta my money like you was some big shot. Leastwise Gallagher paid regular."

Afraid of being caught spying, Sid took a deep breath and walked up the steps and past the two men. He fought to keep from running. They didn't so much as lower their voices, much less notice him.

"Well, you ain't workin' *for* me," said Bayless Sly, as if he were being perfectly reasonable. "There's the difference. We're partners, J.J. You gotta to spend money to make money. We go around lookin' like a couple of dung beetles, we ain't got a chance of gettin' near Gallagher. Man like him ain't gonna be sleepin' with his horse when he can be in a place like this."

Sid slowed down as much as he dared. Sly didn't seem to notice.

"Tell ya what, J.J., we have ourselves a good supper and find out if there's anybody from off the Loulabelle stayin' at the hotel. If we don't flush Gallagher out, then tomorrow we go back into Kansas and ask around. Give it one more chance. We can stop off in one of them side streets and pick up a little money playin' cards or dominoes. If you think I ain't treating you fair and square, you take what we win."

So they haven't found Mr. Gallagher. Sid wanted to linger and hear what the men decided. But he had to keep moving.

Ma always said reading someone else's mail is rude, but he was tempted to go straight to his toy soldier box. He was more than curious to know if he had the letter they were talking about. He had a look, but the envelope was sealed. He'd have to break the seal. He didn't want to do that. He thought maybe he should tell Pa, but he didn't want Ma to overhear. It would worry her. *I'll tell him tomorrow*, he promised himself.

14.

Kansas

The next morning, Ma and Pa took them out to have a look at Kansas City and buy the rest of the things they needed for the trip. It was the busiest place Sid had ever seen. Streets were crowded with shops. There were blacksmiths, people who made harnesses and yokes, a tinsmith, and a general store that had everything from ready-made clothing and fabric to flour and sugar. There were places to buy barrels, wagons, mules, horses, oxen—just about anything you could imagine. And the streets were full of people outfitting for the trip west.

They saw their first American Indians in the crowds. They didn't know enough about native people to identify their tribe; Pa thought possibly Osage or Kaw. There were black people milling around, too. Sid hoped they were free, like Jacob and Daniel.

Some people looked as if they were down to their last dime. Others looked like they owned the world. Sid heard snatches of conversation between people who spoke in languages he had never heard before. It felt like they were going around the world on one crowded street.

After they had a look around, Ma took Jimmy and Cora to a buy fresh eggs and supplies she wanted for the trip. Sid got to go with Pa to buy their wagon and a team of oxen. It looked like Jimmy was going to pitch a fit about going with them until Ma said she needed a man with her. They agreed to meet back at the hotel at noon for dinner.

The first place they stopped to find a wagon, Pa thought the price was too high and the quality too low. "Mighty fine wagon here," said a salesman. "Won't find better. Getcha all the way to Californie and back." The man pressed Pa to make up his mind. "Lot of folk lookin' at this wagon. Best get it whilst you can. You won't beat the price."

Pa looked the wagon over carefully. He was not to be rushed. "Thank you kindly, but I think I'll keep looking," he said at last. Once they were out of earshot, he said, "Well, Sid, it might get to California if we hauled it in another wagon."

The next place where they stopped, Pa found one he liked, looking it over from top to bottom. A tall, lanky man left the large carpenter's bench at the back where he had been working. He extended his hand to Pa. "Name's Douglas Billings. See anything you like, let me know. Take your time." He shook Sid's hand, too.

Mr. Billings started to return to the carpenter's bench when Pa asked, "What about the brakes on this one? We're looking to go to California. From what I know, there's some steep mountain passes along the way. I want to know that the brakes will hold."

"That's a good question," Mr. Billings said. "Let me show you." He invited them to get under the wagon where they could see. "I designed this brake system myself. Use it on all my wagons. I pride myself on giving folk the best that can be bought whether they know all the finer points about what they are getting or not.

"I started out with Hiram Young, over in Independence back in 1851. Brilliant man. He specializes in government freight wagons. Can't find a better wooden-axle freight wagon. I focus on folk like yourselves, who need a good, dependable wooden-axle wagon.

If you want something bigger, I'll send you over to Young."

"Hiram Young. Seems like I've heard that name somewhere," said Pa, crawling out from under the wagon.

"There was some in the papers last year comparing Young favorably with a supplier over in St. Louis and the Pennsylvania wagon makers. Came over from Tennessee as a slave, bought his freedom, and went to work as a carpenter. That's when I met him. Took me on as an apprentice for a couple of years.

"You got over 1500 miles between you and California. Mountain passes are just one hurdle. You'll have some mighty challenging rivers to cross, too. You taking the Oregon Trail or the California Road?"

"Neither," said Pa. "My brother in California advised me to take the Santa Fe and the Southern Route—the old Mexican road. Says it's too risky on the passes in late March on both the other trails. Wouldn't want to get caught in a blizzard."

"If you're heading out end of March, you could get caught in a blizzard on the Santa Fe Trail, but your chances of surviving are better," said Mr. Billings, "least that's what I hear."

"I'll take the wagon," said Pa. "We're due to meet up with our company this week, and truth be told, I'd like to save on hotel and storage bills. How soon can you have it ready?"

"Will this afternoon do?" asked Mr. Billings. "You'll need a water barrel. I can rig it on the side of the wagon. There's a cooper, Eli Smith, just across the way from me. Does good work. You can pick out what you want. He'll send it over for me to fit on your wagon. Now this wagon will haul a substantial load, depending on your oxen. Have you bought oxen yet?" They hadn't.

"There's a fellow right on the edge of Kansas who will give you healthy oxen at a fair price. Name's John Westerly. He likes training 'em, too. He'll give you some tips, if you haven't worked oxen."

"Can't say that I have," said Pa.

"Some folk favor mules. They're bringing them in from Santa Fe every day now. Most of the teamsters use mules. That may be fine for the trip to Santa Fe, but I don't think you can beat a good team of oxen for endurance. You'll need that if you're planning to follow the Mexican road. Westerly will advise you about yokes for your team, too. He works with another fellow so you can get the whole thing outfitted in one stop. I trust him. He knows that part of the business."

It was a done deal. Pa bought the wagon and canvas top. "It was a little more than I wanted to pay," he explained to Sid as they left for the cooper across the road. "But you can see the difference in quality. The wood siding on the wagons at that first place was flimsy. It looked to me like they cut corners on a lot of things, including the axle. This man takes pride in his work. He was glad to talk about it. We got ourselves a good wagon that we can count on. I trust his judgment about the oxen, too. When you find somebody you can trust, they won't send you off in the wrong direction. Anyway, if we can get the wagon this afternoon, we can avoid another night at the hotel. That'll make up the difference."

The cooper was a stout little man. Like Mr. Billings, he introduced himself and invited them to look around. "Name's Smith, Eli Smith." He talked to them as he fitted long oak staves into an iron hoop. Seeing Sid's curiosity, he said, "Reckon makin' a barrel is kind of like putting together a puzzle." As he talked, Mr. Smith kept working, putting one stave in place, trying another, and setting it aside until one met his approval. The hoop was almost full of staves.

"It looks kinda like a barrel already," said Sid.

"That's just the beginning," said Mr. Smith. "But I reckon you folk didn't come for a barrel-making lesson unless you want to become my apprentice. I could use a smart lad like you."

"Mr. Billings sent us over to find a water barrel," said Pa. "It is mighty interesting seeing you work. We had a good cooper back in Alton, Illinois, where we come from, but can't say as I ever saw a barrel made up from start to finish."

"Illinois? I hail from Pennsylvania. I guess just about everybody out here hails from someplace else," said Mr. Smith.

Sid would have loved to watch the process all the way through. But he knew that they had a lot to do.

"One of my standard barrels will hold up to 40 gallons of water," Mr. Smith said, showing them finished barrels. "From what I hear, you can't count on finding water. You'll need all the water you can carry through some of those stretches."

Pa chose a barrel that Mr. Smith recommended. "We'll get this right over to Billings. Anybody tell you about filling your water barrel?" Mr. Smith asked. "Fill up at one of the fresh streams that pour into the Kansas. Be a lot safer than water from the Missouri. Too many folks on the river, they're throwing so much trash in her these days I don't trust her for drinking water. Some of it's coming from the steamboats. Too much traffic. You have to be careful with your water. Some folks think bad water can make a body sick."

Mr. Smith shook Pa's hand. Turning to Sid, he offered his hand. "Change your mind about going out West, I can always use an apprentice."

They headed on through town to find the place to get oxen. "He said on the edge of Kansas," said Sid. "I thought this was Kansas City."

"Well, it hasn't been called Kansas City that long," said Pa.

On the way through the streets, they passed a saloon. Men were sitting at a table outdoors playing dominoes. A tall, thin man with a pock-marked face sat at one end of the table drinking whiskey from a bottle and watching. "How's about puttin' some money down to make it worth your while?" one of the players asked him. Sid flinched. It was Bayless Sly. J.J. Gordon's back was to him, but Sid would have recognized that red hair just about anywhere.

He patted his shirt pocket. In all the excitement he'd forgotten to tell Pa about the letter. But he'd tucked it into his shirt before he put on his waistcoat, meaning to tell Pa. Now wasn't the time to tell him. "You got the money, Swathmore, we got the time," said Sly.

"You take me fer a fool?" asked Mr. Swathmore. "I don't put money down lessen I play, and I don't play lessen I sees all the dominoes first."

"Are they gonna wager on the game, Pa?" asked Sid once they were past.

"Reckon so. I stay clear of that kind of outfit. 'A fool and his money are soon parted.'"

They made their way through the crowded streets. Sid was almost sure he saw Mr. Gallagher in a side street. Before he could get a good look, the man melted into the crowd.

15.

The Right Team

Sid was just about as excited as he'd ever been about anything when they went to pick up their wagon and team that afternoon. Jimmy got to come along. He was bursting with pride at the honor of going with "the men folk." Sid didn't explain that Pa was the only one who qualified as a man. That wasn't how Jimmy saw it. Jimmy looked up to him. Sid didn't need Ma there to remind him that he needed to be a good example.

"We'll see if the wagon is ready first," said Pa.

Mr. Billings shook hands with them. When Mr. Billings extended a hand to Jimmy, Sid thought his brother would pop the buttons off his shirt in delight. "Glad you were able to do business with John Westerly," he said. "It breaks my heart to see some of the poor animals these dealers pawn off on unsuspecting folk. It takes weeks to get them trained. Some of them barely get by. Lord only knows what happens when the going gets rough.

"Thing is, most of your wagon masters will get you to where you're going; but you can't expect them to do anything but show you where the grass and water are. It's a shame, really. Lot of folks are real greenhorns, hardly know the front end of an ox from its rear"—Jimmy burst into a fit of giggling, but Mr. Billings went on without so much as a pause—"They need more than a guide. You meeting up with a group in Council Grove, or are you going with somebody from here?"

"My brother put me on to a fellow name of William Stokes," said Pa.

Mr. Billings' face lit up. "Good man. Now Bill Stokes has been taking the Santa Fe for years. Knows how to run a wagon train, too. He's turned more than one greenhorn into a seasoned traveler. Lot of folks just head west and follow the trails. So many go now, I reckon they figure they can do it on their own. It's still a dangerous trip. You made a good choice."

"Glad to hear you say so," said Pa. "We'll need all the help we can get. Been nice doing business with you, Mr. Billings. We'll get on over and collect our oxen. We'll be back to pick up the wagon."

"The streets are getting so gall-durn crowded these days, I'll have my boy take you and the wagon over to Westerly. You'll want to work your oxen outside town till you're used to them. Getting through the streets to pick up a wagon isn't the best way to get acquainted with your team. The boy will help you put the bonnet up, too. You'll need to give it a good rub with linseed oil to waterproof both layers. Even so, you'll get some leaks if you're caught in a gulley-washer. Some folks buy an extra canvas to lay over their goods, protects them from rain and dust."

The boy, Matt Billings, didn't seem much like a boy to Sid. He stood a good head taller than Pa. He helped them put up the hoops that held the canvas top and stretch it out over them. "Nice thing about it is you can pull back the top in the early morning before the sun gets too hot. And you can store a lot of things by hanging them from the hoops. The double canvas will keep it a lot dryer inside, once you get it oiled up."

"Now it really looks like we're goin' to California, Jimmy," said Sid, putting an arm around him. For the first time, he felt really excited about going West.

"Yeah," said Jimmy, eyes shining.

"Ever driven donkeys?" Matt asked Jimmy as he hitched two little donkeys to the wagon.

Jimmy was beside himself with excitement. "No, but I sure been wantin' to."

"Then you'll haveta give me a hand," said Matt. His eyes sparkled, but he didn't so much as crack a smile. He let Jimmy help hold the reins, giving a running set of instructions as they rode through the busy streets.

Pa and Sid rode in the wagon bed. It was a rough ride. When they finally got to Westerly's place, Pa said, "Thought I would lose every tooth in my head."

"Streets are uncommon bumpy," said Matt. "Had us a good rain three or four days ago, a real gully-washer. Ruts are still there. It was one big mess I can tell you. A loaded wagon will make for an easier ride, though. Shoot, I heard tell some women-folk do their needlework sitting on the wagon seat."

The six big, gentle oxen they picked out that morning were waiting to be hitched together with yokes fitted just for them. "Your Uncle Luke said we'd put more money into getting a team than anything else," said Pa. "I think it will be worth it."

"They're just cows!" Jimmy exclaimed, undisguised disappointment in his voice. "Reckon we ought to take donkeys. I know how to drive a donkey."

Sid couldn't help grinning, but he didn't say anything. Apparently, Jimmy considered himself an expert on donkeys after riding with Matt.

Mr. Westerly laughed. "You're right, young man. They look like just plain cattle, the kind you'd find at home. The difference between an ox and your ordinary cow is training. Let's get them hitched up to the wagon, and you'll see why they are called oxen instead of cattle."

Jimmy watched, a skeptical frown on his face.

Mr. Westerly had the yoke and harness ready. "Hitching up oxen is different than it is for mules or horses, Jimmy. I'll show you if you like, Johnson."

"I'd sure appreciate it," said Pa. One thing about Pa, he was never afraid to admit it when he didn't know something. "How can you learn if you act like you know it all?" he'd say.

"You set the yoke on your animals that will be closest to the wagon first. We'll yoke your lead animals last." He picked up a heavy double yoke so smooth it shone.

"That's gonna be too heavy," said Jimmy.

Mr. Westerly smiled at him kindly. "You think we ought to give them a nice soft collar like those donkeys?"

Jimmy nodded his head in agreement. Sid tried to keep a straight face.

"Seems like a good idea on the face of it," said Mr. Westerly. "It would be a very bad choice for these oxen. See, cattle pull from the neck and shoulders. Horses and donkeys pull from the breast. A soft collar would just make it harder for these good beasts. It would rub sores on their hide, too. We wouldn't want that now, would we?"

Jimmy shook his head but he didn't look convinced.

"Come on, Star and Sampson, let's get you in place first." He fitted the yoke on first one, then the other. When they picked out the oxen, Sid supposed these two would be the lead, but Mr. Westerly said the strongest oxen needed to be closest to the wagon.

Soon all six oxen were yoked and hitched to the wagon. Josiah and Gregg were the middle team. "Know how they got their names, Sid?" Mr. Westerly asked.

"Didn't Josiah Gregg write a book about the West?" Sid faintly remembered.

"He did," said Mr. Westerly. "First book about the Santa Fe Trail."

Mr. Westerly said Josiah and Gregg were a bit lazier than Star and Sampson. The lead team was Cornflower and Promise. "These two are fearless," Mr. Westerly said as he watched Pa yoke them. "Cornflower will be the key to the team. She is the smartest of the bunch, as calm under pressure as any I ever raised. You tell her what to do, and she knows how to pass the information along."

"How's she goina do that?" asked Jimmy, frowning.

"Oxen have their own ways, Jimmy," Mr. Westerly smiled at him. "Cornflower and Promise are both brave and adventurous. They don't have to be stronger than the wheel team; they just have to be able to lead. First time you come to a wide river, these two will plunge in. Sampson and Star are good strong steers, but they'd think twice about crossing a river if it was up to them."

"Where's the bit and reins?" asked Jimmy.

"With oxen there's no bit and no reins," Mr. Westerly explained. "Just this yoke and chain and the driver. I train them to voice, to whip, and to body movement. That's all you have with oxen. No reins, no harness."

Jimmy still didn't look convinced.

"Never use a whip to hurt an animal, Jimmy. Sometimes you have to give an ox a good firm swat on the rear end to remind him you're the boss. Oxen like to know where they stand. In the herd they work it out with their horns, but I establish who's boss when they're too young to do anything about it."

Jimmy's scowl shifted to a grin.

"Use your whip to signal," Mr. Westerly said. "These oxen know how to follow directions. If I was to fall on the ground, my oxen would stop. Many a driver's life has been saved by oxen who know body commands. The whole team has to know the commands, but Cornflower—your nigh ox—will be the leader."

Sid explained, "The nigh ox is the one on the left side of the lead team, Jimmy. That's where the driver walks."

By the time the oxen were hitched to the wagon, Jimmy showed signs of wavering in his commitment to donkeys. He allowed that oxen *might* be almost as good as a donkey team.

"When you figure that with horses you have to cinch under the belly, get the bridle and bit on and what not, you're way ahead of the game with oxen. Oxen are steady, too. They won't run away, and they aren't in high demand by thieves. You got yourself a good team, Jimmy."

Jimmy beamed.

"Johnson, work them out with a short drive every day before your train leaves. Lot of folks make the mistake of overworking their animals at the start instead of easing them into things. From what I hear, once you're out past Santa Fe you'll want your animals in tip top shape. If you treat them right, they'll be able to see you over the mountains and through the desert."

"Sure do appreciate all your help," said Pa, shaking Mr. Westerly's hand. Mr. Westerly shook Sid's and Jimmy's hands, too.

"God bless you," said Mr. Westerly. "I've sent many a team out to California and Oregon. I don't know if I'd have the courage to go west myself."

As he thought about it later, Sid realized that back home in Illinois he hadn't known the first thing about going to California. He just figured they'd get up and go. He had no idea how much work it would take before they left for Kansas. Now that they'd finally arrived in Kansas, there was still more work to do. *I guess Mr. Westerly would say I'm a real greenhorn*, he thought.

Pa led the team, walking while Sid and Jimmy rode in the wagon. "You boys run in and help your Ma and Cora with our things," he said when they got to the hotel. "We'll sleep with our wagon tonight!"

Jimmy raced ahead. Sid let him lead. He knew his little brother was fairly bursting with excitement about the team. To tell the truth, he was excited, too. When they got to the room, all thought of the team vanished. Their room looked like it had been turned upside down.

16.
Terrible News

Jimmy let out a yell. Sid gasped. All their belongings were on the beds and the floor. Cora sat in a corner of one bed holding Serena close and sobbing. Her mouth set in a grim line, Ma brushed up pieces of Serena's smashed basket.

"Cora and I went to the dinin' room to pick up a basket supper for this evenin'. When we got back, the door was ajar. Serena was fluffed up like a brush. Manager's already been here to have a look. Lock's been forced. Get your Pa, Sid." Her even tone didn't deceive him.

Sid sprinted to the wagon. Pa read trouble in his face and handed him the whip. "Wait with the team, Sid." With that he was gone. Sid longed to know what was happening and anxious about being responsible for the oxen. He needn't have worried about the oxen. They waited obediently. After a while

Jimmy came carrying the first carpetbag. "Ain't nothin' missin'," he said.

"Is, too," said Cora. "Serena's basket got smashed." A flood of tears started all over again.

"Don't you worry, Sugar Plum," said Pa, heaving bags into the wagon. "We'll find Serena a new basket. Smashing her basket was a mean thing to do. Probably somebody making mischief when they couldn't find anything worth stealing. Can't think anybody'd be fool enough to leave valuables lying around in a hotel room."

Ma came last; her face was still drained of color. She held a very unhappy cat tightly wrapped in her blanket to keep her from escaping.

Was it Bayless Sly and J.J.? The thought flashed through Sid's mind. He hoped Pa was right. Somebody was making mischief because they hadn't found any money. If they were looking for that kind of thing, they'd picked the wrong room. Pa was too careful. *But what if they do know? What if it was them?* he wondered, feeling guilty that he hadn't told Pa. He patted the letter that still rested safely inside his waistcoat pocket. He couldn't bring himself to say anything about it, not in front of the others.

Still pale when they arrived at the place where their things were stored, Ma resolutely set to work. Jimmy's assignment was ticking off every item on her list as it went into the wagon. Sid's job was to help Pa place things. Ma was so well organized that she knew exactly where she wanted everything. She wasn't far off, either. Even though she didn't have the wagon when she did her planning all winter long, she had a pretty good idea of how much space they'd have. The only thing she didn't have on her list was Serena and her basket.

Serena did remarkably well, better than anybody besides Cora expected. Contrary to any of the cats Sid had ever known, she took to travel—even on the Loulabelle. Now she explored the wagon as they loaded it, jumping from one thing to the next. When all was done, she found a place for herself atop one of the trunks, just out of reach.

Cora was put out. "You have an ever so very nice blanket, Serena."

"Now that the wagon's loaded, I'll go back into town and get Serena a new basket," Pa said. "She knows the blanket's there for her.

Right now, she wants to see what it feels like to ride up top. The important thing is, she's still with us."

That seemed to comfort Cora. She snuggled down inside the wagon near the blanket, thumb in mouth.

"You goina have buckteeth," said Jimmy. "Goin' to California ain't for babies."

Cora pulled her thumb out of her mouth long enough to say, "Isn't," and stick out her tongue. A stern look from Ma put an end to it.

"Leaving everything behind isn't easy for any of us, Sid," said Pa as they set out to find a basket for Serena. "I was hoping to get on over to the Stokes Company by now, but this is important to Cora. Probably more important than we know."

Finding a basket with a lid was harder than Sid expected. But they finally found a trading post that sold everything imaginable, including American Indian baskets. Sid picked one out that had a wide base and a nice round lid with handles woven into the basket. "Cherokee vine basket," said the trading post clerk.

"Are you Cherokee?" Sid blurted out the question.

The clerk smiled, "Half Cherokee," he said, "the better half I think."

"It's a fine basket," said Pa. "Appreciate doing business with you."

At last, they left for the field where the Stokes Company was gathering. There were a little over twenty wagons already there. Pa said Mr. Stokes wanted at least thirty, and they might pick up a few more in Council Grove.

Sid looked out from the bonnet taking everything in. A girl stood on the edge of the field looking forlorn. Beside her stood a black and white dog, its tail wagging.

"Hallo there," Sid called. She looked a bit younger than he was. When he saw the way her face lit up, he wondered if they would be friends.

Mr. Stokes came over to shake hands. Walking with Pa and the team, he showed them where to park the wagon and pasture the livestock. "We'll be having a campfire once it starts to get dark," he said. "Come sit with us and meet the company."

Sid liked him immediately. Mr. Stokes had a stern look, but his eyes were kind. He shook hands with Jimmy, tipped his hat to Ma, and spoke to Cora, who hid her head behind Ma's skirts.

Now a convert to oxen, Jimmy offered a stream of advice on unyoking. "I thought you wanted us to get donkeys," Sid couldn't help teasing him.

"Nah, oxen's more reliable," Jimmy said with authority.

People were a blur of welcoming faces around the campfire. Sid figured it would take a while to get to know everybody in the wagon company. Later, after they'd pitched the tent for Ma and Cora, Sid slipped the letter Mr. Galloway had given him from his pocket and put it back in his box of toy soldiers, grateful that he hadn't left it in the hotel room. Tucking it under the wagon seat, he promised himself he'd tell Pa about it.

Jimmy and Cora were both sound asleep in their tent when Ma said, "In all the excitement over the break-in, I completely forgot the letter!"

Sid caught his breath, *How could*—but Ma interrupted his thoughts. "It's from Mrs. Harold. It was waiting at the hotel, but the man at the desk didn't think to give it to us last night. How about you read it out for us, Sid?"

She broke the seal on the letter and handed it to him.

"Dear Friends," Sid read.

A hasty note in hopes it will reach you at the Gillis Hotel before you leave on the Trail. Something terrible has happened. Miriam, Jacob's youngest, dear, sweet Miriam has been kidnapped and we have yet to find her! The children were playing hide and seek in the orchard (Jacob and Seraphina are settled in your house now) and they couldn't find her. They were told not to go so far from the house, but you know children. Precious minutes were lost before the others realized Miriam was actually missing and called for help. Daniel and Jacob managed to track her kidnappers as far as the Missouri River. Daniel has gone into Missouri after her. Jacob wanted to go, but we convinced him that he must stay and hold the family together. But, oh, how I fear for Daniel and for my dear, dear granddaughter. Pray for us and especially for Miriam and Daniel. What is to become of our Miriam? This is too hard to bear.
Your neighbor,
Leona Harold

"You don't mean it!" Ma gasped.

"And we're not there to help," said Pa, shaking his head in disbelief.

"What will happen to her?" asked Sid, giving the letter back to Ma.

"Unless Daniel finds her, she will be sold," said Pa, brow furrowed. "That's the long and short of it. I wish I could be hopeful. Daniel's smart, but he won't be safe as long as he's in Missouri."

"It's a terrible risk for him," said Ma. "Poor Mrs. Harold must be worried sick. Thank God the youngens weren't awake to hear this. Sid, we mustn't say a word to Cora, ever. I know we can trust you."

But not with everything, Sid thought. *There's a whole lot more they haven't ever told me.*

17.
Mean Mischief

The next morning, Ma asked Sid to take Cora and Jimmy off her hands so she could get set up to make breakfast. The deep circles under her eyes told Sid that she hadn't slept. He didn't mind helping out with Jimmy and Cora. He usually found a way to make things interesting and keep them from bickering. "Let's go on an expedition," he suggested. It was hard to sound cheerful when his mind kept returning to Miriam. *What if it were Cora? Or Jimmy?*

"Reckon there's tigers out there?" Jimmy asked, half believing it.

Thumb in her mouth, Cora's eyes grew big. She didn't say anything.

"Well, I doubt it," said Sid, sweeping aside the cloud that hung over him, "unless it's imaginary ones. If there are, they'll be cousins with Serena, so I expect they'll be friendly. First thing is to find us some big sticks. You can't be a proper explorer without a good walkin' stick."

He tried to focus on what they were doing, but the worry kept crowding in. *What is a little girl like her to do?* There weren't any words for how terrifying and awful it must be for Miriam and for Jacob and Saraphina. *And for Daniel—*

"Here's a stick without too many pokey places stickin' out," called Jimmy, bringing Sid back to the present. When they found two more good, sturdy sticks, they set out toward the meadow where the livestock grazed. Sid figured Cora could pick flowers and he could keep Jimmy busy looking for insects. That's when they spotted the girl and her dog. She looked worried.

Her name was Grace Willis. She'd found a horned toad on an ant den. It was hard for Sid to imagine that somebody hadn't ever seen a horned toad, but she hadn't. "I think Ruby and Junior hurt it," she said. Grace seemed to think they took delight in doing hurtful things.

Sid explained that it was the ants she ought to be worried about. "Horned toads like to eat ants."

Cora wanted to pat the dog. "This is Old Shep," Grace said.

"Put your hand out first so he can sniff it," Sid told her. Old Shep lifted his paw. Jimmy shook it. But Cora threw herself around the dog's neck in a massive hug. Old Shep didn't seem to mind. He wagged his tail.

"She can't be an explorer without a stick," said Jimmy, looking at Grace.

"Then we'll have to find one," said Sid. He soon discovered that Grace was full of ideas and had a great imagination. Except for Cora and Miriam, Sid had never spent much time with girls. The ones he knew back home didn't seem to be interested in anything but walking around the school grounds in packs, arms around each other, giggling over everything in sight. Sid didn't have time for that kind of silliness. Grace was different. She didn't know the first thing about life outside of a city, though.

Sid liked Old Shep, too. He had always wanted a dog. He never understood why they didn't have one on the farm until he found out about Elijah and his mother. They couldn't have a dog barking at people in the night. It would take a really smart dog to know the difference between somebody running to freedom and somebody up to mischief. He figured Old Shep was that smart.

Grace led them to where a whole family of friendly tigers lived in a ditch surrounded by tall sunflowers. Jimmy, who counted on tigers being fierce, was disappointed in imaginary tigers until Grace said they were invited for tea and produced a peppermint stick from her pocket. She broke it into pieces. They all shared, except for Old Shep and the tigers, who had their own imaginary peppermint.

Ma always said, "If you have imagination, you'll never be bored." Sid knew that he wasn't going to be bored with Grace as a friend. She even said she'd like to learn how to play marbles, and she'd teach him how to do cat's cradle.

Their adventure had to be curtailed when Grace's Mamma called her in for breakfast. Jimmy and Cora didn't want to end the expedition, but it was time for them to get back to the wagon, too.

Pa had milked Buttercup by the time they returned. "You were helping Ma, so I figured Buttercup wouldn't mind if I did the milking. Turned out to be a good thing. I met a fellow named Joseph Winkler," Pa said as they gathered around for breakfast. "He's a barber, just learning about farm animals."

"You could stand with a haircut, Ben Johnson," said Ma, "so could you two boys." She was usually the chatty one at breakfast. Now she fell silent.

"Winkler bought a cow in Kansas City off a man who said she was a fine milk cow," said Pa. "Man didn't mention that she's a kicker. Poor fellow. He'd try to start milking her, she'd give the bucket a good kick, and out with the milk. It was sloshing everywhere. I told him you have to establish authority. I said, 'Winkler, you gotta approach her quietly. Give her a pat on the rump. Push back on her haunch. Lean into her.' He doesn't realize—"

Sid looked at Ma; the worry lines around her eyes seemed to soften.

"—a cow with a full udder needs to be milked. She stands for him, she's not trying to run away. It's just the kicking. He's getting the idea. Seems like a real nice fellow. Plans to set up his own shop in California."

"What's her name?" asked Cora.

"His children named her Bossy," said Pa.

"Maybe she wants to be the boss," said Ma, smiling. Suddenly, Sid knew why Pa was going on about a cow at breakfast. He was trying to take Ma's mind off of Miriam and Daniel.

Ma wrote a long letter to Mrs. Harold. Unknowing, Cora wrote a few scribbles to Miriam. Sid couldn't let himself think about what the chances were of Miriam ever getting to read it, even if Cora could actually write it. There wasn't anything they could do. It was a hopeless feeling. Ma tried to reassure him—and herself, Sid figured—"If anybody can rescue her, it will be Daniel. We just have to keep prayin'."

There were so many things going on that Sid didn't have time to worry until well after the noon meal. By then, most folks were having naps or taking a rest in the shade of the wagons. He decided to have a walk around by himself, setting out in the direction of the meadow where the livestock were grazing. He thought of Daniel and the terrible risk he was taking. *What will Daniel do if he's caught?* He couldn't help remembering how Daniel said, "I can't live trapped up." *What we need is the phantom slave stealer*, he thought. If somebody could slip into Kentucky and Missouri to help people escape to freedom, why couldn't that person find Miriam and steal her back?

Two men stood at the far end of the meadow guarding the livestock. Men in the Stokes Company took turns standing watch. Sid was too deep in thought to pay them much attention. He couldn't quit thinking of the pained look on Ma's face and Pa's set jaw as he read the letter from Mrs. Harold. He thought of Miriam and her brothers and sister all waving good-bye as they left for the Loulabelle. Miriam called, "Goodbye Johnsons, we love you!" *How could anybody take a little girl from her family like that?*

A boy and girl sneaking along the edge of the field brought him back to the moment. Ducking low, they were obviously trying to avoid being seen by the men standing watch. The boy carried a long stick. *They're up to something.* Sid darted behind some brush where he could watch without being seen.

Looking both ways, the two stopped nearby, close enough for him to hear. "Ready, Junior?" the girl called in a low voice.

So, Ruby and Junior, he thought. The two crept toward the cattle. He followed as closely as he dared, hiding behind a tree.

Not far away, Bossy stood chewing her cud.

Slowly, carefully, Ruby and Junior crept up behind her. Then, with split-second timing, Ruby grabbed Bossy's tail and gave it a pull while Junior gave her a sharp poke in the behind.

Bossy let out a bellow, lashing out with a back leg. Ruby and Junior were fast, but they barely escaped her wrath. Her foot struck the stick Junior was holding, snapping it into pieces. Turning on them, head down, Bossy charged.

Ruby and Junior worked like a practiced team. He ran in one direction; she ran in another. Bossy didn't know which one to follow. In her moment of indecision, they disappeared behind the brush pile.

Sid didn't have to think twice. The instant they ran, he was on his way to the herd as fast as he could run. Bossy was angry. Buttercup was the first cow in her way. Bossy lit into her, head down. Buttercup was probably at the very bottom of the cow social register. Her tail hung between her back legs. She was terrified. She didn't even try to fight back.

Bossy began butting any animal in her way. It felt like she was embarrassed and wanted to pick a fight to cover up. If she got the animals too worked up, they were likely to run and escape the guards. There was a bit of scuffling as some animals pushed back. The men standing watch flew into action, herding the livestock out of Bossy's way.

The first wave of her anger over, Bossy was breathing hard, though her head was still down. Her back arched in flight or fight position. Sid walked as close as he dared. "Here, Bossy," he said in a soft, quiet voice. "That was a mean thing that happened to you. But you're okay now. Just settle down."

Bossy's back was still arched, but she didn't move. "It's over, Bossy. You're a good cow. You didn't deserve that."

Bossy lifted her head and looked at him. "Good girl, Bossy." Her back dropped. She seemed to relax.

"Reckon what got them so riled up?" asked one of the men who was standing guard.

"You've got me," said the other, still out of breath from running after animals. "Good thing that dog was here. Good herder, that one." Sid looked down to see Old Shep sitting at his side. He had been so focused on Bossy he hadn't even noticed Old Shep.

"Coulda been a bee, or the weather, or somethin' like that," said the first man.

"That your dog, son?" asked the other, giving Old Shep a pat. "You have a good way with animals."

Sid couldn't help remembering the night on the Loulabelle and Mr. Bright, who also said that he had a way with animals. *Maybe I do*, he thought. "Thank you, sir," he said. "Old Shep isn't my dog, he's with the Willis family."

He didn't say what he'd seen. He couldn't think of any good that could come of it. Anyway, Ruby and Junior were long gone.

18.

A Limping Cow

About the time Sid finished milking Buttercup that evening, Mr. Winkler came for Bossy. Bossy wouldn't let him go near. "Guess she's still worked up," said Mr. Winkler. "I heard there was some trouble with the animals this afternoon."

Pa joined them. He had just finished practicing with the team. "Looks like she's limping in that hind leg, Winkler. Let me have a look." He approached Bossy slowly, giving her a pat on the rump. She bolted, stopping just out of reach. "I think it's the foot," said Pa. "We'd better put a rope on her so I can have a look. She's not going to stand still."

Sid watched, pail of milk in hand. A small crowd of men and boys gathered. Somebody handed Pa a rope. He approached Bossy carefully, talking softly. She didn't arch her back or lower her head. That was a good sign. Pa slipped the rope around her neck before Bossy knew what was happening. "Hold on so she won't run." Pa handed the rope to Mr. Winkler.

Sid had never seen a cow's hind leg move so fast. The minute Pa tried to take hold of the leg she began kicking. "We'll have to pull her down," Pa said. "There's something the matter with her foot, but I need to see."

Sid had watched Pa pull a cow down, but he'd never done it himself. He hurried to take the pail of milk to Ma. "Come on, Jimmy. You gotta see this," he called. By the time they got back a group of men and boys were gathered around. Some of them didn't know what Pa was talking about.

"So, Winkler, first thing you have to do is tie her down low to something stable. Looks like that tree over there is just the ticket. You could tie her to one of your wagon wheels—anything strong enough to keep her from pulling free. Make sure you get a good knot on that thing, too."

Mr. Winkler's mouth turned down in a wry smile. "There's a lot of things I don't know how to do, but I can tie a good knot."

Bossy was mildly cooperative. They managed to get her tied to the tree, but she acted as if she'd bolt free at the first chance. "Give her some slack," Pa said. "Once she goes down, she'll need that extra room on her lead so as not to choke."

The next thing Pa did was to slip another lasso around her neck, pulling it out along her back. "Notice that I'm goina let my rope fall down toward her other side." He reached down and took hold of the loose end of the rope, bringing it under Bossy, staying clear of her flying hind leg.

"Okay," said Pa. "The rope needs plenty of slack so I can pull it as far as her withers." He took hold of the rope on her neck, still holding on the loose end. "It's like drawing a line along the top of her back and making a blanket stitch with this long end that I passed under." Pa quickly laced the long, loose end of the rope under the rope along her back and pulled it through. It did look like he was making a big blanket stitch along Bossy's back. "Now you have your first loop."

"See, Jimmy," Sid said. "Bossy isn't puttin' any weight on that leg. You can see it's botherin' her."

"Why's she switchin' her tail?" Jimmy asked.

"She's tellin' us she isn't happy about being tied up," Sid said.

Pa seemed untroubled. He always said that you have to let animals know you are in charge. Bossy seemed to understand, but she didn't like it.

Sid felt proud of Pa. He and Pa had a real advantage over folk who had never lived or worked on a farm. But Pa never made anybody feel like they were stupid because they didn't know something.

By this time, Ruby and Junior were part of the crowd. *They don't look the least bit sorry*, thought Sid. They watched intently, standing on either side of a man who looked like somebody he'd seen before. *Probably around the campfire*, he thought.

"Now I'm drawing out the rope along her back, just like I did before," said Pa. "I'll make a loop right here." He threw the long end of the rope over Bossy. "Toss that back to me under her belly, Winkler. Watch her legs. Don't want you to get kicked in the head."

Mr. Winkler threw the loose rope end under Bossy without getting kicked. Her kicking foot was probably hurting too much to keep kicking. Pa brought the rope up to make a second loop along Bossy's back. It looked even more like a blanket stitch. They did one more loop. "She's making a big fuss, but the rope isn't hurting her," said Pa. "She just doesn't want us bothering her. We want the loops to stay high up here along this side of her backbone. A cow will go down toward the side where the loops are. If we wanted her to go down on the other side, I'd just slide the loops over to the other side of her backbone.

"Okay, Bossy, we're goina help you down." With that, Pa stepped behind Bossy, pulling the rope back a good distance, out of range of her legs. Getting a firm grip on it, he gently pulled. Bossy couldn't help herself. She knelt and was soon lying on the ground. "You do it right and nobody gets hurt," said Pa, catching his breath. "We have to keep this rope taut, or she'll be back up in a flash."

Pa handed the rope to Mr. Winkler. "She can kick even if she is down. Anybody have another rope?"

"Swathmore, you gotta rope," somebody called. He needn't have; the man standing with Ruby and Junior had already stepped forward.

Swathmore! Sid remembered. Mr. Swathmore was one of the men playing dominoes with Bayless Sly and J.J. Gordon in Kansas City. *How well does he know them?*

Mr. Swathmore knew what he was doing. He quickly tied Bossy's legs securely and stepped back out of the way.

With Bossy unable to kick, Pa took a look at her back leg, feeling it gently all the way to her hoof. "No wonder she's so sensitive," he said, pointing to a swollen place above the hoof. He sniffed the hoof. "This looks new. It doesn't smell bad, so I don't think there's an infection. You get an infection in the hoof, Winkler, she'd be in real trouble, so would the rest of the livestock. No cracks in the hoof that I can see. Oh-h, here's the culprit." Pa pulled out a piece of splintered wood wedged between the claws of her hoof. "Must have stepped on a stick."

At just that moment, Sid caught Junior looking at him. So was Ruby. There was something about the way they looked that said they knew he knew how it happened.

"We'd better separate her from the herd. Give this a chance to heal," said Pa. "There's been a bit of bleeding. Don't want her getting an infection. I'm goina need some soap and water, somebody. Sid, run ask your Ma for some honey."

"Honey?" Ruby scoffed. "What'd he want honey fer?"

"Shut your yapper," said Mr. Swathmore. "You might learn somethin'. Man knows what he's doin'. Junior, get him a pail of water and some lye soap."

Sid raced to the wagon in record time, Jimmy following. Ma had plenty of honey. "If there's an infection that's hard to get to, best thing is to clean the wound and apply some honey," she said, pouring a little into a tin cup. "The honey will seep down where you can't reach."

Sid let Jimmy carry the cup. They ran all the way back, afraid they'd miss something. Junior came running with a bucket of water in one hand and a bar of lye soap in another. Bossy's eyes bulged. She tried to struggle, but Mr. Swathmore held the rope to keep her from getting up. That freed Mr. Winkler to help Pa wash down Bossy's hoof.

"There, there, old girl," said Pa, "you'll be good as new in no time." Once the hoof and upper leg were clean and dry, Pa nodded to Jimmy, who proudly handed him the cup. Pa smeared honey in the area above the hoof, rubbing it all around and into the area between the two claws of the hoof where the piece of wood had been lodged.

By this time Grace's father, Dr. Willis, joined the crowd. "Doesn't look like you need me, Mr. Johnson. I couldn't have done any better."

Pa nodded to Dr. Willis as he washed his hands in the bucket. "We'll tether her up by your wagon, Winkler, best keep her away from the herd till she heals."

"Will this hurt her milk?" Mr. Winkler asked, taking Bossy's lead rope from Mr. Swathmore.

"That man don't know nothin'," jeered Junior. He may have been trying to keep his voice down, but it carried. Sid could see Mr. Winkler's cheeks flush.

Mr. Swathmore gave Junior a cuff on the side of the head. "Not everybody knows the same. Don't reckon you know nothin' about barberin'."

"Her milk will be fine, Mr. Winkler," said Dr. Willis.

"Let's get her up," said Pa. "Give her some grain as a reward. You can milk her while she's eating."

Pa pulled the rope from her back. Bossy stood. Mr. Winkler untied her and led her away. Jimmy raced back to the wagon to tell Ma and Cora all about it.

"I know how Bossy hurt her foot, Pa," said Sid. He told what he had seen.

"I'm sorry to hear that, Son. Best keep it to ourselves for now. I can't think how it could do any good for folks to know. Let's hope they learned a lesson from it."

Sid wasn't so sure they had.

19.
Standing Down a Bully

From the moment he awoke the next morning, Sid could feel excitement mounting in camp. New wagons had joined the Stokes Company, giving then enough wagons to leave. Word had it that they were waiting for another family, and they'd leave as soon as their wagon arrived. Meanwhile, a steady stream of traffic passed their camp. Teamsters came and went regularly from New Mexico Territory. People headed out for the trails west: the Oregon Trail, the California Trail, the Mormon Trail, and the Santa Fe Trail.

They had made good use of the time in camp. Sid was beginning to feel expert at getting their oxen yoked and working them as a full team. Pa let him walk them around the meadow for practice by himself, too. They weren't the only ones getting used to oxen. Like Pa, people helped each other as they learned new things and prepared to leave.

Hiram Swathmore had a harder job than some. His animals were not trained. Though Mr. Swathmore didn't seem very likeable, Sid had to admit that he was good to the oxen. In fact, it seemed like he was kinder to the animals than to his family. Junior was having a hard time learning how to work with the nigh ox. Mr. Swathmore explained how to get the yoke on the team, but Junior got all flummoxed and let the nigh ox loose. Once they'd caught her, Mr. Swathmore gave him a good whack across the shoulders with the handle of his whip. "Reckon that'll smack some sense into ya. Now get it right." Sid had no liking for Junior, either, but he cringed when he saw it happen.

Ruby hung about watching everything. If Mr. Swathmore spotted her, he waved his whip at her and told her it was men's work.

Sid was uneasy about Mr. Swathmore. The image of him playing dominoes with J.J. and Bayless Sly was unnerving. He hadn't thought about the letter for days. There hadn't been a right time to tell Pa about it. It didn't seem terribly important when compared to Miriam's kidnapping. After giving it some thought, he decided that Mr. Swathmore didn't pay him any special attention. *No sense frettin' over it. All I have to do is keep the letter hidden away and take it to the Gallagher Trading Post when we get to Santa Fe.*

Miriam and Daniel were another matter. Worry hung over them like a thick fog, though Ma and Pa didn't talk about it. Sometimes he saw Ma wiping her eyes with the corner of her apron.

"If the phantom slave stealer can get in and out of Missouri and Kentucky without leaving any trace, couldn't he find Miriam?" Sid finally got up enough courage to ask Ma.

"Oh Sid," said Ma. "I wish it were possible." That is all she would say.

Pa said the men were meeting that morning to get organized for the trip. Sid hurried to milk Buttercup so he could join them. He was on his way back to the wagon, pail of milk in hand, when someone called, "Think you're smart, dontcha." It was Junior Swathmore, coming up behind him.

Sid spun around, nearly spilling milk.

Junior sneered. "I seen you workin' yer team. I could unhitch 'em in half the time."

"I expect you could," said Sid, trying to keep his voice even. He wasn't sure what to say, but he tried to act the way Pa would. Pa always said, "You don't have to let somebody pick a fight. If you don't fight, it takes the wind out of their sails."

"I oughta knock the snot out of you," threatened Junior.

"Get 'em, Junior!" It was Ruby. Not surprising, the twins were seldom far apart.

Sid ignored her. "Can't think why you'd wanna do that."

"Somebody needs ta take ya down a peg or two," said Junior.

Sid was torn between running for it and having it out with Junior. Neither one would be so easy with Ruby ready to jump in. She would, too.

"Well, I'm shorter than you are to start with." Sid stood his ground, holding the milk pail, making no effort to look like he was going to fight. He looked Junior in the eye. Junior took a step forward, hands held up in fists.

"Let 'em have it, Junior! You got the bulge on 'em." Ruby cheered.

I'm in for it, thought Sid, keeping a grip on the milk pail. He wouldn't fight unless

Junior hit him first. He stood still, hoping it would take the fun out of it for Junior. The question was, would Ruby jump him from behind before Junior knocked him down?

They stood there looking at each other, Junior ready to punch, Sid holding on to the pail of milk. "Pull in yer horns, Junior," Ruby said after a while. "He ain't got the sand to do nothin'."

Junior seemed to think it over. "Sissy. Can't even put up a fist. Ain't worth the trouble it'd take to knock some sense into 'em."

"Anyways, we got better things to do," said Ruby. "Men's started meetin'. Women's goina be listenin' in. Kids is all playin'. Won't get a better chance."

"Yeah," snickered Junior. Dropping his fists, he followed her.

Sid was still shaky when he got back to the wagon. The Swathmore twins were nowhere in sight. Children played around the periphery of the circle made by the men as they gathered for the meeting. Many of the women were there, too. Others gathered in little clusters chatting. Mr. Stokes called the meeting to order. Sid hurriedly put away the milk and rinsed out the pail. He was about to join Pa when, out of the corner of his eye, he noticed something moving near the Winkler wagon. It looked like Bossy, but when he turned to have a better look, she wasn't there. It didn't seem right. He slipped around the wagons to see what was going on.

"Better get that there tether moved, Junior. Ain't far enough down. I'm near ready," Ruby was lacing a rope along Bossy's back the way Pa had done. Junior was busy tying her to a wagon wheel.

"Rope's fine," Junior said. It was easy enough to see that he had not made a proper knot. Ruby seemed to approve, though, pulling the last loop in place along Bossy's back.

Agitated and shaking her head, Bossy lashed out with her sore leg. Ruby jumped back, still holding the rope.

Junior laughed. "Take 'er down, if ya think yer big enough."

"Watch me." Ruby began to pull.

Nothing happened.

She wrapped the rope around her waist to brace herself, pulling again. But Bossy didn't go down. She wasn't tied low enough or well enough. The cow gave a great lurch, pulled the tether free, and took off at a run.

Ruby was thrown to the ground. Still wrapped in the rope, she was unable to get herself free. Bossy dragged her along, headed into the meadow.

Running as fast as he could, Sid caught hold of the rope that was dragging Ruby, placing himself between her and the cow. He was dangerously close to Bossy's hooves. "Whoa, Bossy. Whoa, girl."

Junior stood frozen. He didn't seem to know what to do. "Help me," Sid yelled, panting for breath as he ran. "Have to slow her down—give Ruby enough slack to pull free."

Junior unfroze. Catching up with them, he grabbed the rope behind Sid. Pulling as hard as they could, the two boys slowed Bossy to a walk. All the while Sid talked to her as gently as he could manage, "Steady Bossy—good girl—slow and easy." Maybe it was his tone of voice. Maybe she was exhausted after her burst of energy. Maybe her foot hurt too much to run. Whatever it was, Bossy suddenly stopped in her tracks, throwing Sid and Junior forward so fast neither could keep his balance. Sid fell, landing just short of Bossy's hind legs. Junior landed on top of him with a thud.

Eyes bulging, tail hanging down between her legs, Bossy stood. It was a sure sign that she was still frightened.

Sid struggled to catch his breath and get up. One kick and he'd be a gonner. "Fine—goina be—fine—Bossy," he panted. "Easy, Junior—roll off—easy, to the side. No sudden moves."

By some miracle, Bossy stayed glued to the spot where she stopped.

"You okay, Ruby?" Sid asked, still holding the rope as he got to his feet.

Ruby was unable to reply. She lay flat on the ground, the wind completely knocked out of her.

"Junior, see if she can get up. Get that rope out from around her before Bossy decides to take off again. When Ruby's free, I'm gettin' hold of Bossy's tether and takin' her back where she belongs." Sid held on to the rope while Junior helped a scraped, rope-burned Ruby to get up. The front of her dress was covered with dirt and grass stains.

"Let's keep this nice and steady," said Sid. "Once Bossy's tied up back at the wagon, we'll get that other rope off. "Good girl, Bossy, I'm comin' up behind you now," Sid patted Bossy on the haunches, talking softly as he moved toward her head. She stood still, but she was stressed. He took the tether, patting her on the neck. "You're okay now. We're takin' you back to where you belong. Then I'm goina get you a nice treat.

"Ruby, you best go ask my Ma to take care of those scratches," he said. "We'll deal with Bossy."

Sullen and still trying to catch her breath, Ruby said, "Reckon you goina tell our Pa."

"Tell you what," said Sid. "You don't do anything like this again, and I reckon I don't need to say any more about it. You be kind to these animals. They depend on us, and we depend on them."

"Don't need no sermon," said Ruby.

Sid met her defiant gaze. "Just remember what I said." With that, he led Bossy back to the Winkler wagon and tied her tether with a hitch knot. Then he and Junior carefully unlaced the rope from her back. Junior left without a word, not even a thank you.

"I'll be back, Bossy," said Sid. "I promised you a treat."

Ma said Ruby had been by. "She was a right mess. Looked like rope-burn on her hands and arms, but she wouldn't say. Anyway, she let me clean her up."

After he'd taken the grain to Bossy, Sid returned to tell Ma what happened.

"Well, Sid," she said, "Ruby was one lucky young lady. Bossy could have turned on her. Good she didn't let go of the rope. If Bossy had pulled her from the middle, she coulda ended up with some broken ribs or worse. I'd say the Good Lord was lookin' after all three of you."

"Why do they have to act that way? Junior tried to pick a fight with me. I barely know him."

"Beats me," Ma admitted. "Maybe they've been treated bad. Maybe they just have a mean streak."

"I thought Junior was goina clean my plow for sure, but he walked away."

"A bully is part coward, Sid," said Ma. "He doesn't want to get hurt. Besides, where's the glory in it if the person you're tryin' to best won't fight? I doubt they'll bother you again. But I expect Junior and Ruby are always goina be tryin' to put a spoke in somebody's wheel. Something's itchin' 'em."

"Was I a coward?" Sid asked later when he had a chance to talk with Pa. "I mean, when I didn't fight Junior?"

"No, Son," said Pa, putting his arm around Sid. "It takes a whole lot more courage to stand down a bully than it does to fight. Best thing is, when it came to it, you helped Ruby and Junior. You didn't let your bad feelings keep you from doing the right thing."

Ruby and Junior never bothered him again.

20

The Last Wagon

The Payne wagon arrived that afternoon. Mr. Payne led the oxen. Mrs. Payne followed, holding a baby. A boy and girl sat on the wagon seat. They looked a little older than Jimmy and Cora. But Sid thought maybe they might become playmates. Cora missed Miriam and wrote "letters" to her every day, scribbles in a writing tablet. It was painful to witness, knowing what he did.

Gossip spread like wildfire throughout the wagon train before the Payne oxen were unhitched. Sid hurried to find Grace and tell her.

"Daddy said they were coming," said Grace. "Mr. Payne is a good friend of Mr. Stokes. Daddy says he used to be an Army scout."

"Oh." Sid felt a bit deflated at not being first with the news. "I reckon Mr. Stokes will be introducin' them to the company tonight."

Grace's mamma had her busy helping pack eggs in cornmeal. Sid liked Mrs. Willis. She had a way of making everything fun. He was glad to help. Grace had already put a layer of eggs on a deep layer of cornmeal in a wooden barrel. Sid knew what to do. He'd helped Ma store their eggs for the trip. You had to make sure none of the eggs touched the side of the barrel or each other. When the eggs were placed, more cornmeal was added until they were safely buried. Then another layer of eggs, then more cornmeal. "Every time we need an egg, we'll be digging for treasure," laughed Mrs. Willis. "Either that, or we're going to have a whole lot of scrambled eggs. If that happens, I'll just add some milk and we'll have a barrel of spoon bread."

They were almost finished when they heard a whining voice, "I don't see how I can get everything done, bein' so weak from the baby and all. Mr. Swathmore brought a whole crate of eggs. I ain't got the first idea what to do with 'em."

It was Mrs. Swathmore. Ma said he shouldn't criticize, but Sid thought she was one of the most disagreeable people he had ever met. As far as he could tell, all Mrs.

Swathmore did was complain, borrow things, and pawn her baby off on anybody she could get to hold him.

"We're just finishing," said Mrs. Willis. "I'm sure Sid and Grace would be glad to help you pack your eggs. I'll mind the baby. How about that?"

Grace scowled, "What about Ruby and Junior?"

Mrs. Willis gave her a firm look, "Come, Grace. We can lend a hand. We'll have the job done in no time."

"Sure, Grace," said Sid. "We're expert egg-packers now." If Ruby and Junior knew there was work to be done, they'd be long gone, exploring the riverbank, or lazing about somewhere out of sight. He'd just as soon they stayed out of sight even if it meant packing Mrs. Swathmore's eggs.

The two younger Swathmore children, Myrtle and Otis, watched with wide eyes from under the wagon. Sid and Grace set to work. Mrs. Willis calmed the baby and got Myrtle and Otis involved in a game.

Mrs. Swathmore whined the whole time, making no effort to help. "Did you see that wagon come in?" she asked in her high-pitched little-girl voice. "I can't think why that wagon master let the likes of them join the company, us payin' him good money and all. Least he could do is get good folk. Like as not they's runaways. We'll all be in trouble for lettin' 'em in. Those youngens will be runnin' around wantin' to play with my Myrtle and Otis like they was just as good. I never seen nothin' so disgustin' in my whole life."

Sid bristled. Grace looked at him, rolled her eyes, and went back to work packing eggs.

Mrs. Willis answered softly, "I understand that we've been waiting for the Payne family. Mr. Payne knows all of the country we'll be traveling through. He is a retired Army scout."

"I didn't know they'd let 'em in the Army," scoffed Mrs. Swathmore.

"Mr. Payne is a freed Negro," Mrs. Willis said. Her voice was firm. "His wife was born free. She was a teacher in a famous school up north before she and Mr. Payne were married. I think we're lucky to have them with us."

"Well, I don't think it's right," complained Mrs. Swathmore, "folk like that puttin' on airs."

"I will stand by what I said. I think we are lucky to have them," said Mrs. Willis." I see Grace and Sid have all the eggs packed." With that she handed the baby back to Mrs. Swathmore. "Otis, you and Myrtle come play with Grace anytime your mother says it is okay. The more the merrier."

Sid was glad to get away. Mrs. Swathmore gave him a headache.

"We may not be able to change Mrs. Swathmore's mind," said Mrs. Willis as they left the Swathmore wagon, "but we can give her a chance to change. And we don't have to let her get away with saying bad things about people."

Sid wasn't hopeful. He couldn't erase the memory of the welts on Elijah's back. *People who would do that don't change.* He thought about it later as he stretched out on the wagon seat to take a nap. He doubted Mrs. Swathmore would change. He thought of Miriam. *What if she's sold to somebody like that horrible woman?*

"Come on, Sid!" Jimmy called, urgency in his voice. "Mule train's comin' and it's a big one. Mr. Stokes said!"

"Hurry, Sid! Hurry, Grace!" shrieked Cora. She held hands with Myrtle Swathmore, fairly dancing with excitement.

Sid jumped down from the wagon, still feeling groggy from his nap. He could already smell dust kicked up by the train. Teamster trains came and went every day. This one was coming in with goods from New Mexico Territory.

They hurried to find a place away from the dust where they could keep count of the wagons. They could hear harness bells, braying of mules, cracking of whips, and the call of teamsters before they saw the train.

"I couldn't be a teamster," said Grace. "I'd choke on all that dust."

"I see 'em!" yelled Jimmy.

Wagons began passing. Painted on the side were the words, "Spiegelberg Trading Company."

"I've never seen so many mules in my life," said Grace. They lost count at 63 wagons.

"What you reckon they want all them wagons for, anyway?" asked Jimmy as they crawled under the Willis wagon out of the dust.

"My mamma says they're bringing silver and fur and buffalo hides and all kinds of good things from places like Mexico," said Grace.

"We don't need any of that stuff," said Jimmy.

"Maybe not," Sid said, "But then we're goin' out there where that came from. People living back East probably do need those things."

"Some of 'em got donkeys an' mules," said Otis. "Pa says mules is real strong, and donkeys works hard." Sid couldn't help smiling. It was the first time Otis had volunteered anything.

"They sell some of the mules," said Grace. "They keep some for their trip back to Santa Fe."

"We got oxen," said Jimmy. "Oxen's better 'n donkeys and mules any day." Sid tried to keep a straight face.

Mrs. Willis looked under the wagon, "Time for supper, Grace. Otis, Myrtle, you'd best run along. Sid, I expect your mamma will be looking for you three."

Right after the evening meal, members of the Stokes Company always gathered around a large campfire. That was when Mr. Stokes welcomed new members to the Stokes Company as he had welcomed the Johnsons. Some people had musical instruments. A couple of people had violins, another a guitar. Several men had harmonicas, and a woman had a mandolin. Men and women, boys and girls all sang and enjoyed themselves. Sometimes one of the adults told a story.

Boys and girls played games while the adults talked. Sometimes it was hide and seek or tag. One night, Sid and Grace organized games for the younger children. For the little ones, going west was like a holiday.

It felt like a holiday for everyone that evening. They had been gathering for almost a week. Now they were on the cusp of leaving for California. Mr. Stokes introduced the Payne family. "As most of you know, our last wagon arrived today. We're ready to set out for California!" Everybody clapped. There was some cheering and whistling, too.

Mr. Stokes put up his hand to quiet the crowd. "I've been sayin' we haveta be ready to leave on a dime when the Payne wagon arrives. Tonight, we welcome Jim and Dorcus Payne and their children, Matthew, Lydia and the baby, Anna. We're right lucky to have them join our company. Mr. Payne is an experienced scout who worked for the U.S. Army. He knows most of the country between here and California like the back of his hand—better than I do, and I know it better than most. Mrs. Payne is a schoolteacher.

She taught school in Brooklyn, New York, before she married Mr. Payne."

Sid sat with Ma and Pa, helping keep Cora and Jimmy occupied. Not far away were the Swathmores, though Ruby and Junior were nowhere to be seen—they usually prowled around the camp getting into mischief unless somebody was telling a story.

Mr. Swathmore muttered, "Guess they love the likes of them up there in New York. No reason for him to try and make us love 'em."

The Willis family sat nearby. Grace rolled her eyes.

Mr. Stokes continued, "Now I've never been that far back east, but from what I hear, New York is a mighty big place. Mrs. Payne tells me she will welcome any of the children who would like to sit for lessons once we're out on the trail. No charge. And she has plenty of books, too. Doesn't matter how old or young you are. I might sit in myself, polish up my readin'." He gave Mrs. Payne a broad smile.

After the Payne family was introduced, Mr. Stokes got down to business. "I met with the men earlier today, anticipatin' the arrival of the Payne wagon this afternoon. A wagon train needs to be like a community. Tonight, the men are goina elect a captain who will hold meetin's and be in charge if I haveta go on ahead or can't do my job for some reason. The captain will be my right-hand man. He will keep roll, too, so we know everybody is with us all the way. We'll elect a council—I'd like ten able-bodied men to serve. Council members meet every night to talk about any problems we're havin', if anybody needs help, or to advise me about things that come up. That goes both ways. I'll need advice from time to time and they'll know the members of the company well enough to offer it."

"I don't hold with secret meetin's," Mr. Swathmore called out. "Settin' up a bunch of council members makes some folk think they's better 'n everybody."

His comment created quite a stir. A lot of people seemed to agree with Mr. Swathmore.

"Hiram Swathmore, I think you're missin' my point," said Mr. Stokes patiently. "This isn't about anybody being better than anybody else. The old sayin' is, 'Everybody's business is nobody's business.' This way, we have people responsible for helpin' out. When the council meets, anybody can sit in.

No secrets. Anybody can lend a hand, too. Everybody's had a chance to say what's in our bylaws. Everybody should have had a chance to look at 'em by now, too. I'm askin' the Company to adopt our bylaws. I'm goina have 'em read out so as everybody has a chance to hear before we vote. One vote for each man."

Grace leaned over and asked Sid, "How come it's just the men voting?"

"That's just how it's done," said Sid. He hadn't thought about it before; he guessed it was like voting for the President of the United States or something. "Women don't vote."

"Well, that's not right," said Grace indignantly.

"She does have a point," said Ma. "We're goin' on the trip, too."

A man read out the proposed bylaws. They included things like what to do if anybody got sick and couldn't travel and having every able-bodied man take a turn keeping watch at night. Grace took exception to this under her breath, too.

There was some discussion before a vote was taken. The by-laws were adopted unanimously. Pa and Dr. Willis seemed pleased, so Sid figured it was a good thing.

When it was time to elect the captain, Dr. Willis nominated Jim Payne. At first there was silence, then discussion broke out. Some members of the company thought they didn't know Mr. Payne well enough, since he'd just arrived. Others didn't think a freed Negro should be given the responsibility. The discussion started to get heated, when Mr. Payne asked to speak.

"It's a real honor to be nominated as captain," he said. "'Specially since me and my family just got here. But I think my talents are in scoutin'. As Mr. Stokes said, I'm retired from bein' a scout for the Army. Seems like it'd be a shame not to use that experience to help the company get to California. We'll all have to give our best if we're to get to there safe 'n sound."

"Well, Mr. Payne, you'd make a right good captain in my opinion," said Bill Stokes, "But we'll respect your wishes. Any other nominations?"

By the time the voting was over, Pa had been elected captain and ten men were in place to serve as the council. There was a lot of backslapping, congratulating, and discussion among the men. Sid was proud of Pa.

Mr. Stokes called them back to order. "The last item of business is a word from Doc Willis about dangers on the Trail. Most folk think we're goin' out into the wilderness where we'll be raided by Indians and run over by stampedin' buffalo. We may meet some Indians. Like as not they'll respect us if we respect them. And I hope to see some buffalo—we'll need to do some buffalo huntin' on the trail, but Doc will tell us about some even greater dangers and how we can protect ourselves."

Grace's daddy had been a doctor in St. Louis. They were going to California to start a medical school. Dr. Willis was a kind man, soft-spoken, but firm. People already trusted him.

"The two greatest dangers on the Trail are cholera and smallpox," he said. A hush fell over the company. "We aren't sure, but we think that cholera is caused by contaminated water. I've been advising people about filling water barrels." Dr. Willis had been all over the camp, urging people to dump their barrels back into the river if they hadn't been cleaned properly. He recommended that people use apple cider vinegar to scrub them out.

Dr. Willis continued, "You all know how serious an outbreak of smallpox could be.

Some of the riverboats coming in have reported cases of smallpox, so we have to be on guard. Unfortunately, not all of them report. They're afraid they'll lose business. The best thing we can do is to keep an outbreak from happening. The only way I know to do that is to wash your hands before you eat. Keep your hands away from your nose and mouth—"

"That means you two," Ma said, looking at Jimmy and Cora.

"—don't pick up old bedding, blankets, or anything we may find left along the trail. The pox is spread when you come in contact with someone who has broken out or you pick up things that have been in contact with someone who has the pox. Some of you have had the pox. I survived smallpox when I was a boy. Some of you have been vaccinated. But you cannot assume you are safe if you don't follow proper precautions. If you have any medical problems once we're on the trail, I'll do my best to help.

"I'm not the only one who can help out with doctoring. Mr. Stokes has considerable experience. Right after I joined the company, he gave me a letter from Doctor John Short of Alton, Illinois, commending Mrs.

Benjamin Johnson, who has been his valued assistant for years. He is right sorry to lose her. I've already talked with Mrs. Johnson. She is happy to lend a hand if we need her. She's an experienced midwife, too."

Dr. Willis had Ma stand up. Sid felt a warm glow of pride as she stood.

"One other thing. From what I understand, a lot of deaths happen because of accidents. Be careful of your guns and who can get at them. We'll be having open fires on the trail. Be mindful of the little ones, not just your own, but everyone's. If we watch over one another, we will have fewer accidents."

Mr. Stokes concluded the meeting. "We're here to help each other. Until we get used to breakin' camp and headin' out on the trail every mornin', I advise those of you with little ones to keep them in your wagon until we're out on the trail. Doc Willis, thank you. You didn't sign on to be the company doctor, but we sure appreciate your willingness to help out. We're lucky to have Doc and Mrs. Willis with us. Thank you, Miz Johnson for being ready to help, too.

"We're lucky to have all of you. We have several farming families, a tinsmith's family, a blacksmith, a carpenter's family, a shopkeeper's family, and a barber's family. Some of you are lookin' for a fresh start. There's room for all of us in California. We're goina get there, one day at a time.

"We're movin' out at seven o'clock in the mornin'. Wake up is at 4:00 AM. You'll hear my bugle sound, that is, unless Ben Johnson wants to play a few notes, seein' he's captain."

Pa waved and shook his head, "Not me!" There was laughter all around.

Mr. Stokes brought the meeting to a close. "While the ladies are fixin' breakfast, men will get the teams rounded up, watered, yoked, and hitched to the wagons. We eat at 6:00 AM sharp. At 7:00 we hit the trail. No later. Now, let's have a song or two. Then we'll turn in. We'll need a good night's rest before we hit the trail."

21.
Wagons Roll!

Sid was so excited he didn't think he could sleep. But when the bugle sounded at 4:00 AM, he awoke with a start. He knew exactly what had to be done. He hurried to get Buttercup milked and tethered to the wagon. He tried to stay calm. Mr. Stokes had cautioned the men about remaining calm. "Talk to your animals gently. Last thing we need is to get the livestock stirred up. So go easy."

Pa had the wheel team, Star and Sampson, yoked and was watering Josiah and Greg by the time Sid had Buttercup milked and tethered to the wagon along with Sandy. "We'll saddle you afterwhile, Sandy," Sid patted the horse. "You're goina be carryin' the Captain of the Stokes Company." Pa would help supervise the whole train. *That means I'm going to lead the team.* It was exciting and terrifying at the same time.

"This is the real thing, everybody," Sid told Buttercup, giving her a pat. He hurried back to help Pa who was putting the yoke on Josiah and Greg. Without being told what to do, Sid rounded up Cornflower and Promise. The air was full of the sounds of getting ready. Oxen lowed, horses whinnied, dogs barked, excited voices called to each other.

Ma had breakfast waiting when they brought the team up to the wagon. Jimmy and Cora were so excited they were running around and around the wagon. "Giddy-up! Goin' to California! Giddy-up! Goin' to California!" Jimmy yelled, pretending he was riding a horse. Every now and then, Cora took her thumb out of her mouth to echo, "Goin' to Cal-forna!" as she raced after him.

"They've been like this since you brought the milk, Sid," said Ma, looking at Pa in desperation. "It was either just ignore 'em or spend my time tryin' to get 'em to settle down."

One look from Pa brought the wild ones to a halt. Otis and Myrtle appeared, wide-eyed with wonder. They looked hungrily at the cornbread Ma had waiting for breakfast. Sid wondered if they ever got a proper meal. Ma didn't ask questions. She had the children get on the wagon seat with Jimmy and Cora, giving them each a big piece of cornbread with a blob of creamy butter to eat while they watched the team being hitched up. Between bites, Jimmy offered a running commentary on the proper way to hitch a team to the wagon.

"Now don't you go and miss your breakfast, Ben Johnson," Ma ordered. Pa grinned. He was excited to be off, too.

After breakfast, while the camping gear was stowed, Sid saddled up Sandy. Ma sent Jimmy over to the Swathmore wagon to find out if Myrtle and Otis could ride with them.

Sid felt the excitement like an electrical charge running through him. He picked up the whip, taking his position to the left of Cornflower, waiting for the signal to move. Anticipation mounted all over camp as Mr. Stokes and Pa rode around the circle of wagons making one last inspection.

Sid was proud to be in charge of the team, but anxious, too. The team obeyed him in the field. *But Pa won't be here to help.*

"First line, move out," Mr. Stokes called, leading the way. Mr. Winkler's wagon was first to follow. Bossy was tethered behind, and she wasn't limping.

As soon as the Winkler wagon was out of the circle, Pa nodded to Sid, "Johnson wagon, move 'em out."

"Giddy up!" Sid called to the team. He didn't have to crack the whip; Cornflower was ready. They pulled the wagon forward to clear the circle. "Gee!" Sid commanded. The team moved to the right to follow the Winkler wagon toward the trail.

"Swathmore wagon, move 'em out." Sid could hear Pa calling behind him and the crack of a whip as Mr. Swathmore called, "Giddy up," sounds that echoed around the camp as Pa moved to each wagon, sending it into the line. Pa would be the last one to leave camp.

"We gonna be first, we gonna be first," Jimmy chanted in a sing-song voice as the wagon swung to the right. He and Otis were perched on the wagon seat. They waved at the other wagons as they rounded the camp, with Jimmy acting like the grand marshal of a parade. Cora and Myrtle sat behind the wagon seat with Serena, who was none too happy about being trapped in her basket. They peered out from behind the bonnet, waving. Like most of the grown-ups and older children, Ma walked.

"Giddy up." Sid called to the team, moving them straight forward toward the trail. The Winkler wagon moved into position and halted to wait for the first line to fill in. "Haw," Sid directed. Cornflower and Promise led the team to the left.

The Johnson wagon was assigned to center position, first line. "Easy," Sid called, as they pulled in alongside the Winkler team. "Whoa." They were on the Santa Fe Trail!

As soon as the Swathmore wagon pulled into place on Sid's left, Mr. Stokes rode ahead, signaling the first line to move forward to make room for wagons to line up behind.

Sid was proud of the team. They were untroubled by the team on either side or the sound of whips cracking and drivers calling out orders behind them. *We did it! I did it. We're on the way to California.*

Mr. Stokes rode back to help Pa keep the wagons moving into line. Sid looked around. The Willis wagon was in the second line of wagons, behind the Winkler wagon. Sid wondered if Grace had seen him lead out with the team.

Junior and Ruby were on the other side of the Swathmore team near the nigh ox, too preoccupied to be any bother. Mrs. Swathmore sat on the wagon seat, holding the baby, looking like a martyr being led to execution.

Ma let Jimmy and Otis get down to stand with her and watch. Jimmy kept up his chant, "We gonna be first." It was annoying, but Sid tried to hide his impatience. "Every day we'll have a new line up, so everybody in the company will have a chance to go first," he explained. "That's goina be real important. The wagons at the end have to take the dust from the front wagons. It wouldn't be fair for somebody to be last all the time."

Not all the teams performed as smoothly as the Johnson team. Some of the oxen were still skittish and balked. Some drivers were less confident. Their fearfulness was passed along to the oxen. Bellowing livestock, crying babies, screaming children, barking dogs—all added to the confusion. A cow tethered behind one of the wagons came loose just as the wagon turned to move on to the trail. Pa had her rounded up and back before she had much taste of freedom. Altogether, it looked like loosely organized chaos. But Mr. Stokes seemed untroubled.

As the last of the wagons were leaving camp, Mr. Stokes rode to the front where he paused, looking at his pocket watch. "Seven o'clock sharp," he said, grinning at Sid. "First day and we did it. Your pa will have the others on the trail in good time." Rising to a stand in his stirrups, he took off his hat and waved it, calling in a loud, commanding voice, "Wagons roll!" Then, relaxing into the saddle, he trotted on ahead. The message was picked up and repeated, surging through the line of wagons like waves rolling into shore. "Giddy up!" called Sid, proudly leading the team forward, following Mr. Stokes along with the other two wagons in the first line.

"They'll be eatin' dust all day," Jimmy explained to Otis, as if Otis hadn't heard it himself. Ma walked alongside, keeping the boys back by the wagon and out of Sid's way. Cora and Myrtle went on with their play inside the wagon. Mrs. Winkler and her older children walked, too. Almost everyone walked. Men waved their hats and rows of cheers went up as each group of wagons moved forward. They were off at last into a great unknown, full of hope and fear, following the well-worn trail toward Council Grove.

When it was almost noon by the sun, Mr. Stokes had them halt for "nooning" near a creek at a place called Boone's Fork. "Reckon we've come about six miles so far," said Pa, joining them after the last wagon came to a halt. "That's good time."

Nooning gave them time to eat and take a rest. More importantly, it gave the oxen a break. They were unhitched and allowed to graze. Horses and cows that were tethered to the wagons were turned loose to join them. Grass that had been grazed to the ground the summer before was lush and green from winter's snow and late winter rain.

Women cooked the noon meal over campfires. Ma flew into action as soon as the wagon was in place. She said they wouldn't be having a hot meal every nooning. "We'll be out of these woods soon enough. Uncle Luke says there's nary a stick of wood to be found on parts of the trail." She put Jimmy and Otis to work making a campfire. Sid wondered if Mrs. Swathmore noticed Otis and Myrtle were absent.

He marvelled, watching Ma pat biscuit dough out on her breadboard. It was a wonder how she made such delicious meals without a stove. Some of the women had camping stoves with them. But Ma refused to buy one. "I can cook just as well over a campfire, and I'd rather have room in the wagon for other things."

She put the biscuits in a heavy skillet with a domed lid, setting them near the edge of the fire until it burned down to coals. When dinner was ready, there were biscuits with sorghum molasses and slabs of fried bacon with stewed dried apples and cream for dessert. Sid didn't know he was so hungry until he started to eat.

"Where'd that butter come from?" demanded Jimmy. One of his jobs at home was to churn the butter.

"Didn't you see Ma tie the wooden churn to the back of the wagon this morning?" asked Pa, helping himself to more butter. "The wagon did your work for you."

"Don't worry, Jimmy," said Sid. "There'll be plenty of other jobs." Jimmy made a face.

When Mr. Stokes said nooning would be nearly two hours, Sid thought it would be a waste of time. But by the time all the noon chores were done, and they'd had a little rest, it was time to yoke up, water the animals, and hit the trail again.

Grace Willis came to walk with him. "I was going to walk with you this morning, but Mamma said you needed to have a chance to get used to being on the trail without me getting in the way."

They made good time despite constant traffic to and from Kansas City. They overtook people who were planning to find a wagon company in Council Grove. Others overtook them. Some wagons were alone, some in small groups. Most were drawn by oxen, but some were drawn by horses or mules. These wagons moved along in no particular order. Some wagons fell in behind or alongside the Stokes Company. A buggy drawn by two little donkeys passed them, pulling up alongside Mr. Stokes, who tipped his hat. Sid couldn't believe it when the man told Mr. Stokes that he and his wife were on their way to Santa Fe. *Who would think of crossin' nearly 800 miles of prairie in a buggy with no more than a trunk tied on the back?*

"You're welcome to fall in with us," called Mr. Stokes. "Be glad to have a preacher in our company."

"Thankin' you kindly, but we'll be on our way," said the man. "Me and the Missus are meetin' up with missionary friends at Shawnee Mission. I'm afraid you'd slow us down."

"You could be right," said Mr. Stokes. "But you never know. 'Steady wins the race,' as the old sayin' goes. And there is safety in numbers. Good luck to you."

"May the Good Lord bless you," called the man as he set his donkeys to a steady trot.

After a while Pa took over leading the team so Sid could have a break. One of the other men took Pa's place. Mr. Stokes rode the length of the wagon train every now and then, too, but he was usually at the front, making sure the trail was safe. Even on the well-traveled trail there were places to avoid.

"What happens if a wagon breaks down in the back?" asked Grace.

"Pa says that the wagons on either side send word up along the train," said Sid. "Like Mr. Stokes said, we all work together."

He was glad for a break. Grace thought they should walk the whole length of the train and back. Ma agreed, "If it's okay with Mrs. Willis, but don't go any further than the end of the train before you start back." After that, they walked the length of the train almost every afternoon, sometimes going to the front and walking backwards to see how long it would take for the train to pass them, sometimes making a circle of the train. The oxen were steady, but slow. They didn't have to work very hard to keep up.

Late that afternoon, they came upon a man pushing a handcart piled with provisions. The woman with him led a cow. The cow carried a large pack over her back. The couple made camp with them that night. They were going as far as Oregon Trail Junction to meet a handcart company. From there, they would pick up the Mormon Trail to the Salt Lake Valley. "We are Latter Day Saints, on our way to Zion," said the woman, her face aglow.

"You sound funny," Jimmy blurted out.

"Jimmy!" Ma exclaimed, a flush of pink rushing to her cheeks.

The lady gave them a big smile. "No need. We're from England. We think you sound funny, too."

Jimmy looked amazed. "You do?"

Everyone had a good laugh.

Later, Sid wondered how they would ever make it to Oregon Junction and if they could buy a wagon there. "Some people can't afford a wagon, Son," Pa told him. "It will be a hard trip for them, but if they're willing to give it a try, I'll not be one to tell 'em they can't do it. It's a lot safer on the trails than it was ten years ago. Folks will endure a lot to find a better life and follow their conscience."

"My Mamma says they're followers of Joseph Smith," said Grace, joining them. "We may not agree with them, but that's one of the best parts of being an American. We don't have to agree."

She was right. But sometimes Grace had an annoying way of sounding smug.

22.
Council Grove

Mrs. Payne started lessons their second night on the trail. Only a handful of children came. Most families seemed to think school could wait until California. It turned out to be great fun, though. They didn't really study anything, not like at school. Mrs. Payne had books for everyone to look at. They all had a chance to talk, even the little ones. She wanted to know what interested them.

"Is it true that Indians use sign language?" a girl much older than Sid asked.

"Yes, so Mr. Payne tells me. Frontiersmen and scouts learn sign language so they can communicate with native people. Not all tribes speak the same language, so they use signs to talk with each other."

"Can we learn?" Jimmy asked.

"*May* we," Grace corrected him under her breath.

"My daddy knows sign language," said Matthew Payne.

"I'll tell you what," said Mrs. Payne. "If some of you are interested in learning sign language, I'll ask Mr. Payne if he can teach us. He may be busy, but he might be able to teach us a few words now and then." Everybody seemed to think it was a good idea.

Council Grove was on Sid's mind. Mrs. Payne said it was a famous place. She said Council Grove was probably the most famous spot between the Missouri River and Santa Fe. "Mr. Payne tells me it probably won't look famous, it will just look crowded," she laughed.

"What makes Council Grove so famous?" Grace wanted to know.

"We couldn't travel on the Santa Fe Trail if it weren't for something that happened in Council Grove. In 1825, a treaty was signed with the Osage Tribe," Mrs. Payne explained. "It was one of several treaties that gave the U.S. government a right of way for the Santa Fe Trail to cross the plains.

"Does anybody know how we got this vast land?"

"The Louisiana Purchase." Sid had to be quick to beat Grace to the answer.

Grace jumped in before he could say more, "We bought it from the French in 1803."

Mrs. Payne nodded. "But as far as the native people were concerned, the French didn't own it. It wasn't theirs to own. The native people don't believe anyone owns the land. It is here for all to enjoy."

"But don't different tribes have different parts of the land?" said Grace.

"Yes, but they move about in a large area that they consider their grazing and hunting area. That's different from settling down, building a house, and saying you own the land. At one time all this vast area around here was land of the Kanza people—Kanza means 'people of the south wind.' In fact, Council Grove has grown up on land that still belongs to the Kanza Nation."

"Well, that's not right," said Grace.

"Can anybody guess how Council Grove got its name?" Mrs. Payne asked.

"Trees," Jimmy exclaimed. "Trees in groves."

"Trees," echoed Cora.

"Maybe the people who signed the treaty met there?" Matthew Payne said tentatively.

"All of you are right," said Mrs. Payne. "It was named for a grove of trees and for the council that met to make the treaty with the Osage Tribes."

Jimmy clapped his hands, looking pleased with himself. Cora beamed as if she'd thought of it by herself.

"US Commissioner George Sibley was one of the people who represented the United States. Pa-hu-ska, Chief of the Great Osage Tribe, and Ca-he-ga-wa-ton-ega, head of the Little Osage Tribe, were among those who represented the Osage Tribes. A mountain man who went by the name of 'Old Bill' Williams was interpreter for the meeting."

"Did he talk to the Injuns in sign language?" asked one of the boys.

"I understand that Mr. Williams spoke several *Indian* languages." Ma would have told the boy that saying Injun is disrespectful. Mrs. Payne didn't correct him, but Sid noticed the way she emphasized the word Indian.

"There were several treaties that gave us the right to use the trail through Indian lands."

"Pa said treaties don't mean nothin' to Injuns," said another boy who had been listening intently.

"It's Indian, not Injun," said Grace indignantly, "And my daddy says that the government should be ashamed for making promises and not keeping them."

Mrs. Payne intervened, gently. "I think it may be hard for the native people to see so many people using the trail now. There weren't so many traders driving wagons back and forth or so many wagons going out West when the treaties were signed that allow us to use the tail. That was thirty years ago. Something happened in 1849 that sent droves of wagons west. Anybody have an idea what that was?"

Sid knew the answer. "The Gold Rush. My uncle went to California to find gold, except he didn't find gold."

"A lot of people were like your uncle, Sid," said Mrs. Payne. "They liked California and stayed. As far as the Indian nations are concerned, the problem with so many people traveling on the trail is that every wagon train brings livestock to graze the lands and men with guns to hunt the buffalo. I suppose it seemed like there was an endless supply of grass and buffalo back in 1825. Mr. Payne tells me that it was a vast open land then. You rarely ever met a wagon train. Just think about today—we were hardly ever out of sight of other wagons. Council Grove used to be a sleepy little stopping place. Not anymore."

The time flew by. Sid decided that the nicest thing about Mrs. Payne was that she had a way of explaining things without making you think she was trying to get you to learn something you didn't want to know. And a lot of stuff you might not want to know, she made so interesting that you wanted to know it.

By the time the Stokes Company reached Council Grove a few days later, Sid felt like he knew a lot more about how to be part of a wagon train. He was so absorbed in life on the Santa Fe Trail that he didn't worry so much about Miriam and Daniel or about the letter to Mrs. Gallagher that lay at the bottom of his box of toy soldiers.

Mrs. Payne knew what she was talking about when she said Council Grove was a noisy place. They arrived in time for nooning one afternoon, near the beginning of their second week on the trail. Mr. Stokes had the train stop opposite the main campsite in a grassy spot near the Neosho River. He was very particular about getting the wagon circle in place properly, even more so than usual. He always signaled when the train was to camp for nooning or in the evening, then rode well off the trail, dismounting where he wanted the lead wagons to stop. Sid took over leading the team while Pa directed the wagons off the trail, one row at a time, until they made a circle. Every morning the wagons in the second row led out, and the first in line waited to bring up the rear.

The wagons pulled close. As soon as the last wagons closed in the circle, men began unyoking, beginning with their lead team. Tongues of wagons and chains between wagons made a fence that kept livestock inside. Most nights, the circle was open and, livestock grazed freely outside the circle.

The afternoon they reached Council Grove, Mr. Stokes had everyone meet after the teams were unyoked inside the circle. "We're right here where we can give our livestock a good waterin'. Unless your water barrel is gettin' lower than the half-way point, we'll wait till Diamond Springs to refill," he told the assembled company. "We stopped here because I don't want to be in the middle of some of the mischief that takes place over in the main campgrounds. It's too crowded. We're keepin' our livestock in the circle. I'm postin' a double watch."

"Too many Injuns from what I hear," said one of the men. "Steal you blind."

"Too many of everybody," said Mr. Stokes. "There's too many on the trail who want to do their last-minute outfittin' from other people's goods and livestock.

"Council Grove is the last place you can count on gettin' supplies till New Fort Bent. If there's somethin' you meant to bring, but didn't, we'll be here till after noonin' tomorrow. Far as I know, we don't have any wagons in need of repair and we're well stocked. But there's Seth Hays' Trading Post—it's the oldest—and both the Columbia brothers and the Chouteau brothers have stores. There's a government blacksmith. There's a new post office—it's a year old. I've heard that folk used to leave letters at the Post Office Oak. It's that old oak tree near the post office. I don't know about that. I never left anything myself, but you never know. You young folk might want to have a look and see what you think. Council Grove is a crowded place now. Keep your youngens close. Don't let 'em wander over into the wagon camp. We'd have the little end of the horn tryin' to find 'em."

23.
A Close Call

Ma said Sid could take Jimmy and Cora to mail letters to Mrs. Harold and to Uncle Luke. "Mrs. Willis wants to send mail home. So does Mrs. Payne. You children can all go together if it's okay by their parents. I expect Otis and Myrtle will want to go, too. I'll see if Mrs. Swathmore will let them. Sometimes she gets her back up about them bein' around Matthew and Lydia. Such a shame. They won't have a chance to do anything if we don't look out for 'em—and mind you don't forget to ask if there is any mail for us. I'm hopin' we'll hear from Mrs. Harold."

Sid felt a pang of guilt. He had thought so little about Miriam and Daniel. But Ma hadn't forgotten. He could see the worry lines across her brow and around her eyes.

Cora hurried to the wagon, returning with Serena's basket. "Cora, if you're plannin' to take Serena along, I can tell you it's a bad idea," Sid told her. "Cats don't like being wagged around in a basket."

"Serena wants to go," said Cora stubbornly. "She likes to ride in her new basket." Sometimes Sid marveled at what Cora was able to get away with. She carried the cat around like she was a rag doll. Serena wouldn't have accepted such treatment from anybody else.

"That basket will get awfully heavy," Sid warned.

A loud meow came from the basket.

"See? Serena wants to go," said Cora. She held on to the basket firmly.

"Doesn't sound like that to me," he said, but he knew he was defeated. Ma was already at the Swathmore wagon. She was holding the baby, patiently listening to Mrs. Swathmore whine while Otis and Myrtle happily skipped over to join the fun. If Cora got one of her stubborn streaks, she could hold them up until it was too late to go. "Well, if you take her, don't expect me to carry the basket," he warned.

"Me neither," said Jimmy.

By the time they got to the Payne wagon, Serena had quit protesting. Mrs. Payne had letters for her family in Brooklyn, but she hesitated about letting Matthew and Lydia go into Council Grove without an adult. "It's not that I don't trust you to look after them, Sid, goodness knows, you're almost tall as a man now. But Council Grove is crowded. There's some who might be tempted to put their hands on two little black children."

Mr. Payne gave them a broad grin. "Tell you what, there's safety in numbers. You'll have Grace to help. If everybody promises to stick together, and you go straight to the post office, you'll be fine. Mr. Stokes and I'll be along afterwhile to look in on the blacksmith. If you run into any trouble, look for us. It's close by. The Post Office Oak isn't far from the post office if you want to have a look. Just stick together and steer clear of that crowded campsite. That's where you're sure to find trouble."

"I think we should leave a letter at the Post Office Oak," Grace said. She was always thinking of some adventure. Sid didn't mind waiting while she wrote the letter. She'd be quick.

A plaintive meow came from Serena's basket when Cora set it down. It didn't sound as if Serena was glad to wait.

Soon Grace read the letter aloud:

Dear Person Who Reads This:
We are children traveling to California with the Stokes Company. It is much nicer to be with a wagon train than we thought it would be. We hope that you have a very safe trip and don't get sick or anything bad. If you want to write us a letter, we are stopping at Bent's New Fort and in Santa Fe.
Sincerely,
Grace Willis and Sid Johnson

"Me, too," said Cora, "it's from Serena and me, too."

"You can't write your name," scoffed Jimmy. "How you gonna sign an important letter?"

"Can too," said Cora.

Grace had everyone sign. Matthew and Lydia signed. Otis and Myrtle made some marks. Sid wondered if Ruby and Junior would have been able to sign. He doubted if they had been to school, either. Cora wrote her name and some scribblings. "That's Serena," she said. Sid shot Jimmy a warning look before he could say anything ugly.

It wasn't a long walk to the post office. It would have been quicker if Cora hadn't been carrying the basket. She had to set it down every so often. But she didn't ask anybody else to carry it. Grace started to volunteer, but Sid gave her a look. She grinned. Grace was good that way. She seemed to know without him having to say anything. He felt sorry for Serena, though.

Nobody paid them much attention as they walked along the wide Santa Fe Trail toward the post office. Council Grove was a busy place as people came and went from the main campground. It didn't look much like a town, though. It was a few buildings strung out on either side of the wide Trail.

"I think those people must be from the Kaw Nation," said Grace, as two men came their way. They wore red breechcloths, leggings—Sid thought they were probably made of deerskin—and blankets that were loosely wrapped around them. Some of the Kaw men they had passed on the way to Council Grove wore a headdress. These men wore a single feather in the scalp lock on top of their shaven heads.

Otis pulled Myrtle behind Grace, as if to protect her. *No tellin' what their ma has told them about Indians*, Sid thought. He took their hands, "It's okay," he said, "they probably live here." He could feel little Myrtle tense as the men came closer.

"What's all that stuff they got hangin' from their ears?" asked Jimmy, stopping in his tracks to look.

"Don't stop and stare, it's bad manners," said Sid.

"I think it's for decoration," said Grace. She was much more patient. *But then, she doesn't have to live with him*, thought Sid.

"Huh?" Jimmy scrunched up his nose.

"Like collar buttons or necktie studs my daddy wears," she said. "It's just a different custom."

"Well it looks funny," Jimmy said.

"Like Ma says, 'Different people have different ways,'" Sid reminded him. "They probably think we look funny, too." He couldn't help noticing how some people from the campground moved completely off the wide trail to avoid meeting them or looked at the men as if they shouldn't even be there at all or ought to get out of the way. He wondered how it must feel to see people acting like your home belonged to them. The men passed, looking ahead as if they took no notice of anyone around them.

At the post office, Sid handed the letters over to the postal clerk and asked about mail. "Benjamin Johnson, you say? Care of the Stokes Company?"

"Yessir," said Sid.

"I do have a letter for you," said the clerk, handing him a letter addressed to Ma and Pa.

Cora set Serena's basket down and popped her thumb into her mouth. A loud "Meow," came from the basket.

"You sendin' that basket to Oregon?" the clerk asked, winking at Sid.

Cora removed her thumb. "Serena wants to see the Post Office Oak."

"Oh," said the clerk. "She doesn't sound very happy."

"Serena's happy," Cora said.

"Maybe she wants to leave a message in the rocks by the Post Office Oak," said the clerk, looking very serious.

A steady stream of people came and went from the post office, many of them from the Stokes Company. A rather scruffy-looking man stepped aside to let them exit. His face was shaded by a large hat with a high crown and broad brim like the teamsters wore.

"Well, hello there, young lady." It was Mr. Gallagher. If he hadn't stopped them, Sid would have walked right past without knowing him.

"How is your kitty doing?" Mr. Gallagher asked, stepping back off the path and out of the way. "I see she has a fine new basket."

A low, angry rumbling came from the basket the moment they paused.

"Serena's basket got smashed," said Cora.

"Did it?" Mr. Gallagher said. "How awful for Serena."

"Somebody tried to steal our stuff," said Jimmy.

"You don't mean it!" said Mr. Gallagher, eyes widening in surprise.

"We was in Kansas," said Jimmy.

"Before we left Westport." Sid intervened. "Somebody broke into our hotel room and made a right mess. Fortunately, nothin' was missin'. Pa said we were lucky nobody was in the room at the time."

"Yes, I think so," said Mr. Gallagher, brow furrowed. "I'm sorry to hear it. It sounds like Serena wasn't so lucky, Cora."

"Serena likes her new basket," said Cora.

"It's a very nice basket," said Mr. Gallagher. As they started to leave, he touched

Sid's arm. "Might I have a quick word?" He sounded troubled.

"Wait up a minute," Sid called to the others.

Mr. Gallagher spoke quickly, in a low voice. "I am afraid I put your family in danger in Westport without knowing it. I planned to stay at the Gillis House Hotel, too, but changed my mind. Is the letter still safe?"

"It is," said Sid.

Mr. Gallagher let out a long, slow breath. "Thank God. Unfortunately, two men who used to work for me found out about it. That's why I changed my plans. They must have discovered that there was someone from the *Loulabelle* who registered, and thought it was me trying to hide from them by using another name."

"There were two men at the hotel that I saw on the *Loulabelle*, but I didn't recognize anybody else," said Sid. "One was great big with red hair and the other—"

"Thin and weaselly looking," Mr. Gallagher nodded his head. "It's the letter, Sid. They are after the letter. I wasn't entirely forthcoming when I asked you to carry it. If it were an ordinary letter, I could send it by post. But the letter contains important history about my wife's family—history that she feared was lost to her. Bayless Sly, the weaselly one, is a dangerous ruffian."

The thought flashed through Sid's mind that he should tell Mr. Gallagher about overhearing him on the *Loulabelle*, but he didn't want to interrupt.

"It's a long story. But for some reason, Mr. Sly imagines the letter tells secrets that will lead to some vast treasure. He managed to bring the other man under his influence. They've been dogging me all the way from St. Louis. That's why I asked you to deliver the letter. I knew they might find me. The letter is precious to my wife—more precious than any gold or treasure Bayless Sly can imagine."

"Would you like it back now?" asked Sid. "We're camped just on the other side of the main campsite. You can come get it."

"Keep it for me, Sid, if you will. When I met you on the *Loulabelle*, it was clear that you are an honest young man from a good family. I knew I could trust it to you. But I never intended you or your family any harm.

"Put it away among your things and forget about it until you get to Santa Fe. I frequently travel the Santa Fe Trail on business, so I may cross paths with you before you get there. I doubt your family will be bothered again. If Sly suspected, he'd have tried to find you on the trail before you ever got to Council Grove."

Sid nodded. The others were getting restless. He could hear Jimmy starting to complain.

"If I have reason to think otherwise, I'll send someone to get the letter. I know for a fact that at this very moment, Sly is playing dominoes at the campground. Otherwise, I wouldn't have stopped you. I think—I'm hoping—that Mr. Gordon may have signed on with a teamster train. I hated to see him get mixed up with Sly."

"Yessir," said Sid. "If someone else comes for the letter, how will I know they're really from you?"

"Esteban's Cross. They'll say 'Esteban's Cross.' What will you say in return, just so they know they have the right young man?"

What a curious— Sid's thought was interrupted as Cora called, impatiently. "Come on Sid, Serena wants to go."

"Serena's basket." He said the first thing that popped into his head. "I'll say 'Serena's basket.'"

"God bless you," said Mr. Gallagher. Before Sid could ask him anything else, he faded into the crowd.

"We wanna see the Post Office Oak," Jimmy called.

"Then off we go," said Sid, trying to sound lighthearted. They began retracing their steps. They had passed the Post Office Oak on their way to the post office. It was an unmistakably big tree with a pile of stone around the base of its broad trunk.

"Looks like a place for hidden treasure,"— Matthew pointed to a hollow in the trunk— "if it wasn't so high up."

"Yes, but Mr. Stokes said letters were left in the rocks," said Sid.

"Oh, Matthew!" Grace clapped her hands. "It does look like a place for secret messages. Maybe there was a rope ladder and people climbed up to leave money or jewels or treasure maps."

"Nothin' here," said Jimmy, poking in the rocks.

Lydia was usually quiet. When she said something, it was worth paying attention. "If there was a ladder, everybody would know about it. So, you couldn't leave secret messages."

"You're right, Lydia," said Grace. "There must be another way up."

Sid eyed the hollow. "Matthew, what if I lifted you up. Could you reach it?"

"What about me?" Jimmy said.

"Matthew's taller than you are." Sid tried to hoist Matthew up to the hollow. It didn't work. "You'll have to stand on my shoulders, Matthew."

"So how will we get him up on your shoulders?" asked Grace. "Could we make stair steps?"

"That'd take about a hundred years," said Jimmy.

"No, I mean what if we help him step up," said Grace, patiently. "Sid could sort of squat down. Matthew could step on you, then Lydia and me, then up on Sid's shoulders."

Otis was content to watch. The little girls lost interest and began turning over every rock under the tree that they could lift.

After Grace, Lydia, and Jimmy made several attempts to hoist Matthew up, Sid said, "How about I lean up against the tree and Matthew, you hold on to the trunk to support yourself while they lift. That way, you don't lose your balance, and I don't get strangled!"

Lydia was just enough shorter than Jimmy that she couldn't be much help to Grace. She lost interest, too, and joined Cora and Myrtle looking for messages in the rocks around the massive tree trunk. Soon they were out of sight.

Matthew managed to get one foot up on Sid's shoulder. Grace and Jimmy hoisted the other foot up, while Matthew steadied himself against the tree, taking some of the weight off Sid. He walked his hands up the trunk as Sid slowly stood up. When he was finally standing, Matthew could almost reach the lower branch of the oak tree, but not quite. Sid wished he had asked Matthew to take his shoes off. They were digging into his shoulders.

"Oh no!" said Grace, "Just a few more inches..."

"Looks like you youngens need a hand," said a kindly voice from behind. It was vaguely familiar. "Reckon I can boost him up a little higher."

It was a welcome thought, especially with Matthew's heavy shoes. When Sid turned his head to look, he was so startled he nearly dropped Matthew. August Mean, the bounty hunter, was smiling like he meant to be helpful.

After that, everything happened all at once with blinding speed.

Cora shrieked, "No, no, NO!"

Arthur Mean threw a rope around Matthew and yanked him to the ground.

Thrown off balance, Sid fell, knocking Grace to her knees. He hit his head against the tree—it didn't knock him out, but he couldn't get up.

Roscoe grabbed Lydia yelling, "Got her!" She was too terrified to do anything but go limp.

Myrtle and Cora froze with fear. They were too scared to cry out again or even to run.

Matthew kicked and yelled, but he didn't have a chance to wrench free. In a flash, a dirty bandanna was stuffed into his mouth, and his hands were tied behind his back.

Only minutes before the trail had been alive with people walking or riding between the main campground and the trading posts. Now, there was nobody in calling distance. Sid was too dazed and out of breath to do anything.

Grace stood. Without even taking time to brush herself off, she put her hands on her hips. "Don't you *dare* take our slaves!" she demanded in a big, stern voice, stamping her foot. "My daddy is Doctor Willis. Their mamma belongs to us, and so do they. He will have the law on you if you take our property." Her voice rose to a shout, "THEY'LL HANG YOU. Don't you think for one minute that my daddy won't find you, either."

Sid could hardly believe it. He had never seen Grace pitch a fit. Now he witnessed her full-on fury, like one of the storms that swept over the wagon train unexpectedly, hurling lightning and thunder. Her face was red, fists clinched at her sides as she stamped up and down with her feet.

"I'm going to start screaming, and I'm not stopping until you let them go." With that she let out a piercing scream that went straight to Sid's spine, setting his teeth on edge. He'd never heard anything like it.

The men were momentarily confused. August stepped back, knocking Serena's basket over. The lid flew off.

Hair standing on end, Serena—Sid allowed later that she'd already put up with more than anybody ought to expect of a cat—threw herself at Mean. She struck, hitting his upper leg and sinking her claws in. Back arched, looking like a cat from a horror story, she pulled back and slashed again. Screaming in pain and letting out a string of curses, Mean tried kicking her. He missed. Thrown off balance, he dropped Matthew, tripped over the rocks, and fell flat on his face, narrowly missing Matthew, who'd managed to roll out of the way. "Give me a hand, you fool," he yelled at Roscoe.

Serena backed off, hair still fluffed up and tail looking like a bottle brush. Grace kept up her ear-splitting shriek.

By this time, Roscoe had Lydia tied up so she couldn't move. He set her down to help Mean. Catching his breath, Sid pulled himself up.

Roscoe bent over, trying to help Mean to his feet. Mean yelled, "Look out!" just as Sid gave Roscoe a shove from behind, sending him sprawling on top of Mean.

Tossing his pocketknife to Grace, Sid yelled, "Grace, cut Matthew free. I'll get Lydia. Everybody run! Back to the post office, fast as you can go. Jimmy, help the youngens. Don't wait! Go, NOW!"

Cora wasn't going anywhere without Serena. Looking at the two men with disdain, she scooped Serena up in her arms. "My cat don't like you, Mister," she said, running after the others.

Grace freed Matthew in an instant. "Run!" Sid yelled, pulling the bandana out of Lydia's mouth. There wasn't time to untie her. Picking her up and carrying her, he followed Grace and Matthew as fast as he could go. It wasn't easy. His head wasn't clear.

Behind him, Sid could hear the bounty hunters struggling to their feet. Roscoe yelled something that he couldn't quite make out. It sounded like "Damn the whelps, if Besser gets loose, we're done for. He's worth more than a dozen of these ..." Slowed by Lydia's weight and still reeling from his fall, Sid tried to go faster.

24.
Signs of a Scuffle

Sid didn't know how much longer he could carry Lydia. Suddenly, she started calling, "Daddy, Daddy, Daddy!" He was never so grateful to see anybody in his life as Mr. Payne and Mr. Stokes running their way.

The little ones reached them first, breathlessly interrupting each other trying to tell what had happened. Mr. Stokes knelt, putting his big, protective arms around Cora, Myrtle, and Otis all at once. Jimmy even let himself be hugged. Mr. Payne hugged Matthew and took Lydia from Sid's arms. Grace and Matthew helped unwind the rope wrapped around her.

"Grace saved the day," said Sid, breathing hard.

"And Serena," said Cora.

"And Serena," he said, still panting, "have to go back for her basket." It felt like things were whirling around him.

"No," said Otis. Little Otis held the basket in one hand and the lid in the other. His eyes shone as Mr. Stokes praised him for quick thinking.

Tears in her eyes, Grace said, "I'm sorry Mr. Payne. It was all I could think to do. My Daddy and Mamma don't hold with owning slaves. And I don't either."

"But those two men didn't know that did they?" said Mr. Payne. "You acted with right good sense and quick enough to distract 'em."

"I couldn't think how else to get their attention," she said. Tears spilled over and made their way down her cheeks.

"She sure can scream," said Jimmy.

"I shouldn't have let you youngens come in without a grown-up," said Mr. Payne. "This place is far too crowded now."

"Wasn't any crowd at the Post Office Oak," said Jimmy.

"No, not when you needed one," said Mr. Payne.

"So, what about that hollow in the tree?" asked Mr. Stokes. "Be a shame to go to so much trouble and leave without havin' a look."

The others jumped up and down in excitement, except Lydia, who still clung to her daddy and Matthew, who stuck close to his side. Sid wasn't jumping either. He felt like he was walking on the deck of the Loulabelle again.

The bounty hunters were nowhere to be seen when they got to the tree. "Sid, you're just about the right height to reach the hollow, if you aren't too winded for me to give you a boost," said Mr. Payne.

"No Sir, best let Matthew—awful headache," said Sid just before he collapsed.

The next thing he knew, his feet were propped up on a rock. Mr. Stokes was pressing a wet handkerchief on his head. "You with us, Sid? Sit up and take a sip of water."

Sid's head hurt, but things had stopped spinning around him. "What happened?"

"You passed out for about a minute there," said Mr. Stokes. "You've been mumblin' about bees or somethin'."

"It's what Roscoe Bones yelled. We were runnin' from 'em. I couldn't quite hear. It sounded like 'Damn the whelps, if—Besser?—maybe he said 'Besser gets loose.'"

"So, you know these bounty hunters?" His eyebrows knit together, and the set line of his jaw suggested that Mr. Stokes was both troubled and angry.

Sid told him everything he knew about the two men.

"Mr. Payne, maybe you oughta go ahead and help the chil'ren? Keep'em occupied while I take a look? Take it easy, Sid. Don't try to stand up just yet. I'll be back directly." With that, Mr. Stokes began examining the tracks left by the bounty hunters.

There was very little chance of Sid getting up unchallenged. Grace sat next to him, watching him like a hawk. She helped him to sit up, leaning against a tree with the wet handkerchief on his head. They watched as Mr. Payne lifted Matthew onto his shoulders.

"Mind you, don't stick your hand in and bring out an angry opossum," Mr. Payne directed. "Best poke a stick around in there first."

Jimmy passed a stick up to Matthew, who straddled the branch. "Nothing livin' here," Matthew called, poking into the hole.

"What about our letter?" asked Grace, taking it from a pocket. "Maybe we can leave our letter in the hollow. Don't you get up till Mr. Payne says so, Sid."

Jimmy hurried over to get the letter from Grace. Matthew put it in the hollow and the job was done.

"Come here, Jim," Mr. Stokes called. He was squatting down at the edge of the oak and maple grove nearby.

"Looks like just the two of 'em," said Mr. Payne as the two men returned. "They came out of that stand of woods that backs up to the campground."

"That's what I read," said Mr. Stokes. "You're a better tracker. I'm not discountin' your years as an Army Scout, but with this outfit loose, I don't want you goin' off alone where you can't be seen."

"If you miss anything, I'd be surprised," said Mr. Payne. "Mr. Stokes is one of the best I know," he added, looking at the children who had gathered around them.

Mr. Stokes disappeared through a grove of trees, returning in a few minutes. "Tracks lead to where a wagon was pulled over up on the other side of those cottonwoods; mule drawn."

Mr. Payne frowned. "Must be tryin' to pick off anybody they can. Probably mean to haul 'em back to Independence to the slave auction."

"Signs of a scuffle," said Mr. Stokes. "Looks like they took somebody before they came after our youngens. Nothin' more we can do. Tracks leave off. They're long gone by now."

As they made their way back to camp, they saw a small crowd just outside the main campground. They were gathered around two boys. One boy, smaller than the other, was taking a real pounding. A stream of blood ran from his nose, yet he didn't quit. "Give it to 'em Billy boy, give it to 'em!" somebody yelled. A cheer went up every time a blow was landed.

There were four grown-ups watching, but they didn't seem to be helping. In fact, a man with his back to them elbowed his companion. "Reckon that one knows how to fight," he said, admiration in his voice.

The man turned slightly. Sid cringed. It was Bayless Sly with another man. He didn't see J.J. Gordon anywhere.

"That's not an equal fight," said Mr. Stokes grimly. "I wouldn't ordinarily interfere. . ." his voice dropped off as he pushed through the ring to seize both of the fighting boys by the collar.

"That's enough, boys. I hate to see a fight that isn't equal. There are better ways to settle differences."

Sid held his breath. If the boys in the circle chose, they could take Mr. Stokes down in a hurry. He wanted to see, but he was also afraid Bayless Sly might see him. Mr.

Payne moved them back, though, well away from the crowd. Cora and Myrtle hid behind them, burying their faces in Grace's skirt, afraid to see the fight. Lydia still clung to her father.

He needn't have worried about Mr. Stokes. Bill Stokes spoke with such authority that the crowd of boys began to move away. "Son, you run along and get a plaster on that nose." He sent the smaller boy off. Before releasing the other boy, he said, "Young man, I don't like to see an unfair fight. You're bigger than that other boy. With greater strength comes greater responsibility."

Suddenly, a tall man who had been watching from the periphery, stepped into the dwindling circle. Sid couldn't make out his features. He was at least a head taller than Mr. Stokes, "I'll thank you kindly not to interfere," he said politely. "Boys will be boys. They have to learn how to settle their differences like men. We're keeping an eye on them. Best take your slave," he paused, looking Mr. Payne's way, "and get on about your business." He used some other words for Mr. Payne, too, that were best not repeated.

Several people turned to look at Mr. Payne, including Bayless Sly. Sly looked straight at Sid. His gaze swept past without so much as a flicker of recognition crossing his face. He looked momentarily at Mr. Payne, Lydia, and Matthew, as if sizing them up, before disdainfully looking away. Sid let out a sigh of relief. Sly didn't know him from anybody else.

"Glad to know you were watchin' the boys," said Mr. Stokes pleasantly. "I don't know the particulars of the fight. But I know a fair match when I see one. Can't think of many circumstances that would call for a bigger boy to give somebody smaller than he is a thrashin'. But I didn't come to make trouble with anybody. My *good friend* and I will be on our way."

As they hurried back to camp, Mr. Stokes said, "Some of these wagon trains let youngsters run wild. They can make life miserable for anybody who doesn't join in their mischief. I won't have it. Travelin' on the trails is hard enough without havin' a bunch of young hoodlums creatin' chaos. Sorry about that man's language."

"I've heard worse," said Mr. Payne. "When I hear that kind of talk, I figure it's a mark on the person sayin' it, not on me."

Sid felt like he'd let everybody down. He hated telling Ma and Pa about what happened in Council Grove. They didn't scold him. "Those bounty hunters would have had Matthew and Lydia off so fast we'd never find 'em," said Pa.

"Good for Grace," said Ma.

"They're casting a wide net," said Pa. "Sheriff McDown must have really put the fear into them. Maybe they've quit working the border and moved up here. Now that the Kansas-Nebraska bill's made Kansas a territory, there's a big push to bring Kansas into the Union as a slave state. That means opportunity to low-lifes like Mean and Bones."

When Sid remembered the letter the post office clerk gave him, Ma shut her eyes for a moment and took a deep breath. "Let's pray there is good news, it's from Mrs. Harold." Ma usually had somebody else read. She seldom put down her work. Her hands were always busy mending, knitting, or doing something to get ready for the next meal. But she didn't wait to hand the letter to someone else. Looking around to make sure neither Jimmy nor Cora was within earshot, she quickly opened the letter and read:

Dear Ones,

Trust that this finds you well.

No good news to report. We had a message from Daniel. He picked up Miriam's trail over in Missouri. They're following the river. She was still alive and hadn't been sold. The deeper into Missouri that Daniel goes, the more concerned we are for his safety. Keep praying for them and for all the captives. We live on hope and prayer.

I am enclosing a note that came addressed to me. The stamp was from the Province of Canada up in British North America.

Faithfully,
Leona Harold

Ma handed Sid a small piece of paper with "Sid" in neatly written script. It was folded twice. It read, "Dear Sid, We and our family in Ontario are well and hope you are the same. Sincerely Yours, Elijah." That was all it said.

"That is wonderful, Sid!" said Pa, like he'd just read the family a three-page letter full of details. "Elijah wouldn't want to give anything away that might compromise stations. I reckon they heard us say Mrs. Harold's name."

"Nobody asks for family names," said Ma.

Pa nodded in agreement. "That note may be short, but it tells us a lot. Now we know for sure that Lula and Elijah made it out of the US and into British North America. They are with family in Ontario. So that means they were able to meet up with their guide and other family members. We know they're safe. That's a blessing. It's more than we ever heard before."

Sid wished that he knew more. But it was a relief to know that Elijah was safe. It felt like somebody had taken a big load off his back.

He had been wrestling with an idea since the Post Office Oak, wondering if he should tell Ma and Pa. The note from Elijah made it even more urgent. "Pa, if August Mean and Roscoe Bones are in Council Grove, maybe they're the ones who kidnapped Miriam. Maybe she's here. Mr. Payne said he thought they were picking up slaves to take to the auction in Independence. Couldn't we try to find her?"

"I don't know, Sid," said Pa. "It seems like a big stretch. It doesn't make sense that they would bring her all the way past Independence, then take her back again to sell her at auction. It grieves me to say it, but if they kidnapped her, they wouldn't have passed up the markets in Independence and Westport."

Ma took a good look at Sid. She made him put a cold wet cloth on his head and lie down. That was when it came to him. *Roscoe Bones wasn't sayin' Besser. He was sayin' Belteshazzar!* The phantom slave stealer. He was bursting to tell somebody, but Pa was on guard duty and Ma was helping Mrs. Swathmore. *It wouldn't do any good anyway,* he told himself. *They'd just say that if there is such a person, it's better not to talk about it.*

"How are you feelin', Sid?" It was Mr. Payne. "Mrs. Payne sent some of her fried pies over for your supper. It's her way of sayin' 'thank you.'"

"Have you ever heard of Belteshazzar?" Sid took the fried pies, setting them down with Ma's cooking things.

"Belteshazzar? Can't say as I have. Sounds like a Bible name. The Misses would know, why?"

"It's what the bounty hunter said, 'Damn the whelps, if Belteshazzar gets loose we're done for. He's worth more than a dozen of these'—and that's all I heard."

"Well, I reckon you could ask her about it," said Mr. Payne. "Now would be a good time to ask, before she gets busy makin' supper, that is, if you feel like it."

"Belteshazzar? Why do you ask?" Mrs. Payne looked up from a stocking she was mending.

"Because of what happened at the Post Office Oak," said Sid. He told Mr. and Mrs. Payne how he first knew the bounty hunters before they ever left for the Santa Fe Trail. "Ma and Pa know somethin' they aren't tellin' me, somethin' about this Belteshazzar. Roscoe called him a phantom slave stealer. I think I have a right to know what they've been hiding from me."

"A right?" Mrs. Payne raised her eyebrows. "If your parents are keeping something from you, Sid, I daresay it is for your own protection and to protect the people who help those who are escaping to freedom. Granted, if there is such a person as this Belteshazzar, and they've captured him, he'd be a great trophy."

"Shouldn't we try to rescue him?" Sid asked. "Maybe they have other children.

Maybe they even have Miriam. Maybe they brought her here instead of to the slave market in Independence."

"I expect your Pa is right," said Mr. Payne. "I'm sorry to have to say it, but if they were plannin' to sell her it would be in Independence. She'd be in high demand as a house slave."

"These people make their living by selling," said Mrs. Payne. Brow furrowed, she sighed. "I'm so sorry, Sid, but there would be no reason to bring her past the best markets in Missouri."

"Sid," said Mr. Payne gently, "the chances of findin' Miriam all the way out here on the Santa Fe Trail are, well, they amount to zero. There isn't anything connectin' the bounty hunters you met today with your friend's daughter. I don't know what those men planned to do with Lydia and Matthew. I just thank God that you and Grace were so alert. There's no way to ever thank you enough for that."

Sid blurted it out before he could stop himself, "But what about Miriam's mamma and daddy? What about Seraphina and Joseph Harold? Wouldn't they be grateful for somebody to rescue her?" It was a disrespectful outburst. His could feel his face flush red.

Tears welled up in Mrs. Payne's eyes. "I am so sorry, Sid. I am so sorry."

Sid felt tears burning in his eyes, too, as he returned to the wagon. He hadn't ever felt so dejected in his whole life.

"Are you still feelin' poorly?" asked Ma when Sid turned down a fried pie.

"I'll eat it," said Jimmy.

"No," said Ma, "you've already had your share."

"Haven't neither," said Jimmy.

Ma gave him a look. "The evidence says otherwise, young man. Mrs. Payne would never send over four pies when there are five of us. And, you have crumbs down the front of your shirt. Get on with you and don't try my patience."

Jimmy hurried to get under the wagon where he liked to hide when he knew he was in trouble.

"I'm okay, Ma," Sid wasn't quite truthful. As soon as he had a chance, he got the family Bible. *Mr. Payne said Belteshazzar is a Bible name.* Maybe if he found it in the Bible, it would give him some clues. He didn't need to look at the Table of Contents. He'd had to memorize the books of the Bible in school. *Genesis, Exodus, Leviticus—Leviticus has lots of hard names.* He opened to the book of Leviticus. It was hopeless. He figured he could read all day and still not find the name. He thumbed through the Table of Contents trying to decide where to look next when his eye fell on "Daniel". *Daniel is a Bible name, too. Maybe it's in the book of Daniel.* He fumbled with the pages; finding the book, he began reading. It wasn't until he came to chapter three that he found what he was looking for: "The king ordered Ashpenaz, the chief of his court officials, to bring some of the Israelites from the royal family and from the nobility. . . young men without any physical defect, good-looking. . ."—he skimmed ahead—"capable of serving in the king's palace. . ." *Nothing yet.* "Among them, from the descendants of Judah, were Daniel, Hananiah, Mishael, and Azariah. The chief official gave them other names: he gave the name Belteshazzar to Daniel—" *There! There it is.*

For a while, before they left for the Santa Fe Trail, he'd thought the phantom slave stealer might be Pa, especially when he learned Pa slipped out at night with his gun. Suddenly it all made sense. *It is Daniel! The phantom slave stealer is Daniel. It has to be him.* He put the Bible away where he had found it.

"Do you feel well enough to return Mrs. Payne's plate?" Ma interrupted his thoughts. He wanted to tell her what he'd found, but something held him back. He didn't feel like seeing Mr. or Mrs. Payne just then, either. But he couldn't say no to Ma, or she'd think he was sick.

"I was just about to come get you," said Mr. Payne when Sid got to their wagon. "There's somethin' we want to show you."

"This may be important, Sid," said Mrs. Payne. "After you left, I looked up the name Belteshazzar in the Bible. It isn't so easy to remember all those Bible names. It's a Chaldean name. Some of the Hebrews who were taken into captivity in Babylon—"

"I know!" said Sid, interrupting in his excitement. "It's Daniel. It's our friend Daniel. He's the phantom slave stealer. He was trying to find Miriam and they've caught him."

"There are lots of people named Daniel," said Mr. Payne.

"Daniel is Belteshazzar. I'm sure of it! And Ma and Pa know—"

"Or suspect," injected Mr. Payne. "They may not know, but they wouldn't wanna share their suspicions to protect him, *whoever* he is."

"Daniel's gone a lot," it came out in a rush. "He said he works at the docks. When the bounty hunters were trying to capture Belteshazzar—before we ever left for the Santa Fe Trail—it was Daniel who came walkin' across the field. And they have him now, which means they have Miriam."

"If he's your Daniel," said Mr. Payne, "it does put things in a new light. Let's go talk with your Ma and Pa. Mrs. Payne, supper will have to wait."

"James Matthew Payne," said Mrs. Payne, "you be careful. And you, too, Sid." But she didn't ask them not to go.

25.
The Ugly Shadow of Slavery

"**O**h Sid, I don't want you to be disappointed," said Ma. "Your Pa and I know that there's a guide they call Belteshazzar who works all along the border states. He used to send people our way. We never asked about him. Sometimes they let the name Belteshazzar slip. But Sid, there are lots of men named Daniel. Belteshazzar may not even be named Daniel. It may be a code name picked at random. As to a *phantom* slave stealer, your Pa and I have both heard some talk, back in Alton—"

"But it was mostly from anti-abolitionists," Pa finished her sentence.

"Really and truly, Sid," Ma's face was drawn up in worry lines. "We don't know anything specific about any such person. It may be more than one person. Whoever they are, God bless 'em and keep 'em safe."

"I've been thinking on it, Sadie," said Pa. "What happened this afternoon may have nothing to do with Daniel and Miriam. But those bounty hunters can't be allowed to get away with preying on children. Matthew and Lydia won't be safe as long as they're out there. We'd better get going if we're going to find them. I think we ought to talk with Bill Stokes first, though."

"I was thinkin' the same thing," said Mr. Payne. "No need to signal our business to everybody in the Company, though. Too many people get involved and they'll get in the way. I figure we've got another couple of hours before sunset, so we'd best make tracks. You talk with Stokes. I'll take Sid with me. Meet you at the Post Office Oak. You'll need your horse."

"You can't possibly be thinking of taking Sid!" said Ma, undisguised alarm in her voice.

Sid's heart sank. "Please?"

Pa intervened. "We may need him, Sadie. He's near a man now. I trust him in a tight spot."

Ma let out a long, slow breath. "You be careful, then, you two. Same goes for you, Jim Payne."

"Sid, get your gun," said Pa, and he was off to find Mr. Stokes.

The sounds of laughter, children at play, and people doing evening chores belied the tension Sid could feel building within as he followed Mr. Payne out of camp. On the other side of the Santa Fe Trail, sounds from the nearby main campgrounds mirrored and multiplied those coming from the Stokes Company. People were going about business as if there were nothing else to think about beyond getting ready for supper and an evening around the campfire.

Mr. Payne studied the ground by the Post Office Oak all the way to where the bounty hunters had left their wagon when they tried to kidnap Matthew and Lydia. He seemed to be able to look at ordinary dirt and pull meaning from it. Sid couldn't have made anything out of the tracks on his own.

"Not all these hoofprints are alike, Sid. It helps to know when you're trackin'. Lot of mules pass through Council Grove. We gotta know *these* mules. Once we're away from here, we'll need every bit of information we can get. We'll be lucky to find anything left on the trail, too much traffic."

He pointed to the dirt around the wagon tracks. "Three men, Sid. What do you think this mark means?" The pebbles and dirt looked as if someone had been sweeping the ground in short brush strokes.

Sid took a guess, "Maybe a rope or chain brushin' on the ground?"

Mr. Payne's mouth was set in a grim line. "A chain. Rope would leave a softer line, blurred more at the edges. One of 'em is shackled. Means he's black, you can count on it. See how his footprints sort of slide together, like he can't walk full stride?"

They followed the faint tracks a few yards back from where the wagon had waited. "Here's where they caught him," said Mr. Payne. "Signs of a scuffle. See how the dirt and rocks are kicked up here? He was comin' up from behind this stand of trees. He wasn't in shackles then. Wonder what made him take such a risk?"

"Miriam," said Sid. "He's been followin' her all the way from home."

"Could be," said Mr. Payne. "Somethin' or somebody made it worth the risk."

They didn't have to wait long for Pa. Mr. Stokes was with him. "We were all thinkin' along the same lines, Sid," said Mr. Stokes. "You were the only one with the good sense to say we oughta do somethin' about it."

Furrow lines were traced across Mr. Stokes' brow. "I talked to Seth Hays up at the Tradin' Post before he closed shop this evenin'. Most of what's goin' on gets talked about at his place. There's a lot of activity with slaveholders from Missouri comin' in. They don't plan to settle. They just want to be here long enough to bring Kansas Territory into the Union as a slave state."

"Bunch of 'em came over and voted in the election in March," said Mr. Payne, "then went back to Missouri. They'll be back for the next election. All kinds of shenanigans goin' on from what I hear."

"Hays has a slave, Old Sally," said Mr. Stokes. "He brought her with him when he first came out here, so there's no mistakin' his sympathies. He doesn't know of any markets hereabouts like you'll find in Westport and Independence. Says most slaves in Kansas Territory are for housework and farmhands, or they teach 'em a trade and hire 'em out for smithin' or work like that. Kansas isn't ever goina be plantation country."

"But why would they want Matthew and Lydia?" asked Sid. "If they can't trade 'em?"

"Hays says that there is some tradin' that goes on," said Mr. Stokes. "Sometimes people ask him where they can get a slave as company for their youngens—probably what those bounty hunters want the chil'ren for. He thinks tradin's all amongst owners who are already here. Their slaves have chil'ren, and they sell or trade the youngens off among themselves."

Like they were cows or chickens, thought Sid. Even though he'd grown up in the ugly shadow of slavery, he still couldn't imagine such a thing.

"We can skip lookin' in the campgrounds." said Mr. Stokes. "If the men are holdin' captives, they aren't likely to advertise it by campin' there. Too many abolitionists goin' West. If I was a gamblin' man, I'd bet on them crossin' the Neosho, settin' up somewhere close by where they can make contact with folk who are homesteadin' on the Kaw Reservation."

"There's a place I hid out when I was scoutin' for the army," said Mr. Payne, "a cave this side of that bare hill over there across the Neosho. That was before they built the Kaw Mission School that side of the river. I don't reckon the cave's much of a secret now. Still, it would be a good place, especially with the Mission School openin' up that old

Indian trail. Thomas Huffaker—he runs the Mission—is a slaveholder. Word has it he works Indian boys same as slaves. Cave's about 10 minutes from here on horseback."

"Let's get to it," said Mr. Stokes. "What's the plan when we get there?"

"We're goina have to make up the plan as we go," said Mr. Payne. "Let's see what we find."

Sid sat behind Pa on Sandy. They forded the Neosho River a short distance from the campgrounds. The trees grew more densely on the far side of the river where campers hadn't thinned them out. Not far from the river Mr. Payne pulled up his horse, signaling for them to wait while he dismounted. He studied the ground where a smaller road split off the Santa Fe Trail to the north. "This is the road up to the Kaw Mission," he said. "They came this way."

Mr. Payne led his horse, halting about five minutes later. The trees were thinner here where the land began to unfold into prairie. The grass-covered hill loomed large to their left. There was very little cover, apart from an oak grove that stood between them and where the hill had eroded, leaving a limestone bluff with brush and trees at its base.

"They turned here," said Mr. Payne. "Hasn't been anybody since. We'll leave the horses in that grove. I expect this path goes up the side of the bluff. Wasn't a path when I was here."

"Your call," said Mr. Stokes, dismounting.

Mr. Payne didn't hesitate. "Get the horses back out'a sight. I'll have a look up ahead, then we decide on a plan."

They walked the horses into the oak grove, where they tethered them well out of sight. "Waitin's the hardest, Sid," said Mr. Stokes. "Sometimes it's the most important thing a body can do, though."

"Wagon's pulled over in the brush where the trail leads up to the cave." Mr. Payne returned so quietly he gave Sid a start. "It's our bounty hunters. There's a man in shackles and at least half a dozen youngens, maybe more. I didn't take time to sort out the tracks."

"Children?" Pa's brow furrowed.

"Makes sense," said Mr. Stokes. "They pick off youngens like Matthew and Lydia. Easier to handle. They may be plannin' to set up a supply chain to serve the new territories. Youngens make good house help, do chores around the farm. They can be taught a trade. Bring in money. It fits."

Pa shook his head, brow still furrowed in anger. "Probably think children can't do much to stop 'em either."

"Anybody thinks youngens can't do much hasn't been around 'em," said Mr. Payne.

"Just so everybody knows, we can't afford to make any mistakes," Mr. Stokes said. "Law says you can hang people in Kansas Territory for helpin' slaves escape. And you don't have to have a sheriff's blessing.

"So, what do you think, Payne?" Mr. Stokes asked. "I go in on this side, and you come in from above? Johnson follows as back up behind me?"

"Too risky. They'll shield behind the youngens," said Mr. Payne.

"What if you pretend you want to buy slaves?" asked Sid. "Couldn't you get 'em to come out that way?"

"Might draw 'em out," said Mr. Stokes. "What do you think, Johnson?"

"I've had dealings with those two scoundrels," said Pa. "They might recognize me."

"Stokes, you're the 'buyer,' then—it's a good idea, Sid. We go in, Johnson," said Mr. Payne. "You take the near side. I'll work my way over to the other side. Stokes, you and Sid wait here. Once we're in place,

Stokes comes up the path, makin' plenty of racket—you don't wanna get shot. Draw 'em out of the cave, and we surround 'em. If there's any buyers on hand, Johnson and I will decide if we can take 'em or if we need to wait. We'll have to see how it plays out. Sid, you keep watch on this end. If anybody shows up from down here it could throw the whole thing off. If that happens, we drop back and try again later."

"What's our signal?" asked Pa.

"Mourning dove?" Mr. Payne cupped his hands as if he were going to imitate a dove call. "Long, short, long. Anything goes wrong, three short."

Sid watched Pa and Mr. Payne disappear into the undergrowth. It didn't seem fair. It was his idea, but he had to wait behind.

"Thing that has me worried, Sid, is buyers," said Mr. Stokes. "There's a few settlers scattered through this area—illegal squatters; they're slowly eatin' up the Kaw Reservation. Some of 'em are slave holders. Government looks the other way. Squatters are bankin' on the Kaw bein' pushed out. Could get some traffic from the wagon camp, too."

"Then what if I climb up that tree where I can see the path both ways?" asked Sid, eager to do something besides wait with the horses.

Mr. Stokes eyed the tree. "Not a bad idea, Sid. See how it looks from up there. Branches start a little high. I'll give you a boost up."

The tree was an old oak, maybe as old as the Post Office Oak. Its branches reached out over the path leading toward the bluff. Sid straddled a limb well above Mr. Stokes' head and directly across the path. It was sturdy and high enough to get a good view. "I can see the trail goin' on up to the Mission, the horses, and this path far as the bluff. But I can't make out where the cave is."

"Tell you what," said Mr. Stokes, "I'll throw you a rope. You may be up there awhile. You'll be safer if you loop it around a branch and around your middle." He unloosed the rope Pa carried on Sandy's saddle and tossed it up to Sid, who caught it. "Get a good loop shround that branch and another around your middle. If you fall, grab the rope so it takes the pressure off your middle. You'll have one heck of a rope burn, but it will break your fall."

The mournful call of a dove came from one side of the bluff, long, short, long. It was answered from the other. "Good luck, Sid, we're countin' on you." With that Mr. Stokes mounted his horse and started for the bluff.

Sid watched as Mr. Stokes reached the brush some distance ahead and disappeared. He busied himself with the rope and waited, hoping all was going well, wondering what would happen if it didn't. *Shoulda had Mr. Stokes hand me my gun.* He considered climbing back down to get it, but he was afraid it would take too long, and he would miss something important.

It felt like he was suspended in time. Nothing happened on the trail to the Kaw Mission. There were no more dove calls from the bluff. The sun dropped behind the hill. *Maybe I should go find out*, he thought. Yet he'd been told to wait. *What if they're in trouble?* With night coming on, it would be hard to find them. Conflicted, he slid out of the noose that was around his waist and reached for the solid branch where he'd tied and anchored the rope, trying to suppress the fear that welled up inside. I *have to find out.*

Before Sid had a chance to untie the rope, the faint but unmistakable sound of Roscoe yelling curses came his way. *So they got 'em!* Relief flooded through him. He strained to see through the darkness surrounding the bluff as the cursing grew louder. Three figures emerged from the brush.

26.
Nearly a Hero

"Keep movin'," Roscoe yelled. "I ain't got all night. Supposed to meet Huffaker up to the Mission near an hour ago. I miss a good sale and I'll beat ya till ya won't be fit for nothin'—both of ya."

Sid felt his flesh creep with horror. Coming toward him were Jim Payne and Daniel Harold. Roscoe Bones followed on a mule; his gun aimed at their backs. Both men were shackled together at the neck, at the wrists, and the ankles. They had to move like they were in a three-legged race. Mr. Payne's hat was gone. Daniel was stripped to the waist. "We'll see how ya like workin' with a bunch of Injuns, you no good—"

He had to stop Roscoe. But how, without his gun? He felt for his slingshot. It was there along with three or four smooth stones. *No good. Too many branches in the way*, he thought. He couldn't climb down to get his gun. Roscoe would be sure to see him. *I'll*

*have to wait and follow at a safe distance.
Then maybe I can pick Roscoe off with the
slingshot.*

He pulled his legs up on the branch in
case Roscoe looked up. But in his haste, he
dropped the rope. It hung directly in the
path below like a hangman's noose where
it was bound to give him away. Sid began
slowly pulling the rope back up, hoping the
movement wouldn't catch Roscoe's eye.

He needn't have worried. Roscoe carried
on, "Uppity Freed—nothin' more disgustin'. Ain't so free now." He gave Mr. Payne
a whack with the end of the rope he was
holding. "And Belte—shaz—zar,"—he drew
it out like the name left a nasty taste in his
mouth—"if it was up to me, we'd be on our
way to Missouri. But no, 'Get 'em off our
hands,' August says. 'He ain't clever 'nough
to be no Belteshazzar. Nobody's ever been
able to catch the phantom slave stealer,' he
says. Well I caughtcha—didn' I?

"I'm getting' fed up with August Mean
bossin' me around. Don't care how many
times ya denies it, boy, I know. I been followin' ya too long, ya—" He let fly another
string of foul language. Lowering his gun and
placing it across his lap, he began lashing

Daniel with the knotted end of a rope. Daniel stood tall under every blow, making Roscoe even angrier, "Damn ya! Ya ain't human." With that, he turned on Mr. Payne and began hitting him. Mr. Payne didn't so much as cry out.

The rope! Suddenly Sid knew what to do. If he timed it right, he could drop the looped end of the rope around Roscoe and yank him from his saddle. At the least, he might distract him long enough for Mr. Payne and Daniel to escape. With one end of his rope securely tied to the tree, he didn't need to be stronger than the bounty hunter. He just had to get the rope around him. *I'll only get one chance.* Pulling the rope out into a wide loop he poised, calculating when he'd have to drop it. *Just before Roscoe comes under the branch—have to give the rope time to fall—I'll drop it then.*

Holding his breath, Sid prayed inwardly as the men closed the distance to the tree. *Five. . . four, three. . . .*

Mr. Payne and Daniel passed under him. That was when Sid saw the blood on Daniel.

It was caked and matted over his shoulders and back the way Elijah's had been. Fresh blood marked where Roscoe had hit him with the rope.

Sid was so startled, he lost his balance, dropped the rope, and fell. Wildly grasping at branches with his free hand, he clung to the rope with the other. Gravity was against him. The branches broke under his weight, slowing, but not stopping his fall. Frantically grabbing the rope with both hands, he skidded down like some primeval jungle man swinging from a vine. It happened so fast Roscoe didn't have time to do more than look up before Sid smashed into him, knocking him off the mule.

The mule bolted and ran. Roscoe's gun went one way, and he went another, hitting the ground with a thud.

Stopped by the loop at the end of the rope, hands burning with searing pain, Sid dangled a few feet above the ground. It felt as though his hands were permanently fixed to the rope. He couldn't let go.

Mr. Payne and Daniel didn't stop to ask questions. Moving as one person, despite their shackles, they reached Roscoe almost before he hit the ground. In one smooth sweep Daniel had his gun.

In almost the same instant, they turned to Sid, sandwiching him between them. "Let go, Sid, we've got you," said Daniel. As they supported him with their shackled bodies, Sid forced his hands loose from the rope and slid to the path, jarred and shaking.

Roscoe began moaning. Mr. Payne and Daniel whipped back around, aiming the gun at him. Their ankle and wrist shackles gave them just enough slack to move their arms and to walk, but no more. To take aim with the gun, Daniel had to lift both his arms. Mr. Payne's had to move with him. Unless they were well coordinated, one of them was sure to fall pulling the other with him.

"Get your gun, Sid," said Mr. Payne, "We haveta get him tied up before he gets his fight back."

Roscoe quit moaning, going limp. "You want to play opossum?" said Daniel. "Fine. Don't even think about moving unless I tell you to."

Sid ran for his gun, longing to know about what was happening up at the cave. There wasn't time to ask. Nobody needed to tell him that Roscoe was still as dangerous as a cornered wildcat. He loaded his gun before he left the horses. A shot rang out. Terrified, he crept back through the trees. Mr. Payne and Daniel were flat on the ground looking up. Roscoe had a revolver pointed at them.

"Now where was we?" Roscoe said, an ugly, self-satisfied smirk on his face. "Recognize my nice new Third Model Colt Revolver? Been thinkin' on buyin' one since we first met. Sure appreciate you savin' me the trouble.

"Where'd that danged boy go? I owe him. One of these here shots is fer him."

Heart pounding, Sid raised his gun and took careful aim, suddenly realizing that he couldn't do it. He had to either kill Roscoe or seriously wound him. Otherwise, he risked taking a shot that could ricochet on the hard ground and rocks, hurting Daniel and Mr. Payne. This was not a job for his gun. Carefully setting it down, he reached for his sling. Slipping his index finger into the loop at one end and grasping the knot at the other end, he placed a stone in the pouch. Stepping out from his hiding place, he made one quick overhand shot. The stone hit its mark sending the revolver sailing from Roscoe's hand. Roscoe yelled, dancing back, and waving his hand in pain.

Mr. Payne and Daniel struggled to their knees, grabbing the revolver. "Hands up, high," ordered Daniel.

Sid came out of the brush, gun aimed at Roscoe. "Want me to shoot him?" He tried to sound as if it were something he did every day. He wasn't sure that Roscoe recognized him back at the Post Office Oak. Roscoe recognized him now. Eyes blazing with hatred he looked Sid up and down.

"Kick his rifle out of the way where he can't reach it," said Mr. Payne. "Watch he doesn't throw sand in your eyes. It's how he got us."

Sid eased around behind Roscoe. It would be just like Roscoe to try to grab him as a shield. He kicked the rifle out of the way. "He'll have a knife on him, too," said Sid.

"Get him tied up, then," said Daniel, never taking his eyes off Roscoe. "Hands up high, Bones. You so much as flinch, and I'm leaving you for the vultures."

Once he had Roscoe tied up and his knife collected, Sid found the key to the shackles in Roscoe's waistcoat pocket. Roscoe rewarded him by spitting in his face.

Pa would say, 'Don't give him the pleasure of reacting,' Sid thought. Without comment, he wiped off the spit with his sleeve. Then he unshackled Mr. Payne and Daniel. They put a gag in Roscoe's mouth, put their wrist and ankle shackles on him, and tied him to a tree well off the path.

"Where's Pa and Mr. Stokes?" Sid couldn't wait any longer.

"Taking part in an auction," said Daniel.

"Shouldn't have gone in without lookin' over the whole hill," said Mr. Payne. "Been too long since I was here. Set us up for trouble. Let's get back up there and see what's happenin'. I gotta make this right."

This time Sid got to go along. "That sling may come in handy, Sid," said Mr. Payne.

"He's dead accurate," said Daniel. "Handles himself like a man under pressure, too." Sid felt his face flush at the praise.

Once they reached the underbrush at the base of the bluff, Mr. Payne and Daniel were silent as the night shadows around them. Sid felt as clumsy as a wild hog, cringing at every twig he snapped. They came out in the brush where they could see the cave without being seen. A campfire burned. Around it sat a group of children—boys and girls all about Matthew's and Lydia's ages. Mr. Stokes and Pa were busy unshackling them along with a man they didn't recognize. August Mean was nowhere in sight.

Mr. Payne cupped his hands and blew, "Coooo-coo-coooo."

"Come on out, Payne," said Mr. Stokes.

"Glad we won't have to stop off at the Kaw Mission and get you two on our way back to camp."

Pa introduced a stranger. "This is Fredrick Dickson, an abolitionist who lives in Lawrence, Kansas. He's been tracking a boy kidnapped while their wagon was noonin' just past Shawnee Mission a few days ago."

"I had just about given up hope of ever findin' him," said Mr. Dickson. "I spotted the wagon headin' out of Council Grove this afternoon. Followed them up here. I was waitin' until nightfall. Didn't know they had an auction set up till men started showin' up. I figured I'd have to go back to Council Grove and try to round up some help, then these two good men came along. I knew Ben Johnson immediately, met him this afternoon at the Tradin' Post."

"One of the homesteaders coming for the auction caught Jim Payne right after he gave me the 'all clear' call," said Pa. "There are two paths down the bluff. Mean sent Roscoe off to the Kaw Mission by one path about the time Mr. Stokes was coming up the other." He grinned. "Our wagon master sized things up and introduced himself as a US Marshall. Said it's illegal to buy and sell slaves at auction in Kansas Territory, but he'd let the homesteaders go if they left quietly."

"Is it illegal?" asked Mr. Dickson.

"You've got me," said Mr. Stokes. "Things change fast, and news gets out slow. They didn't know the difference."

"So, when did you become a U.S. Marshall, Bill Stokes?" said Mr. Payne, looking at Mr. Stokes, eyebrows raised.

"I'm not," a guilty smile spread across Mr. Stokes' face. He opened his waistcoat, flashing a silver star pinned to his shirt. "Had this star made up specially. Comes in handy. If you read it, the badge says, 'Wagon Master.' Crooks don't get close enough to read it."

"That's not the whole story," said Mr. Dickson. "Mr. Stokes flashed his star, and somebody hurled a rock at August Mean. He's just now comin' to. It was the children. The minute those squatters started leavin', the youngsters rose up and started hurlin' rocks. Sent them scatterin' in a hurry. They'd been quietly squirrelin' away rocks, just waitin' for the right opportunity. I don't know if those squatters were more afraid of the law or takin' a poundin' from the children."

"We got the keys to the shackles off of Mean," said Pa as he finished unlocking the shackles holding the last child. "It's getting dark. These youngsters need a proper meal."

"Dickson is goina to take 'em all back to Lawrence," said Mr. Stokes. "They'll head out in the mornin'. Group of abolitionists will take 'em in while he tries to find their families."

"Except this one," said Daniel, patting a little girl on the head who was leaning into him.

She shyly smiled up at Sid. "Miriam!" He cried. He could hardly believe it was her. She was bony as a skeleton. Her hair was all matted, her clothing in tatters, and she was barefoot.

August Mean was clamped in the shackles that had held one of the boys he had kidnapped. "Let's decide what to do with the bounty hunters," said Mr. Stokes.

"I reckon we can take care of 'em," said Mr. Dickson. "Soldiers from Fort Riley are stoppin' by Lawrence pretty regular now that tension over the question of slavery is buildin' up. Feelin's are runnin' pretty high. Abolitionists are preparin' for an explosion. It's bound to come sooner or later. Pro-slavery forces are goina try and run us out."

"From what I hear," said Mr. Stokes, "you can't count on soldiers out of Riley bein' sympathetic to your cause. There are some officers up there that own slaves. You'd be on shaky ground tryin' to hold 'em."

"If I can get them back as far as Westport, I can get passage on a steamboat back to Illinois," said Daniel. "I know the captain. I trust the sheriff in Alton. I can't testify against them in a court of law, but I know who can."

"I don't know about that, Daniel," said Pa. "Gettin' these two to Westport wouldn't be that easy for anybody, but for you travelin' alone? I wouldn't want you to risk it."

"With the right teamsters it would work," said Mr. Stokes. "Teamsters are a generally a trustworthy lot, but there are a couple of companies out of Santa Fe that I'd stake my reputation on. Gallagher Trading Company—"

"Gallagher! I—we know Mr. Gallagher," said Sid. "We met him, Pa, remember?"

"William Gallagher's a good man," said Mr. Stokes.

Some of the children were too weak to walk. They had to be carried to the wagon. Their arms and legs were rubbed raw from the shackles. "Shootin's too good for any-body who'd do that to a little child," said Mr. Stokes as they watched Daniel drive the wagon out of sight. Mr. Dickson and Jim Payne rode alongside the wagon.

The bounty hunters were shackled together and taken back to Council Grove under Mr. Stokes' supervision. He wanted them to spend the night chained to his wagon so they would be under the watchful eye of the men taking guard duty.

By the time they reached camp, Daniel was well-scrubbed. He wore one of Pa's clean shirts, a bit short at the cuffs. It wasn't tucked in at the waist. Sid figured his back was too painful. His neck was raw from the shackle, too.

"Jimmy got in trouble," Cora tattled. "He said Miriam had a bird's nest in her hair."

Ma gave her a look. "Miriam was a wel-come sight no matter how she looked."

Miriam was clean, wearing one of Lydia's dresses, and her hair perfectly plaited. "I had to call Mrs. Payne over to do that," said Ma, bending down and giving Miriam a kiss on top of the head.

Miriam and Cora sat with their arms around each other. Sid felt as though he was smiling from inside out and all over as he watched them.

The whole Payne family came over as they were finishing supper. Mrs. Payne brought enough extra fried pies so they could all have dessert together. "Oh dear, I'm one short," she said.

Ma gave Jimmy a look. "No, some of us got ahead of ourselves."

The girls were sent off to bed in the tent shortly after dessert. Lydia was allowed to sleep over with Cora and Miriam. Sid wasn't sure how Serena was going to take to being loved on by three adoring girls all at once, *But Serena has her ways*, he thought.

"Sure do thank you for your help, Mrs. Payne," said Daniel. "You got Miriam looking more like herself."

"Poor thing," said Mrs. Payne. "Her hair was so tangled; I was afraid I'd have to cut it off. What must she have been through?"

As they reviewed the events of the evening, Mr. Payne said, "It was Sid who saved the day on our end. If he hadn't been up that tree, Daniel and I would likely be dead."

Jimmy and Matthew's eyes were big with admiration as Mr. Payne told what Sid had done. Sid's face flushed hot. He didn't feel brave or heroic. "I was tryin' to drop the rope around him," he said. "But I fell. It was dumb luck."

"Dumb luck or clever plan," said Mr. Payne, "it came to the same thing."

"It's what we do with what we're given that counts, Sid," said Mrs. Payne. "You turned a mistake into an opportunity."

Mr. Payne nodded in agreement. "It wasn't dumb luck when you used that slingshot."

"Sid's always been good with the slingshot," said Ma, beaming. "But we mustn't heap too much praise on him. We don't want him to get a swell-head."

Sid felt his face going red again. He had hit the mark with his slingshot. It was something to feel good about.

Mrs. Payne invited Jimmy to sleep under their wagon with Matthew. "Please Ma?" begged Jimmy. Sid knew he was feeling glum about the girls getting to be together in the tent while he was doomed to an ordinary night.

"As long as Mrs. Payne promises not to give you any pie," said Ma. "You had your share."

27.
On the Trail Again

They sat around the campfire a little longer that night, watching the embers glow, glad to be together and safe. It was a bittersweet moment. Tomorrow the wagon train would leave. With any luck, Daniel and Miriam would leave for home, too. There was little chance that they would ever see each other again.

Sid found himself blurting out the question that had haunted him since before they left Illinois, "Daniel, are you the phantom slave stealer, the one they call Belteshazzar?"

"Sid! Manners," said Ma, frowning.

"It's all right, Mrs. Johnson," said Daniel.

"Belteshazzar was Daniel's name in the Bible," said Sid.

"Lots of folks named Daniel, Sid. Can't all of us be called Belteshazzar."

"Well, I've been thinkin'," said Sid, still unable to restrain himself despite Ma's disapproval. "When I was out huntin' that mornin' and those bounty hunters were waitin' for Belteshazzar, they called him 'the phantom slave stealer.' It was you that walked up. I reckon you were bringin' a group up from Missouri like they thought, but you had 'em hidden somewhere out there in the field. You were makin' sure it was safe for them before you crossed the creek."

"Sid—" said Pa firmly.

"Let him be, Mr. Johnson," Daniel interrupted. "No harm in hearing him out."

"Well," said Sid, a bit more slowly and deliberately now, "the way I figure it, you don't really work at the dock in Alton all the time. You're gone because you're helpin' people get out of slavery in Kentucky and Missouri. That's how come you had enough nerve to set out after Miriam. You know how to hide and how to escape."

"I didn't exactly escape those two at the Post Office Oak, did I?" said Daniel. He paused for a minute as if he were deciding what to say. "Think about it this way, Sid. If I am Belteshazzar, the phantom slave stealer, I can't really talk about it, can I? And if I'm not Belteshazzar, I can't deny it because that would risk exposing the actual

Belteshazzar or Belteshazzars—there could others using that code name. The important thing is that somebody is helpin' captives find their way to freedom. So as much as I trust you, I can't say anything either way."

It was not a satisfying answer. But he knew it was all he would get.

"There's something else," Sid figured he might as well put all his suspicions out at once. "I used to think you were the phantom slave stealer, Pa. That's because sometimes you went out at night after everybody was asleep. You took your gun with you. Then you came back close to daylight. So, if you weren't the slave stealer, what were you doing?"

"There was that fox that was always getting after our chickens," said Pa tentatively.

Sid wasn't buying it. But before he could say anything else Ma intervened. "I don't reckon it will hurt Daniel to know." she said.

Daniel? It wasn't what Sid was expecting.

Pa looked at Daniel. "Last fall, after that freed family up on the other side of Alton was attacked in the night, there was a group of us worried about your family. A boy about Sid's age is the only one who escaped. The others haven't been seen since. You can bet they are in slavery again. So, a group of us decided to patrol that stretch along the creek between our two properties at night until things settled down."

"Your Pa was just takin' his turn, Sid," said Ma.

"We didn't want your family routed in the middle of the night and hauled off to be sold," said Pa. "Things seemed to settle down around Alton and we eased up on the night watch."

Sid didn't know what to say. Daniel was silent. They sat watching the coals die down. Pa got up and banked the last of them. Darkness closed in over the camp. Stars hung above, so close it looked like you could reach up and pick them.

Finally, Daniel spoke. "Don't think we don't appreciate what you all were trying to do. But we have to be able to look out for ourselves. We've been bolting the doors at night since the little ones came along. Even Mamma Harold sleeps with a gun at hand."

"Lord have mercy!" said Ma.

"When your barn was set on fire, the only thing that surprised us was that it wasn't our house," said Daniel.

"I reckon you and Jacob have to walk a fine line," said Ma. She spoke slowly as if she were thinking it through. "I know Mrs. Harold—and Mr. Harold, when he was alive—wanted y'all to be part of their family, but they didn't want you and Jacob to ever forget the mamma and daddy who were killed trying to get you to freedom. She's always been afraid you'd end up feelin' like you don't belong anywhere."

"Lot of resentment of freed Negros has been building up," said Pa. 'It's why the Illinois legislature passed that Anti-Immigration Act."

"Illinois doesn't want us," said Daniel. "I was against Jacob and Seraphina moving up to your place right now. It wasn't because some people don't want black folks living in Illinois—we've grown up with that. But war's coming. When it starts, Seraphina and the youngens need to be with Mamma Harold, because Jacob and I will be on the front line when the shooting starts. I'm grateful we have neighbors who will be there with us."

"I guess that was the hardest part of leavin'," said Ma, "feelin' like we are lettin' you all down by not bein' there to do our part."

"I'm not saying you aren't missed, Mrs. Johnson," Daniel said, "but I'm mighty grateful you happened to be in Council Grove when Miriam and I needed you."

"We've been mighty grateful for you, too, through the years, Daniel," said Ma. "You've pulled Sid out of more scrapes than he can remember, not to mention when the bounty hunters had him."

Sid was exhausted. Even so, he lay awake for a long time after they turned in for the night. He was unable to shut his mind off. He'd been a near hero, maybe even heroic. He had a lot to tell Grace Willis tomorrow when they set out on the Santa Fe Trail again. She had no idea what they'd been through since Matthew and Lydia were nearly kidnapped. She might act like a little "know it all" sometimes, but the good thing about Grace was that she'd be too curious to hold a grudge just because he knew more about something than she did. *I won't tell her about Belteshazzar, though. Daniel's right about that.* Grace knew a lot about slavery, but she didn't have any first-hand experience the way he did. *And I don't really have first-hand experience,* he reminded himself, *not like Miriam and Daniel and Elijah. I can see what has happened to them, but it's not the same as having it happen to me.*

When they set out for the Santa Fe Trail, Sid thought they were leaving the struggle over slavery behind. Seemed like it was everywhere they went. *I wonder if we'll ever be free of it?* How many times had he heard Mrs. Harold say, "Like my dear husband used to say, 'until all of us are free, none of us is really free.'" At the time, he hadn't thought about what she meant. It was just something the grown-ups went on about. Now he was beginning to understand. *Wonder if it will be different in California?*

Then another, unrelated thought crossed his mind: the letter to Mrs. Gallagher. *Gosh! I hope I never see Bayless Sly and J.J. Gordon again.* It wasn't exactly the kind of thought that would let a person go to sleep. He flopped over in his bedroll under the wagon. On one side, Pa was beginning to snore, not so much as it would wake anybody, but enough to know he was fast asleep. If Jimmy were between them, as he usually was, he'd be going crosswise. In the morning he'd have his head burrowed into Pa's side and his feet touching Sid. On his other side Daniel was breathing the short, steady breaths of sound asleep. Coyotes yapped along the Neosho River. Somewhere, far from camp, a wolf's chilling howl rode on the night wind.

Well, Sid reassured himself, *the thing is, Bayless Sly didn't recognize me this afternoon. Besides, that whole main campground was swarmin' with boys. They must belong to three or four different wagon trains. Even if they did know me, they'd have one dickens of a time pickin' me out of all the rest of the boys headed west. So, there's no reason to go worryin' about it. Mr. Stokes said Mr. Gallagher is trustworthy. I'm glad Mr. Gallagher knows he can trust me.* With that he let out a big sigh, turned over and fell fast asleep.

The next morning the trail was alive with activity. Wagons and buggies began leaving camp at dawn. Sid was up in time to see the Dickson wagons leave for Lawrence. Mrs. Dickson sat next to one of the boys who had been in the cave. Now he drove the wagon that had held him captive. Mr. Dickson was alongside with his team of oxen pulling the Dickson's covered wagon.

Sid could see why Mr. Stokes said they would wait and leave after an early nooning. By seven o'clock the trail was bedlam as wagons lined up to cross the Neosho River. Companies that were getting organized for the first time added to the confusion. Wagons jostled with each other to get in line. From what Sid could make of it, in some of the trains your position depended on how fast you got in place. It was hard to tell one train from another as wagons crowded the trail. A cloud of dust hung over the campsite for the rest of the morning. Teamster wagons came and went. About mid-morning, a wagon train arriving from Santa Fe pulled up along the trail by the main campsite. It seemed almost too good to be true when they read the sign painted on the wagons, "Gallagher Trading Company, Santa Fe New Mexico Territory."

Daniel spoke to the man who headed the train. It was bound for Independence.

Soon the two bounty hunters were each tethered to the back of a teamster wagon. Ma gave Daniel a fat letter to take to Mrs. Harold. "Well Sid," Daniel said, shaking hands as they got ready to leave, "we've had another close call together. Maybe I'll get out to California to see you one day. You never know."

They waved to Daniel and Miriam until they could no longer hear the mule harness bells jingling. "When I grow up, I'm goina drive a teamster train," Jimmy explained to Otis and Matthew. "I'm good at drivin' donkeys."

"Those are mules," said Matthew.

"Don't matter." Jimmy was unabashed. "Oxen, donkeys, mules—I can drive any of 'em."

Sid was eager to get back on the trail. As they hitched the oxen to the wagon, he felt almost as lighthearted as the first day on the trail, even though the Johnson wagon was going to be in the last group this time. Mr. Stokes was already directing wagons across the Neosho River, one at a time, when Pa called for the last row to fall in line.

Pa had Sid wait to take their wagon across the river last. Jimmy sat next to him on the wagon seat while Ma rode inside with Cora and Serena. Up ahead, he could hear shrieks coming from the Swathmore wagon as it crossed. There was no telling what kind of mischief Ruby and Junior were up to. Mr. Swathmore's loud, "Shut up your infernal yammerin'," brought the screaming to a halt.

When Sid directed the team to the bank of the Neosho, Cornflower didn't have to be asked twice. She and Promise were already expert at crossing rivers. How many more are there to come? Sid wondered, as they pulled out of the river. Water streamed from the oxen and the wagon bed. He guided the team back in place, following the line of wagons moving forward. They were on the Santa Fe Trail again.

Council Grove was barely out of sight when Grace and Old Shep came back to walk with him. Grace was bursting with news. "I couldn't wait to see you! Where were you yesterday afternoon? You'll never guess what happened after we got back from the Post Office Oak. You know those two men who tried to capture Matthew and Lydia?" She didn't wait for him to answer. "Well, I saw Mr. Stokes bring them over to our camp. They're being held prisoner. Mr. Stokes posted an extra guard just to watch them last night. There was a man over at the main campsite who captured the bounty hunters and rescued a whole wagon load of boys and girls. Can you believe it? That's what would have happened to Matthew and Lydia. My Daddy says that they left for Lawrence, Kansas this morning. They're going in the opposite direction from us. Mr. Stokes met them in Council Grove and said he'd keep watch over the prisoners till morning. That's why he brought them over here last night. I hope they go to jail."

"Really?" said Sid, smiling to himself. "You don't say!"

"My Daddy says we're in buffalo country now. I wonder when we'll see buffalo. Mr. Payne says there used to be buffalo once you crossed the Missouri River. Now they're mostly in short grass country. We're in long grass country, but we'll be in short grass country soon. Buffalo must like short grass better." Grace kept a steady stream of conversation going. He didn't mind. Sid didn't feel much like talking. There were too many feelings that seemed to be flying at him all at once. So much had happened in the few weeks since they left Alton, Illinois. He knew things that he didn't know when he left home *– some of it I wish I didn't know*, he thought. He was glad for Grace's company and her happy supply of chatter.

"Mr. Payne says we'll have to hunt buffalo. Do you think you'll shoot a buffalo? I wouldn't want to. Prairie chickens aren't so plentiful on this side of Council Grove as they used to be either. There are too many people on the Santa Fe Trail nowadays. Mamma says they are actually grouse. We just call them prairie chickens." Grace paused for a moment.

"How's your head? My daddy says you have to be careful. You might have a concussion. I guess that's why I didn't see you yesterday afternoon. I wanted to check on you, but Mamma said I should leave you alone and let you rest."

"I think the land is getting flatter than before Council Grove," Sid said, avoiding the subject. He pointed to the rolling hills before them where the trail stretched toward the far-away horizon. "That's where we're headed, Grace, out way past where we can see, and then some."

The sky above looked bluer than any he had ever seen. A strong, warm wind from the southwest picked up, driving dust away from the trail and bringing the sweet smell of prairie grass. Sid took in a deep breath, savoring it. He was glad to be on the Santa Fe Trail again.

The term "slave stealer" was in use in the 1850s. While I do not know how widely used it was in southern Illinois in 1856, it suited my purposes. Sometimes slave stealers took slaves to resell them. But slave stealers were also men and women who risked their lives to help freedom seekers escape from slavery. Some of them were former slaves who had found their way to freedom. Although slaveholders called such people "slave stealers," it is not a correct label. As Pa puts it in the story, "it isn't stealing to give somebody back what was theirs in the first place."

Slave stealing is often associated with Jonathan Walker, known as "The Man With the Branded Hand." Walker was caught trying to help seven freedom seekers get from Florida to the British West Indies where slavery was against the law. He was fined $600, put in public stocks for an hour, and his right palm was branded with S.S. for slave stealer. He spent nearly a year in jail before Northern abolitionists rallied behind him and paid his fine. After that, he worked to bring slavery in the United States to an end. As bad as his treatment had been, Walker wanted people to know that it was far worse for people held in slavery. Four of the seven freedom seekers he had tried to help were paddle whipped and released to the slaveholder. We don't know for sure what happened to them after that.

Another character important to the back-story is the abolitionist The Reverend Elijah Parish Lovejoy. Lovejoy was a Presbyterian minister and fearless advocate for the end of slavery. He published a newspaper and wrote a column that promoted human dignity and freedom for all. His printing press was destroyed more than once. Each time he relocated it. An anti-abolitionist mob burned his press and killed Lovejoy. He died in Alton, Illinois on November 7, 1837, defending his beliefs and in defense of a free press. In this book, the abolitionists, Mr. and Mrs. Harold, are fictional characters who supported Lovejoy's work.

You can learn more about the real people and places that appear in the story on my website: https://fschoonmaker.com. While you're there, sign up for my mailing list. You can message me from the website, too. I love to hear from readers of all ages.

About the Author

Frances Schoonmaker is the award-winning author of *The Last Crystal Trilogy*. Book three of the trilogy, *The Last Crystal*, won the 2019 Agatha Award for Best Middle Grade/Young Adult Mystery. Schoonmaker spent her early school years in Western Oklahoma and graduated from high school in Washington state. After teaching in elementary school for a dozen plus years, she joined the faculty of Teachers College, Columbia University where she was Professor in the College's historic Department of Curriculum and Teaching. She retired in 2009 and was granted the title Professor Emerita. When she isn't writing, she enjoys making school visits to meet with girls and boys, traveling, reading, walking, her garden, and three mischief-making cats. She divides her time between Baltimore, Maryland and Stratford-upon-Avon in England. You may contact her at her website: https://fschoonmaker.com where you will find more about her and her books.

Acknowledgments

When I finished writing *The Black Alabaster Box*, I had it piloted with boys and girls in very different classrooms. The good news was that they liked it—really liked it. Even better news was that they had some very good suggestions for me, suggestions that I took seriously. They also asked that the next book be about going all the way to California. Thank you to them for reminding me that historical fiction can be as exciting to young people as historical fantasy. Sid Johnson doesn't get all the way to California in this book, but he is on his way with promise of more to come.

I am indebted to historian, Leo Oliva, whose research focuses on 19th century Kansas, for invaluable advice along the way and for feedback on the final draft. I am grateful to those who read early drafts: Marie Swaby-Rowe, Wendy Pollock, Jon Dunlap and his 4th and 5th grade class, and Nancy Schoonmaker. Special thanks to Chloé Rayban, author and consultant, Jericho Writers.

www.ingramcontent.com/pod-product-compliance
Lightning Source LLC
Chambersburg PA
CBHW071401200726
48294CB00002B/269